SECRETS

BRANTLEY WALKER:

SECRETS

BRANTLEY WALKER: OFF THE BOOKS, 6

NICOLE EDWARDS

NICOLE EDWARDS LIMITED

A dba of SL Independent Publishing, LLC
PO Box 1086
Pflugerville, Texas 78691

SECRETS
Brantley Walker: Off the Books, 6
NICOLE EDWARDS

COVER DETAILS:

Image: © vvvita (39327653) | 123rf.com
Design: © Nicole Edwards Limited

INTERIOR DETAILS:

Formatting: Nicole Edwards Limited
Editing: Blue Otter Editing

AUDIO DETAILS:

Image: © vvvita (39327653) | 123rf.com
Narrators: Tor Thom & Charley Ongel

IDENTIFIERS:

ISBN: (ebook) 978-1-64418-049-5 | (paperback) 978-1-64418-050-1 | (audio) 978-1-64418-051-8

BISAC: FICTION / Romance / Gay
BISAC: FICTION / Romance / General

CHAPTER ONE

Friday, September 3, 2021

BRANTLEY WALKER WOKE UP ON FRIDAY MORNING with renewed energy.

It was the first time in months that he hadn't had a restless night. One without a headache or a nightmare, both of which always left him feeling off come morning. The migraines had been extra brutal these past couple of months, knocking him to his knees at least three days a week, so the fact he'd been headache-free last night, sleeping soundly, had made all the difference.

No nightmare, no headache, just rest after a round of amazing sex with the man he loved.

It was almost like, for the first time since that fateful day when the world had literally crashed down on him, he was living a normal life.

Brantley smirked even as he gently shook his head. Normal wasn't something he would've ever considered himself. As a Navy SEAL, normal didn't apply. And while his career in the military had officially ended, he hadn't exactly left the excitement behind him.

With a sigh, he pushed himself up, rubbed the subtle ache in his leg, grateful it hadn't gotten any worse in recent months. The scar from where the rusted rebar had torn through his flesh was an ever-present reminder of that horrific fucking day. It was also a reminder that he was alive and breathing and that he had so much to be thankful for.

Maybe he risked jinxing himself, but Brantley was not going to question his good mood or look too closely into what spurred it. Especially since he knew what the day was going to bring. Now that Sniper 1 Security had officially absorbed the Off the Books Task Force and they were up and running relatively smoothly, they'd spent the past two weeks working to fill the vacant positions they'd been outlining since April. Today they would finalize all their efforts, which meant they could finally push forward rather than continue to move in circles.

After making a pit stop in the bathroom to take care of morning business, Brantley returned wearing shorts and a T-shirt, socks on his feet.

He sat on the edge of the bed, shoes in hand to finish getting ready for his run, while the man who'd rocked his world last night slept soundly on the other side.

Looked like he was going to have to be a little more aggressive to get Reese out of bed this morning.

"Today's gonna be a good day," he said aloud, pulling on his shoes.

"Did you say somethin'?" Reese grumbled, snuggled beneath the navy-blue suede comforter that had just appeared out of nowhere one day last week.

"Time to get up," he told the grouchy man.

Reese's response was a grunt.

Brantley glanced over his shoulder, then patted the mattress, urging Tesha to hop up there. If anyone could get Reese out of bed, it was the man's canine partner.

"I tried," he told the dog with a shrug. "Now it's your turn. You wanna go for a run, you gotta wake him up."

Tesha's excitement came in the form of a full-body wag and the little hop she started around Reese's legs.

No way could Reese sleep through that.

"Better get up," Brantley told him. "She's gonna sulk and mope for the rest of the day if you don't come with us."

Another grumble, but at least Reese stirred enough to sit up, his long legs swinging over the edge of the bed, bare feet smacking the hardwood.

Reese grunted. "You have somethin' against sleepin' in?"

Brantley knew it was rhetorical, but still it made him laugh.

"I'm leavin' in five," Brantley said on the way to the door.

Reese muttered something he couldn't understand, making him laugh as he strolled out of the bedroom.

Sure enough, just shy of the allotted time, Reese appeared in the kitchen. He'd pulled on shorts and a T-shirt, shoes on his feet. He still looked half-asleep, but Brantley intended to fix that with ten miles of pounding pavement on a warm September morning.

"I hope you know, I was gonna seduce you," Reese complained, falling into step with him on the way to the front door.

"Next on the agenda," Brantley promised.

"Like hell. After this, I'm goin' back to bed."

"We can do it *in* bed," he quipped. "Wherever you like. But right now…" Brantley opened the door, stepped outside.

"Son of a bitch." Reese glared at him. "Why the hell didn't you tell me it was rainin'?"

More like drizzle. Or maybe just the ridiculous humidity that'd been blanketing Coyote Ridge for the past couple of months.

Brantley smiled. "Where's the fun in that?"

Less than a minute later, Reese was at his side cursing him, Tesha trotting along in front, tail wagging.

Damn fine way to start a Friday.

When they returned to the house nearly an hour later, Brantley felt even better than when they'd left. His heart was pumping strong, and the fresh air had cleared his mind.

"Not your best pace," Reese said when they walked into the house.

Brantley peered over, barked a laugh. "Maybe that was because I was keepin' *your* pace."

He found himself smiling wider when Reese glared at him as he made a beeline for the refrigerator.

Brantley was ready when Reese tossed him a bottle of water, catching it with one hand while he admired the man. The good news was, the sleep had worn off and, in its place, a grumbling man desperately in need of a shower. Exactly where Brantley hoped to have him in the very near future.

"You want breakfast?" Reese offered, tossing his empty bottle into the recycle bin—something *else* that had just miraculously appeared in the house recently. "Not right this second, I mean. But before—"

"Shower first," he interrupted, finishing off his water and pitching the empty into the allocated bin.

Reese turned back to the refrigerator, opened it. "I'll wait till you're done."

Brantley turned and started walking backward, grinned again. "The hell you will. You're gonna join me in the shower, Tavoularis. Right. Fucking. Now."

Reese peered around the refrigerator door. "I'll make breakfast."

"Keep up with the excuses, and I'll make you work for it."

"Work for what?" Reese groused.

"Get your ass in the shower," he commanded, still smiling. "Now."

Reese finally gave up, stomping in the direction of the bathroom. "Anyone ever tell you you're too damn chipper in the mornin'?"

"It's gonna be a good day."

"So you keep sayin'."

Once they were in the bathroom, Brantley figured it was time for less talk, more action. After turning the water on, ensuring it wasn't too cold and not too hot, he began stripping his clothes off, piece by piece. He knew Reese was still sulking near the sink, but he figured that wouldn't last much longer.

If he knew anything about Reese Tavoularis at all, he knew the man couldn't resist him when he was naked.

DAMN IT.

Reese knew he should've stayed in the kitchen. At least if he'd had any intention of resisting Brantley's charms. Because here and now, with Brantley stripped bare, his heavy erection in his hand as he moved to stand beneath the spray of water, Reese felt his blood begin to pump faster and hotter.

Funny thing, considering they'd just beat feet for ten freaking miles. He should've been exhausted, ready to sit down, to rest, but *oh, no*. His body's natural response to Brantley's naked form was to stand tall and take notice, which made it impossible to resist the man. And Brantley knew it, too.

Rather than give Brantley what he so obviously wanted, Reese decided to sulk a little more, crossing his arms over his chest and leaning against the counter openly ogling all that sleek, toned flesh.

Christ, the man looked good wet.

"You can keep watchin' if you want. But you're still gonna get in here with me."

"That so?"

Brantley smiled.

Damn him.

Reese stood his ground, arms crossed, wondering when the hell he'd become so damn easy. At one point in his life, he could've resisted any woman on the planet for as long as necessary.

Then again, Brantley wasn't a woman, and no woman had ever turned him on like this man could.

It shouldn't have surprised him that Brantley would pull out the big guns, planting one hand on the tiled wall and gripping his cock in his fist, stroking slowly, steam beginning to drift up, molding to his ridiculously nice body.

They were at a standoff, and there was no doubt in Reese's mind who would win, but for the time being, he was going to hold out for as long as—

Ah, hell, his cock was so hard it hurt. But he was stronger than that damn appendage, damn it. He would just focus on...

Brantley's big, bulging biceps...

Those thick shoulders...

Rippling pecs...

Washboard abs...

Fuck me, I'm doomed.

As if he could sense Reese's ongoing mental battle, Brantley turned, relaxing back against the wall, jerking his cock more firmly, his chest and arm muscles flexing.

For fuck's sake.

"Fine," Reese bit out as he shoved away from the sink. "You win."

"I know I do. Now strip and get your fine ass in here."

It wasn't the fastest he'd ever disrobed, but it was damn close. And then he was in the shower, beneath the hot spray, chest pressed up against Brantley's, their mouths fusing together.

And just like that, all was right in the world. The fog from sleep, the exhaustion from their run, even the damn guilt Reese had been battling as of late faded away like mist, and his brain and body came alive. All of that thanks to Brantley's skilled hands as they traveled urgently over his back, gliding effortlessly down to his ass, gripping firmly, teasingly.

"Do you know how hard it is to resist you?" Brantley mumbled against his mouth.

Oh, he had some idea, but Reese asked the question anyway. "How hard?"

Reese cocked his head to the side when those firm lips went on a sensual journey along his jaw.

"I could fuck you ten times a day," Brantley growled softly against his skin.

"Could you?"

"Easy."

"What stops you?"

"Don't wanna scare you off."

Reese moaned when Brantley sucked on his neck. "Think we're long past … can't scare … *fuck*." He leaned in to get closer. "Don't stop doin' that."

His eyes rolled back when Brantley continued to lick and suck the sensitive skin beneath his ear.

"I could do this all damn day. Every. Fucking. Day."

And Reese could let him because he wasn't sure anything had ever felt so good, so right. The man had the ability to soothe him in ways he'd never experienced, and he did so simply by being there.

"I want you," Brantley continued. "Want to taste you, touch you … *fuck* you…"

Reese groaned, not caring that he was so fucking easy when it came to this, to him. Everything about this man made him feel wanted, desired. Safe.

It was then, as he slid his arms around Brantley's back, holding tight, that he realized Brantley was his safety net. The one thing he could hold on to and manage to remain upright, both literally and metaphorically. When it had happened, he didn't know, and whether or not it was a good thing was something he would have to think long and hard on, but not here, not now.

Shifting, he cupped Brantley's cheek, urged his head back up, so their mouths melded together once more, and he leaned into him, getting lost in him.

"I love you," he whispered when their lips parted.

It felt good to tell him that.

Brantley pulled back, his hands sliding over the sides of his face and holding his head. Their gazes met, held. "Love you right back."

Oh, yeah, he could get lost in those blue-gray eyes, that raspy, dark voice, the strong, skilled hands.

And once again, they were leaning in, tongues twining, the pace leisurely.

Hands stroked, wet skin against wet skin.

As much as he wanted this to last all day, they did have to get to work, had things to accomplish. And right now, slow became counterintuitive to what his body needed. Soft moans became louder, more guttural, laced with an eager desperation.

"My turn," Reese said firmly, sliding his hand into Brantley's hair and tugging so his head shifted back, their eyes met.

"Your turn," Brantley whispered, his surrender insanely hot.

All thought ceased, and sensation took over as Reese took control, turning Brantley around, working them both into a frenzy with roaming hands. He teased Brantley with probing fingers until the man was begging for more. Because he demanded so nicely, Reese gave him more, sliding deep inside him.

"Christ…" Brantley planted his palms against the tile, pushing back against him. "Fuck me, Reese. Fuck me *hard*. You feel so … damn … good."

Brantley always said shit like that, and in the beginning, Reese had thought they were simply filler words. A plea to get him to hurry up, move things along. But he realized that wasn't the case because Brantley never tried to rush him. It was as though he was surrendering, something the man did so rarely.

Gripping Brantley's hips, Reese positioned him for a better angle as he began pumping his hips, sliding into the blistering-hot depths of his body. Slow at first, then faster until the world seemed to have paused and the only thing moving was him as he drove himself to completion, spurred on by Brantley's deep moans and sexy grunts.

"Fuck ... gonna ... oh. Fuck. Yes." Brantley growled low in his throat. "Come."

The last word and the tight clasp of Brantley's ass on his cock triggered his release. Reese slammed home as he let out a deep, bellowing roar to signal the orgasm that all but obliterated him.

An hour later, Reese found himself sitting beside JJ at the breakfast bar while she and Brantley razzed one another over who should be allowed to keep Reese in the long run. Like he was a pet to be passed around.

"It's only fair, Walker," JJ argued. "You get to keep him Monday through Friday. I should have him on the weekends." She picked up a piece of crisp bacon, bit off half of it, spoke again. "I deserve someone who'll cook for me."

Brantley barked a laugh. "Do you now?"

"Yes." She smiled over at Reese. "You wouldn't mind, would you?"

"If I understand correctly, Baz cooks for you," Reese countered.

"He does," she agreed, nodding. "But it's not the same."

"Why's that?"

JJ's gaze dropped to her plate, and she shrugged.

Reese knew better than to interrogate her about her on-again-off-again relationship with Sebastian Buchanan. At the moment, things between her and Baz were tense, and he knew it had everything to do with Molly Ryan, the woman who was having Baz's baby. With only six weeks until the due date, Reese had noticed JJ was beginning to pull away from Baz, if not physically, then at least emotionally.

Add to that the trauma JJ had endured back at the first of the year when her ex-boyfriend had attacked her in her own home. Reese knew she was still dealing with post-traumatic stress. Not that she'd said as much, but Reese had come to understand her in the short time they'd been friends. Plus he knew firsthand what the signs were. After all, he suffered from PTSD himself.

"What do I get out of the deal?" he asked.

JJ looked up, wagged her eyebrows playfully. "I dunno. What'd'ya want?"

"Sex," Brantley answered for him. "He wants sex. From me," he tacked on when she wagged her eyebrows again.

Reese laughed. It seemed like forever since he'd seen JJ relax enough to joke around. The past six months had been hell on the task force, everyone attempting to find their new normal. Although rationally they knew they weren't responsible, they each carried the guilt of Kylie Walker's death on their conscience. They'd been after Juliet Prince, the woman who had kidnapped Kate Walker, for months, and because they hadn't found her, the woman had circled back around and taken them by surprise. Because they hadn't done their job and located her before then, she'd killed someone close to them, and their lives would never be the same.

But with the help of some very resourceful, not to mention ruthless people, Juliet Prince had gotten exactly what she deserved, and she was no longer a threat to anyone. The bullet to her brain had ensured that.

Since then, the members of the task force had focused their efforts elsewhere, trying to pick up the pieces and move forward. Between their monthly trips to Dallas for training and the cold cases they had agreed to keep when the governor disbanded them, they were working hard but had little to show for it.

"At the very least," JJ noted, "I think I should be invited to breakfast every Friday."

"I'm sure that can be arranged," Reese told her.

"If you eat, you take your turn cleanin'," Brantley added.

JJ's lips pursed as though she was considering it. A second later, she was shaking her head. "Maybe the diner's a good place to go on Fridays."

Reese laughed, watching the interaction between the two friends while he finished off his breakfast of eggs and bacon. He'd caved to Brantley's demands after that wicked bout in the shower despite the fact he'd feel sluggish for most of the morning thanks to the heaviness of his choices. But he couldn't deny the smile he'd been gifted with when he agreed to cook Brantley's favorites was worth it.

"Why *are* you here so early?" Brantley asked JJ.

"Baz had to run an errand. I asked him to drop me off first."

That familiar crease formed between Brantley's eyebrows. "What errand?"

"Don't know," she muttered, picking up her coffee. "Didn't ask."

Which meant it had to do with Molly.

Hoping to avoid a meltdown, Reese changed the subject. "How're we doin' on the new hire positions? You get the ball rollin'?"

Brantley looked between them. "What ball?"

JJ sighed and peered over at Reese. "Does he really think we just snap our fingers and everything happens? Or is this just an act?"

Reese smirked, pushing to his feet and carrying his empty plate around to the sink. "I don't think it's an act."

"The paperwork for the new hires," JJ explained to Brantley, her tone laced with amused frustration. "You know, all that pesky stuff that goes on behind the scenes."

"We haven't nailed down the logistics," Brantley noted.

"Maybe not *officially*. But I know you, B. I know exactly who you're gonna hire."

"Do you?"

Reese was intrigued, watching the interactions as he washed the dishes. They'd started with a rather extensive list of potential candidates and had managed to narrow it down, but not without significant effort. Everyone had their own opinions, and it wasn't always easy to incorporate them all. Eventually, they'd had to determine the most qualified and focus on those. Their final list included a variety of computer specialists to a tenured homicide detective.

"I do," JJ confirmed. "I can even tell you who you'll pair together."

"I'll bite." Brantley leaned a hip against the counter, sipped his coffee. "Who?"

"You'll put Trey with Evan Vaughn because Evan's gonna be one of our strongest people, and Trey's eager to continue learning. He'll get the most from working side by side with a former homicide detective."

Reese glanced over his shoulder, saw Brantley cock an eyebrow, his lips twitching as though he was impressed.

JJ continued with, "They'll have Darius Frost as their analyst."

Reese shut off the water, snagged the dish towel to dry his hands. "Why Darius?"

"Because he's the best at what he does." She smiled. "Well, besides me, of course."

"And Luca?" Reese mentioned.

"Yes, and besides Luca." She huffed as though put out. "Trey and Evan'll need someone to keep up with them, so Darius is the best choice."

Brantley nodded slowly. "Okay. Keep going."

"You'll have Slade Elliott work with Allison Bogart. She's smart, she's tough, and she can handle a flirt like Slade." She smiled brightly. "And that's the same reason they'll have Rebecca Richter working with them. Slade could use a couple of ladies to keep him in line."

Reese laughed. Looked like she had Slade pegged already.

"That leaves...?" Brantley asked, clearly to move her along.

"Charlie to pair with Decker Bromwell. They'll work with Jay Hernandez."

Now standing beside Brantley, Reese waited for her to explain her reasons there.

"I think Jay's gonna need to focus, and you've got Charlie, who's used to being the lead partner. She'll be able to work alongside Deck in the field and keep Jay busy digging into the details."

Brantley glanced over at him, smiled. "She nailed them all pretty accurately, huh?"

Reese nodded, grinning at JJ. "Yeah. She's good."

He wouldn't bother to tell Brantley it was basically a recap of the conversation Reese had with her last night before they quit for the day. He didn't mind letting her have the credit for it.

CHAPTER TWO

TREY WALKER ARRIVED AT HQ BEFORE ANYONE else for the first time since he started working for the task force last October.

And okay, fine. He wasn't the first because he'd seen Brantley, Reese, and JJ having breakfast inside the house when he'd walked past on his way to the barn. He could've stopped, chatted for a couple of minutes, had some coffee, been ... sociable. Instead, he decided it was better for him to look busy. He'd seen the sideways glances Brantley'd given him every day this week when he had strolled in after everyone else. Sure, his brother would say he didn't care the hours they kept as long as they got the job done, but that didn't mean Brantley wasn't silently passing judgment.

In Trey's defense, he'd been indulging in some late nights these past few months. Six months to be exact. But it was only once or twice a week—three at the most.

Four last week, but who's counting?

Christ.

His thoughts drifted to Magnus Storme, the damn dog trainer who'd been plaguing his mind and occupying his bed as of late. Didn't help that he'd encountered Magnus and his cocky smile again last night when he'd been heading out. Evidently, Thursday evenings were at-home training days for Tesha. Probably be wise to remember that so he could make himself scarce the next time.

Even now, he thought about Magnus and how the man had shown up on his doorstep last night. As usual, Magnus had sweet-talked his way right into Trey's house, then damn near directly into his bed. It was something the guy was good at. No matter how hard Trey tried to resist the much younger man, it never worked.

It usually meant he needed a couple extra cups of coffee to keep his eyes open.

Not that he was obsessed with Magnus and his cocky smile. The guy was merely a distraction, a way for Trey to forget about all the shit that had gone wrong in his life these last few years. Namely his divorce and the epically bad relationship choices after.

And yes, he could admit it, he had an addictive personality— or so he'd been told—which he liked to believe was why he tended to fixate on certain things. Like booze and sex.

Granted, he'd kicked the booze, but the sex … damn, that was a difficult habit to break. Especially since Magnus could rock Trey's world like no one else.

As long as it remained only about sex, Trey was willing to enjoy the few hours they had together, which was why he'd stopped trying to fight it. He was indulging in something that wouldn't go anywhere, and he saw no reason not to enjoy it while it lasted. It wouldn't be much longer, he figured. When the sex became routine, it would be over for both of them.

Trey booted up his computer then headed to the kitchen to start a pot of coffee. It was always there for him when he arrived, so it took a minute to figure it out. Once he got it brewing, he paced the floor, glancing at the empty desks, thinking about all the interviews they'd been doing, the people they were going to hire to fill them, what this place would look like once they did. They'd tossed around names the past few days, so he had a pretty good idea who they'd settled on, but he wasn't going to pretend to know what to expect. This was all new to him and every damn day seemed to throw another curveball his way.

He thought back to when Brantley had offered him the job. Trey'd been working as a security guard for a high-end hotel, going through the motions. He'd just started up a very intriguing relationship with Cyrus Jernigan, a good friend of Brantley's, and he'd mistakenly believed his luck was shifting. New job, new man.

And then last November happened, and Cyrus opted to take a job in California just so he could skip town without so much as a *see ya later*. When he did, Trey'd been a little shaken. No. Scratch that. He'd been hurt. That was what he'd been. Hurt by the fact Cyrus could so easily dump his ass like he was yesterday's news.

Not that he'd been heartbroken or anything. Trey hadn't fallen in love with the guy, for fuck's sake. They'd just been having fun. Indulging, like Cyrus had said. And no, Trey hadn't been ready for it to end, but Cyrus hadn't given him a say in the matter.

"Pouting doesn't suit you," he muttered to himself, heading for the kitchen when he heard the coffeemaker coughing its completion.

He wasn't pouting, damn it. He was … reflecting. Yes. Reflecting. That was all this was. He no longer thought about Cyrus because he was enjoying his time with Magnus. The guy had come along at a time when he'd needed him. And the sex? Off. The. Fucking charts. That was all it was.

Trey poured a cup of coffee, added one packet of Splenda, then made his way to his desk. He took a sip as he was taking his seat but reversed course immediately and headed back to the kitchen. He grabbed two more Splenda, dumped them in the cup, and prayed no one gave him shit for fucking up the coffee.

Right now, he needed to focus on important things.

Like this cold case he'd been working on for the past couple of months. He hadn't gotten as far as he would've liked, but he wanted to believe he was making progress. Probably would've been wise to use the case during the interviews when they'd gone the interactive route, giving their potential new hires a glimpse at their day to day. He could've gotten someone else's perspective on it. Maybe Baz could take a look, see what Trey was missing. After all, he was the novice here. Luckily for him, the others were willing to forgive his idiocy and help him along. He wasn't sure that would be the case when they were fully staffed.

Movement across the room caught his eye, and he looked up to see the image of Brantley, JJ, and Reese moving across the big screen mounted on the wall. The heads-up allowed him time to pretend he was busy, flipping to his email just as he heard the faint beep of the keypad outside the door. A second later, the lock disengaged.

"Mornin'," he greeted, reaching for his coffee and hiding his wince when he took another sip. Yep, he'd definitely fucked it up.

"Saw you get here. Why didn't you come in and grab somethin' to eat?" Brantley asked.

"Ate at the house," he lied easily. "Plus, y'all looked mighty cozy."

Reese's eyebrows popped, as though telling him that things did appear to be settling down. Good thing, too. Trey was starting to suffocate on the tension. God knows he had enough stress in his personal life. He damn sure didn't need any help with more.

DOING HIS BEST TO PRETEND IT WASN'T a huge deal that Trey was there before he was, Brantley plastered a smile on his face and accepted a cup of coffee when Reese passed it over.

"What's got you all bright-eyed and bushy-tailed this mornin'?" he teased his brother.

"Is that what I am?"

"Looks like it." He motioned toward Trey's computer, took a sip of coffee, winced. "What the fuck is this shit?"

The slow smirk that formed on Trey's mouth told him everything.

"You are *not* allowed to make the coffee," Brantley barked. "Ever."

Trey laughed, looking up at him as he pushed his own mug away. "It's horrible, huh?"

"That's one word for it."

"I'll make more," JJ said, giggling as she watched them.

Brantley handed over his cup when she reached for it. "Besides makin' shitty coffee, what're you doin' up and at 'em before the rest of us?"

"Maybe y'all are just slackin' this mornin'. Ever think of that?"

A slow smile formed on his mouth as Brantley thought about the ten-mile run, the half-hour shower with Reese. "Nope. Don't think that's it."

Trey held up a hand, blocking him from view. "Nope. I don't even wanna know what you're thinkin' right now, little brother. Keep your perverted-ass thoughts to yourself."

"I'm not one to kiss and tell. You should know that by now."

Trey pretended to gag, making Reese laugh.

"Uh-oh," Charlie said when she stepped into the barn. "What'd I miss?"

"Besides the world's shittiest cup of coffee?" Brantley joked. "Nothin'."

"Absolutely nothin'," Trey agreed, "and don't you dare get him started."

Brantley laughed, shaking his head to tell Charlie she honestly hadn't missed a thing.

"Mornin'," Reese greeted. "Your smile's wider today. Somethin' to share?"

Brantley swore he saw the color rise in Charlie's cheeks.

Ever since Charlie had come to Coyote Ridge back when they were looking to hire her nearly a year ago, she'd been spending quite a bit of time here. Not only at work, either. From what he'd seen, things were getting serious between Charlie and Autumn Jameson, the woman who'd taken over managing Walker Demolition after Brantley poached Reese to be his partner.

"Nothin' to share," Charlie said with a chuckle. "Nothin' at all."

Like everyone else on the team, Charlie preferred to keep her personal life private. As much as she could, considering. Brantley knew firsthand that wasn't an easy feat. For any of them.

Six months ago, when the Off the Books Task Force had officially been acquired by Sniper 1 Security, Brantley'd sat down with his new boss, Ryan Trexler, known by everyone as RT, and laid out a plan to keep his team up to date on training. He'd committed to bringing them to the Dallas offices three days a month for the foreseeable future in order to do that, and ever since, they'd been putting the team through the paces. In a couple of weeks, they'd embark on their sixth training session and he was hoping they weren't overdoing it. Not only because Reese had been hovering on the verge of a panic attack the last time but also because Brantley'd seen some fraying around the edges of other team members.

Jessica James, a.k.a. JJ, was in a similar position to both Reese and Brantley, suffering from PTSD brought on by her incident back at the first of the year when her ex-boyfriend Dante Greenwood and his accomplice had rendered her unconscious, then set a gruesome scene in her house. JJ'd come through the ordeal with minimal physical damage, but the mental stress was taking its toll. Not to mention she and Baz were going through *something*—again.

Sebastian Buchanan, known to his friends and family as Baz, wasn't enduring any mental stress brought on by physical trauma. Not unless a one-night stand with a woman who now claimed to be pregnant with his child counted. No one on the team had actually met Molly Ryan, but the woman Baz had slept with on New Year's was thirty-five weeks pregnant with his child, due on October eighth. Initially, Baz had thought Molly was pulling a stunt, pretending to be pregnant when she wasn't, but that turned out to not be the case. According to him, Molly was most definitely pregnant, and she still claimed Baz was the father, although she would not allow him to go to the doctor's appointments with her.

Then there was Charlotte Miller—a.k.a. Charlie. Besides her budding relationship with Autumn, it appeared Charlie's personal life wasn't drama-free either. Brantley had learned three months ago that Charlie's mother was suffering from dementia, a fact she'd kept to herself until he'd all but pried it out of her. Her mother's episodes were growing more frequent, and now they involved random disappearing acts. The last one, three weeks ago, had required them to pull out all the stops. Thankfully, they'd located the elderly woman—who had been disoriented outside of a convenience store—but not until a Silver Alert had been issued.

It was safe to say, they each had a lot on their plates, and that didn't include everything that was going on with the new and improved task force. Add in the new hires, who were adding their own personalities to the mix… Elana Buckley, JJ's new assistant, was their most recent hire about to finish her second month with the team. She was catching on quickly and already asking for more tasks to take on. Elana had actually been brought on to take over as JJ's assistant when JJ decided that Holly Switzer, Brantley's initial pick as JJ's sidekick, was far too talented and needed to be moved into an analyst position on her team.

Of course, there was Holly's brother Luca—the bane of JJ's existence, according to her. Luca, having heard JJ's proclamation, took extra-special care to give her shit even as he settled into his new role as her teammate.

Oddly enough, the only person on the team who seemed even remotely stable was Brantley's brother, Trey. In the past few months, Trey's demeanor had shifted, and he'd gone from the brooding, unhappy man to one who whistled while he worked. Fucking *whistled*. Brantley had a feeling it had to do with a secret relationship Trey was indulging in, but his brother was keeping it close to the vest, and Brantley had more than enough to deal with to pry.

Fortunately this morning, it seemed some of the strain had lifted off their shoulders, and Brantley was tempted to throw a big thank-you up to the man upstairs. After all, someone was responsible for this shift in mood.

Of course, Baz was still missing, and once he got there, he figured JJ's mood would quickly decline. But maybe he was wrong. Maybe she would continue to pretend she only wanted to be friends with Baz, pretend that it wasn't shredding her heart that he was having a baby with another woman.

"Any word from Baz?" he asked, directing the question at JJ.

"Not yet," she answered with a forced smile.

Yep, still pretending.

"I'm sure he'll be here shortly," Trey added. "He's an overachiever like that."

"Well, I don't think we need him to get started. He sent me his notes on the candidates, and based on what I heard last night"—Brantley glanced at JJ—"I think we're all on the same page as to who we're hirin'."

"I thought we had some more interviews to do today," Trey said, leaning back in his chair and sipping from the new cup of coffee JJ delivered.

"If we need to, sure." Brantley glanced at Reese, then to Charlie, Holly, Luca, Elana, and finally to JJ. "What do y'all think?"

"I've got Allison, Evan, and Slade comin' in today for another day of it," JJ said. "But I think we're all in agreement, so there's no need to drag it out any longer if we don't have to."

"Maybe we could do one final rundown," Trey suggested. "Just to make sure we're all on the same page?"

"I'm good with that," Brantley said, looking around to see if anyone disagreed. When they didn't, he continued, "All right then. Holly, why don't you give us a high level of the analysts we've decided on."

Holly spoke up without hesitance. "We were originally looking to hire only two analysts, but we ended up going with three. Rebecca Richter, Jay Hernandez, and Darius Frost. Each one will be assigned to an investigative team and be the direct point of contact for anything that team needs while in the field."

Brantley had to admit, he was impressed by Holly. When Brantley had initially hired her as JJ's assistant, he'd done so without JJ's approval and if he was being honest, he hadn't been sure it would work. After all, Holly had come around shortly after JJ's attack, when they had utilized Luca's skills to find who had supposedly kidnapped the governor's son. But in the months since, Holly had proven her worth, starting out by handling the menial tasks, but they'd soon learned her skills were too great to be ignored. Now she was the third on JJ's team.

Brantley gave a nod. "When will they be starting?"

"Rebecca, who prefers to be called Becs, will start on Monday. Jay and Darius will both be starting the following Monday, on the thirteenth, right before the next training session in Dallas on the seventeenth."

"Perfect." Brantley looked at Luca. "And the investigators? Who'd we decide on?"

Luca lifted a finger to tap one of the keys on his laptop. "Based on our conversation last night, it looks like we've decided on Evan Vaughn, Allison Bogart, and Slade Elliott."

Luca's laid-back, couldn't-care-less demeanor was a facade, Brantley knew. While he reclined in his chair, acting as though he wasn't paying attention, Luca could likely tell you every little detail of what had happened in the past few minutes.

"Trey, give us a high level on Evan?"

Without missing a beat, Trey chimed in. "He lives just a few miles down the road in Round Rock. Has an eight-year-old daughter who lives with him, as does his grandmother. He moved here from Florida six years ago, right after his wife passed. Prior to that, he spent a decade in Miami as a detective. Currently works for Round Rock PD as a homicide detective."

Of all the potential new hires, Brantley saw Evan being the most promising.

"Elana, what've you got on Allison?"

"She's a former SVU detective for the Dallas Police Department who's spent the past several years working an undercover assignment posing as a teenager to lure internet predators."

"A role she's suited for since she looks closer to fifteen than thirty," Luca offered.

JJ chuckled. "Which explains why she was on that undercover op. According to what little she told me, they used her in the field quite a bit."

Brantley knew that Allison Bogart was rather impressive on paper, but he had some concerns about her demeanor, ones he'd only shared with Reese. Despite those concerns, they'd decided she would be a strong addition, and he only hoped she proved them right.

"And last but not least is Slade Elliott," Trey said, offering up the final investigator they were looking to hire. "He's a bounty hunter."

"But you knew that about Slade," JJ added, "since he's your cousin."

"By marriage only," Brantley assured them. "He's one of my aunt Lorrie's nephews."

"Don't forget Decker Bromwell," Holly said. "He'll be the fourth investigator added."

"He will," Brantley agreed, referring to the man who'd helped them out in Port Isabel when they went in search of Juliet Prince back in March. "He'll officially start working with us at the beginning of October. He's finishin' up his current assignment with Sniper 1." He looked around at his current team. "Anyone have any questions or concerns about these people?"

Trey shook his head and said, "I'm good. I'd just like to know who I'll be paired with."

Brantley glanced at Reese, who had been silent throughout the entire meeting. "Care to share who you decided on last night?"

Reese's grin said he knew Brantley was calling JJ out from earlier.

Reese looked at Trey. "You'll be paired with Evan Vaughn and you'll utilize Darius Frost as your analyst."

Trey smiled as though he'd been hoping for that. "Works for me."

Reese glanced at Charlie. "You'll be with Decker Bromwell. Jay Hernandez will be your analyst."

"Sounds good."

"We'll come up with something in the interim," Brantley added. "Until Deck comes on board."

Charlie nodded.

"That leaves Slade Elliott and Allison Bogart," Luca said. "They'll be paired together?"

"They will, yes," Brantley confirmed. "With Becs as their analyst. Reese and I will utilize Holly, with Luca and JJ overseeing and assisting in other areas as needed. Any questions?"

"What about Baz?" JJ asked, her gaze concerned as she looked at Brantley.

"For the time being, he'll be solo or working with one of the teams. He's going to spearhead the social media scam for a while, so he'll have plenty to do."

Brantley could tell that hadn't eased her concerns, but for the moment, he couldn't relay more. With a baby on the way, Baz had requested to be held back. At least until he knew how things would work.

"Anyone else?" Brantley asked.

No one spoke up this time.

"Good. I'll let RT know I'm signin' off on the four new investigators, including Deck."

Brantley noticed JJ peering behind him, her expression going from pleasant to neutral in less than a second, and then she was making a beeline for the kitchen. Before he could glance at the monitor to see what had caught her attention, he heard the beep of the electronic keypad outside the door. A second later, Baz was walking in.

His expression was priceless when he glanced at all the faces staring at him, then down to his watch with a frown.

"I know I'm late," Baz muttered.

"That you are." Brantley gave a chin nod in greeting. "If you're not early, you're late."

Reese snorted. "That's not a rule."

"In the Teams it is," Brantley countered.

Baz strolled over to his desk. "What did I miss?"

"We were just finalizin' the new hires." Brantley took a sip of his coffee. "Any concerns?"

Baz looked around again, then his gaze settled on Brantley. "Depends. Anything different from what we discussed last night?"

"Nope."

"Then I'm good. We puttin' them to work today?" Baz asked.

"Depends," Reese remarked, echoing Baz as he turned to Luca. "Do we have cases lined up?"

"I've got several, yes," Luca confirmed. "I figured Baz can finalize them this mornin' so you can give 'em your approval."

Brantley shook his head. "Don't need my approval. I trust y'all to handle it." He pushed to his feet. "With that said, Reese and I have a conference call with the Sniper 1 team. Holler if you need anything."

He didn't wait for anyone to call him back, eager to get out of the building for a little while. They'd spent the majority of the week inside, discussing their potential candidates, doing interviews. Give him a mission of any kind and Brantley was all over it. Force him to do interviews and ... well, he'd rather shoot his own foot with his .45.

But he was fairly certain there was one thing worse than interviewing potential employees and that was conference calls.

REESE WAS THANKFUL THE CONFERENCE CALL SCHEDULED for this morning had only lasted half an hour. It had been slated for a full hour, but they'd been able to tie everything up quickly, ending the call with time to spare. Always a good thing considering Brantley's overall view of conference calls in general. Reese had tried to assure him they would lessen in frequency over time—at least he hoped—so they just had to endure until RT was comfortable they had everything they needed.

Reese knew the quick call contributed to Brantley's good mood. So far, their morning had gone better than expected, and because Brantley was smiling more, Reese knew there was one thing that would ensure it stuck around for a bit.

Well, two things really, but since they'd already indulged once today, he figured some time at the range would be a welcome interruption. And while the idea of some down and dirty sex was rather intriguing, Reese knew they wouldn't find the privacy necessary. Here at the house, there were too many people waiting for them, and unless they were going to get a hotel room or attempt to contort themselves in the truck, they had very few options. Plus, neither of those set the mood, no matter how spontaneous.

So sex was out of the question. For now.

He got up from his desk, walked across the open area to Brantley's office, leaning on the doorjamb.

"I've got a suggestion," he said, keeping his tone teasing.

"Yeah?" Brantley's eyes widened.

"Somethin' you love to do," he baited.

Brantley leaned back in his chair, smirked. "Oh, I do love to do you."

No matter how hard he tried, Reese couldn't keep his cheeks from heating. He should've been used to Brantley's sexual innuendo by now, but it still got him every time.

"Let's go to the range for an hour," he said, chuckling when Brantley's face fell.

"The range? Seriously?"

"Yes."

Brantley sighed heavily, and Reese couldn't help but smile to himself. He knew what Brantley was hoping for, and Reese had every intention of getting them both naked in the near future, but first things first. An hour at the shooting range would give Brantley time to center his focus, which would hopefully help him to deal with the new hires they would encounter later this afternoon. As far as Reese was concerned, everything flowed better when Brantley was centered, which was why he worked so hard to help out.

"Fine," Brantley finally stated, closing his laptop before rising from his chair. "But *after* the range…"

Reese chuckled.

Most definitely *after*.

An hour at the range turned into two, but it had been worth it. Not only did they get time with some paper targets, Reese also had the opportunity to talk to Matt Logan, the owner of the place. With so many new people on the task force, Reese had been hoping to get Matt on board with allowing them to block time each month for those who needed it, as well as implementing a contract for pricing that was fair for both Sniper 1, who would be footing the bill, as well as for Matt. To Reese's relief, Matt had been more than happy to oblige, assuring him they would have first dibs on the underground range and giving him a more than reasonable dollar amount.

"Where to now?" Brantley asked when they were once again back in the truck.

"Like it or not, we've got to make an appearance at HQ. You do have to make the official offers if you want to hire these people."

Brantley did not appear pleased by that.

In an effort to keep him in a decent mood, Reese added, "But I was thinkin' we'd invite them out tomorrow night. Moonshiners? Give us a chance to get to know 'em better."

Another sigh from Brantley, but this one wasn't quite as distraught. "Dinner. Our house."

Reese frowned. "What?"

"You cook."

Reese stared at Brantley as though he'd lost his mind because there was a good chance he had. "You want me to cook dinner for all of them? Tomorrow?"

"Why not? You're the one who wants to spend time with them. Plus, you've got a grill."

"The bar is more convenient," he countered.

"Our house is more ... personable."

"Yeah? And where do you suggest we seat them?" he asked, a subtle reminder they had yet to put a table in their dining room.

"We'll go shoppin' in the mornin'."

Reese barked a laugh. "You want to go shoppin'?"

"I like to shop."

"You do not."

Brantley smirked. "I like to shop with you."

"No, you don't," he stressed.

"But I will if you ask nicely."

Reese sighed, realizing he was the one who'd set this all in motion. Teach him to make suggestions again. A night at Moonshiners, a few beers, some laughs ... that was a far cry from him cooking dinner for the new task force.

But he would do it because Brantley had suggested it.

And he could only hope the lack of notice would have at least a few of them unable to make it.

CHAPTER THREE

Saturday, September 4, 2021

BRANTLEY HAD TO ADMIT, HE HADN'T EXPECTED Reese to pull off a get-together so quickly. He'd said it as a joke, trying to get a rise out of Reese. Instead, the man had agreed to a cookout for the entire task force.

Guy was a saint, that was for damn sure.

Then again, Brantley hadn't expected every single member—new and old—of the team to agree to dinner at their house. He'd honestly expected at least half of them to decline for one reason or another.

Nope. Even Decker Bromwell had driven down from Dallas specifically for this event.

And now their usually empty house—complete with what Reese referred to as a brand-new dining room suite—was full.

If Brantley was being honest, it wasn't as awkward as he'd expected it to be. Even now, as he sipped his beer and casually watched everyone interacting, there was what he would call a *relatively normal* vibe to the organized chaos.

Evan Vaughn was standing half in the kitchen, half in the living room, watching as his daughter, Sophia—who had turned eight last month—had an animated discussion with Rebecca Richter's seven-year-old daughter, Carly. From the instant the two girls had been introduced, they'd been chattering away about things only little girls understood.

Standing near the back door, Holly and Elana were laughing about something on Holly's phone. At the breakfast bar, Jay, Allison, and Charlie were deep in a discussion about some of their more exciting moments doing police work. On the back deck, Trey, Luca, and Slade were talking Reese's ear off while Reese manned the grill. In the yard, Tesha was keeping JJ busy throwing the ball, while JJ talked to Darius and Rebecca, a.k.a. Becs, about things only the geek squad was familiar with. And last but not least, Baz and Deck were sitting at the patio table, drinking beer and watching everything around them.

They'd gone from three members originally, then quickly to six, then on to nine, and now to sixteen in just under a year, and Brantley couldn't deny he was looking forward to seeing what they could accomplish. Last night, he'd called RT, updating him on the status. Brantley's boss had seemed relatively impressed that the team had come together so easily. Brantley wasn't sure *easily* was the right word, but it had come together, and in the coming weeks, as the newbies started to trickle in full time, they'd be off and running.

He figured it was too early in the relationships to determine whether or not this group would result in a cohesive unit. Only time would tell that, but if they were lucky, it would work itself out. He'd already picked up on a few distinct personality traits— Allison liked to believe she was in charge, Slade enjoyed the flirtatious banter that could very well cross a line if they weren't careful, and Becs was the mother hen. But Brantley knew all too well how those personality traits could give way to others as a group of people tossed together became a team.

"What exactly is an L-O-L, anyway?" Slade asked, stepping up beside Brantley.

Brantley took a swig of beer, frowned. "How the hell should I know?"

Slade nodded at the two little girls playing with palm-sized dolls with a dozen accessories scattered on the coffee table. "They said it. Not me."

Brantley couldn't even pretend to translate little-girl speak. He'd listened to them earlier and hadn't followed a single word. It was like being around his nieces, which was nice, but it always left him feeling a tad overwhelmed.

Slade stepped in front of him. "I wanted to say thanks, you know, for givin' me this opportunity."

"Wasn't nothin' given," he told the man. "They think you're a good fit for the team. Now it's up to you to prove yourself."

"I'll give it two hundred percent."

Brantley knew he would. Slade had been the one to approach him, taking a brief moment after Kylie's funeral to introduce himself and let Brantley know he was around if they needed anything at all. Although they'd grown up in the same small town, he didn't know Slade all that well. Since Slade was five years younger, they'd never run in the same circles but had interacted a time or two at various family functions considering his aunt Lorrie's family was as ingrained in Coyote Ridge as Brantley's own.

"Did you and Reese hang out when you were kids?" he inquired, realizing they were roughly the same age.

Slade's dark brown eyes shifted to the sliding glass doors and beyond. "He was a grade higher. I remember him, but we didn't hang out, no."

One never knew in this town.

"Hey, boss," Charlie called out. "Reese is looking for you."

Brantley excused himself to join Reese outside. He was then relegated to carrying in the food, put to work dishing it up, too. He should've known his man wouldn't let him sit back with his feet up. Not that he minded doing a favor for Reese.

After all, he had every intention of calling in that favor later tonight.

"Looks like you might have another mouth to feed," Evan informed him when he took a plate loaded down with French fries that Charlie had kindly cooked in the oven.

Brantley looked up, saw Magnus Storme talking to Reese on the back deck. Tesha had strolled over to him, clearly wanting to greet her trainer friend. Brantley watched as Trey took a few steps back, putting distance between them but never taking his eyes off Magnus. He recalled the conversation he'd had with Trey when his brother first showed interest in Magnus. He knew curiosity when he heard it, and his brother had certainly been curious about Magnus. The question was, why?

As he watched Trey watching Magnus, he thought back to New Year's at Moonshiners when Magnus had flirted ruthlessly with Trey. Had they…? Surely not. What could those two possibly have in common?

Brantley's thoughts dislodged when he noticed Jay Hernandez approaching.

"Hey, man, thanks for inviting me," the man said with a smile.

Brantley turned his attention to the newest of their analysts. "Next time you should bring the wife and kids."

Jay glanced over at the two little girls playing with their dolls. "I will, definitely. But my boys'll likely run roughshod over everybody."

"I've got a nephew," Brantley told him. "Plus, I've got three brothers. They can't do nothin' I ain't seen or done myself."

Jay smirked, a dimple forming in his clean-shaven cheek. "I might have to take that bet."

Brantley laughed, passed him a plate with a burger and fries.

He couldn't remember the last time he'd gotten together with a group of people who weren't his family. Back when he'd been in the Teams, no doubt. In those days, whenever they were stateside, they made a point to hang out. Wives, girlfriends, kids. Although Brantley had usually been the odd man out—no wife, no girlfriend, no kids—no one had given him shit about it. Not too much, anyway. It had been a good time all around.

As much as he missed those days, those people who'd been an extension of his family, this was his life now. These were his people.

His gaze swung to Reese, who was laughing at something Trey said.

Yes. This was his life now.

And to be honest, he wouldn't trade it for anything.

JJ LINGERED AT THE PARTY LONGER THAN she'd originally intended to.

Before they arrived, she and Baz had decided they would make an early night of it, go back to the apartment and watch a movie, have some popcorn. It had become their routine on the weekends. Friends enjoying one another's company. Usually, they had a good time unless Molly called and interrupted, which she did regularly. When that happened, JJ had no choice but to face reality and the fact that Baz was having a baby with the woman. Baz was going to be a father, something she knew he would excel at. And because he would dedicate his whole heart to his child, their friendship would become an afterthought.

"You okay over there?" Baz asked from the driver's seat of his truck.

JJ glanced his way. "Of course. Just thinkin' ... about the party."

No way would she tell him that she was once again thinking about Molly Ryan and how that woman had come along and derailed JJ's life entirely.

Not that Molly was at fault. Not even Baz. Everything that happened was because JJ had pushed Baz away for so long it finally took, and he went walking right into the arms of another woman. And then the universe had decided to pay JJ back for being so stubborn by impregnating Molly with Baz's baby.

Just the thought of Baz with another woman made her stomach churn.

"It was a nice party." Baz's voice was low in the quiet of the truck. "Better turnout than I expected."

"Yep," she said absently, staring out the window.

"Talk to me," Baz urged. "What's wrong?"

She forced a smile, looked his way. "Nothin'. Really."

"I can tell you're not thinkin' about the party."

When he reached over and his fingers brushed her wrist, JJ didn't pull away. Instead, she slid her arm closer, allowed Baz to link his fingers with hers. It was something he'd been doing as of late, touching her like that. Sweet gestures here and there, something to solidify what was transpiring between them.

Not that they'd picked up where they'd left off last year, but they had found their way back to a point that was comfortable for her. They still had separate bedrooms, but from time to time, JJ would find her way into his bed, and Baz always welcomed her with open arms. The sex between them was off the charts, even if it wasn't nearly as consistent as she would've preferred.

But it always circled back to Molly and the fact that Baz was no longer JJ's for the taking. He had other commitments, ones that were far bigger than a relationship with JJ.

JJ rubbed her chest over her heart. Even thinking about it hurt.

For the longest time, JJ had tried to convince herself that Molly was lying, that her erratic behavior was of a woman who was hiding something. Unfortunately, that hadn't been the case, and Baz had finally confirmed for himself that she was in fact pregnant. Very pregnant by the time he was able to get past her constant avoidance. And now they were counting down the last five weeks before the baby was born.

Pretty soon, JJ would have to move out of Baz's apartment, find a house of her own again. She no longer had any excuses because the insurance had come through; she'd gotten a check to cover the value of the house after it burned to the ground. She'd even gotten a check for the SUV that had been a casualty as well. However, she had managed to put off getting a place and even another vehicle because she had come to rely on Baz to be there for her. They both pretended not to notice that JJ was terrified to be alone, but it was the truth. She wasn't sure she could stay somewhere by herself, but she wouldn't know until she tried.

"You still wanna watch a movie?" Baz asked as he was pulling into the apartment complex, winding his way around to his building.

"I think I'm gonna call it a night," she said, staring out the window once more. "I'm tired."

"Okay."

Just like every time, Baz didn't push, didn't encourage her to spend time with him. He was always there to support her, never asking for more than she was willing to give.

And that in itself saddened her more than anything.

Two hours later, JJ was still tossing and turning in her bed, unable to fall asleep. When she'd gotten inside, she'd gone straight to her bedroom. She'd washed her face and taken a shower, then pulled on one of the oversized T-shirts she slept in. This one was Baz's, a Guns N' Roses one she'd snagged out of the laundry when he wasn't looking. When she closed her eyes, she immediately saw images of Baz and the baby he would soon have. It had pained her to the point she couldn't close her eyes any longer, so she'd settled for staring at the ceiling fan, counting backward from one hundred. She'd done that five times.

Now here she was, staring at the crack beneath the bedroom door. She could see a light flicker every so often, knew Baz was in the living room with the television on. If she had to guess, he had fallen asleep with the remote in his hand. Knowing him, he would've showered, then emerged from his room wearing only a pair of shorts, his muscular chest bare. Thinking about his chest gave way to thoughts of other parts of him, leading to rapid breathing and more irritation.

Before she could talk herself out of it, JJ swung her legs off the bed, pushed to her feet. She padded across the room, out the door, down the short hall, and came to a stop when she saw him exactly as she'd expected. His long, lean body, clad only in a pair of athletic shorts, was laid out on the couch, his legs crossed at the ankles, bare feet propped up on the arm. He had the remote in his hand, resting on his chiseled stomach, his head cocked at an unnatural angle. The lights had been turned off with the exception of the flicker of the television, but it was enough for her to see him clearly.

It would've been best for both of them if she could've turned around and gone back to bed, pretended she wasn't attracted to this man on an intrinsic level, that she didn't want him with every breath she took. They wouldn't be able to do this for much longer, so it made sense that she would cut it off now, find a way to have a friendship with him since he would be otherwise entangled with Molly for at least the next eighteen years.

But she didn't turn around, and when she took a step closer, she obviously made a sound, because Baz's eyes opened slowly, his gaze lingering on her as she approached.

His smile was genuine, as was his reaction when he set the remote on the floor before opening his arms to welcome her down to him.

Without thinking, JJ settled over him, her chest to his, her knees straddling his hips. Her lips found his in a dance they'd been doing for months now. Baz allowed her to lead in the beginning, giving her the option of setting the pace. And when things heated up, when the sexual tension between them became a conflagration, he took over, flipping their positions so that she was beneath him, his knee settled between her thighs.

"JJ," he whispered against her mouth. "God, JJ."

She knew how he felt, knew that this was what they both needed. This connection was undeniable, albeit unsustainable. And it seemed the closer and closer they got to Baz becoming a father, JJ wanted him more and more. She wanted to sate this urge so that when they separated indefinitely, she wouldn't be left with the cold, lonely ache that she had when she wasn't with him.

Baz shoved her T-shirt up to her neck, his hand cupping her breast, kneading firmly, roughly until she was writhing beneath him, grinding herself on his steely thigh, begging him for more. He finally offered more when he pulled her panties down her legs, tossing them behind him before he shouldered his way between her thighs, his tongue finding her wet, aching center. Baz worked her like only he could, bringing her to the pinnacle, forcing her to drop back down before taking her higher again.

Only when she came, only when she screamed his name and clawed his back did he move over her, settling between her thighs and driving into her in one deliciously punishing thrust. There were no barriers separating them anymore. They'd stopped using condoms months ago, promising that for as long as this went on, they wouldn't be with anyone else. JJ had welcomed the closeness, relying on birth control to keep them from going down a path neither of them was ready for.

"JJ," Baz moaned, thrusting his hips, driving deep inside her. "Baby…"

JJ held on, her nails clawing down his back because she couldn't seem to get close enough. She stared up into his face, and he pushed up on his hands, shifting the angle, the penetration, as she wrapped her legs around his hips and let him take them both right up to that razor-sharp edge and then over the cliff into erotic ecstasy.

Neither of them whispered the three words that would change their lives forever, but they hung there between them.

Unspoken.

Never spoken.

CHAPTER FOUR

Monday, September 6, 2021

A STRONG STORM ROLLED IN SOMETIME DURING the night, waking Reese in the early-morning hours.

The man beside him tossed and muttered, trapped somewhere in his mind. Reese knew all too well what Brantley was enduring because he had his own nightmares, some of them growing more intense in recent months.

"Brantley," Reese whispered, placing a firm hand on Brantley's chest, trying to soothe but not crowd.

He knew better. If he didn't want to get a fist to the face or strong hands wrapped tightly around his throat, he had to give the man space and time to emerge from the terror that gripped him in his dreams. The nightmares Brantley suffered, the ones spurred by storms, were usually violent, more so than even the ones Reese succumbed to on occasion.

He kept on, nudging Brantley, urging him to wake up until he was all but shouting.

Tesha came to investigate, leaping up onto the bed, sitting on Reese's feet, keeping a safe distance from the action.

"Brantley, it's a dream." He brushed a hand over Brantley's shorn hair. "Wake up. I've got you."

Suddenly, the thrashing and groaning stopped, leaving the room eerily silent, only Brantley's harsh breaths surrounding them.

Reese didn't move, didn't lean in. He knew all too well how disconcerting the nightmares could be. He'd had his fair share this past year. Ever since he'd found those women locked in that windowless room, chained to beds, trapped in a living hell, he'd been reminded of his own hell. The months he'd spent caged in a six-by-six concrete tomb partially buried beneath the ground, believing that would eventually be his coffin. He could still hear the grating sound of the generator as it powered the camp. He could sometimes smell the food they'd cooked but refused to share.

Lying there in the dark, Reese refused to go back there. He reached over, touched Brantley's arm, grounding them both for the moment. They were safe. Here, together, they were safe.

And when Brantley turned to him in the dark, Reese clung to him, letting their bodies take over, driving out the fear, the anger, the *secrets* from so long ago, replaced with an emotion he knew was stronger than all that, one he refused to let go of. In the dark, he loved Brantley, accepted his love in return. And when they used passion to burn off the residual fear, Reese held on to him, once again reminding them both they were safe.

When dawn arrived, Reese dragged himself out of bed. He never knew what to expect from Brantley after one of those nightmares. This morning, he seemed calm, relaxed. Almost too much so.

Reese didn't press, didn't urge him to talk. It was an understanding they had between them. They'd suffered their own individual hells, and one day they'd share, but until then, they gave each other space. But not too much.

A ten-mile run, showers, and breakfast went a long way to bringing order to chaos. They didn't say much as they went through the motions, but the silence wasn't oppressive. No, this morning it was necessary.

And by the time they headed over to the barn, things were returning to normal.

Well, normal was relative, he figured.

The entire team was slated to come in this morning. Even a couple of new people were starting today. The arrangement they had, at least for the time being, was that as long as there wasn't a pressing case, they would have the weekends off. Reese figured that would likely change once they were running at full speed, and they'd have to take downtime when they could. At the moment, they were still attempting to build their client list, working with Sniper 1 Security to establish a reputation for the task force dedicated to finding missing people. Because it was a new venture for the established security firm, it was taking time.

Trey was already there looking bright-eyed and bushy-tailed. Too bright-eyed. Too bushy-tailed. Reese remembered the man who'd come to work for the task force. In the beginning, Trey had been quiet, reclusive almost, borderline depressed. These days he was opening up, taking charge, and proving he was a damn good investigator. In fact, he was quickly becoming the best of them since he was the one who had closed the most cold cases—seven to date.

"Becs and Slade are startin' today," Brantley reminded Trey when they joined him in the barn. "Need to make sure they've got all the access they need."

"Elana's already workin' on it," Trey replied. "And I got a confirmation date from Evan. His official start date'll be the thirteenth, although he said he'll make himself available if we need him."

Reese knew Evan had given notice, but with active cases underway, they'd figured it would take a few weeks to get him over here. The same with Jay and Darius, both having to give their employers notice. However, JJ suspected Darius would be showing up sooner rather than later, since his employer would likely invoke the confidentiality clause, letting him go rather than risk him learning more and potentially leaking information. According to her, that was standard practice in roles such as his.

So Jay, Darius, and Evan were to start next week, then Allison the week after. That only left Deck early next month. As long as everything worked out, they'd be fully functional by the beginning of October. That was definitely good news as far as Reese was concerned. He hated being in limbo, knew Brantley did, too. Getting the team focused was their next priority, and the sooner the better.

Reese glanced over at the fancy electronic board RT had supplied them with, saw the screen was open to the list of investigators. Dates had been added. Had Trey done that? Or had JJ updated it yesterday?

His attention shifted to the television screen mounted on the wall showing the security camera. Luca Switzer was rolling in now wearing what might just be a brand-new pair of Levi's. The work boots on his feet weren't new, rather worn and weathered, as was the ball cap with the rounded brim. Reese wouldn't go so far as to say Luca was a good-looking man, but there was something about him. Charisma and charm, maybe. Whatever it was, his dark blue eyes always glittered with mischief, and a smile generally announced his arrival.

Aside from his reputation as the good ol' boy popular with the ladies, Reese didn't know Luca all that well, though he'd seen him around Coyote Ridge. Like Reese, the man was born and raised here. His family even had a small farm on the outskirts of town. From what Reese had heard, Luca was estranged from his father, the two of them usually butting heads in town whenever they ran into one another. Since father and son were both very vocal and equally hot-headed, he figured their encounters were like throwing gasoline on a fire.

"Howdy," Luca greeted, smiling down at Trey as he passed.

"Mornin'," Brantley said in return. "Grab some coffee, take a seat. When everyone gets here, we'll get caught up for the mornin'."

Luca nodded, eyed everyone speculatively, then headed to the kitchen.

Not five minutes later, JJ and Baz walked in, together but not together.

There was something different about them this morning, Reese realized.

"Mornin'," Baz said with a smile, this one actually reaching his eyes.

Definitely something different.

Reese nodded his greeting at the same time Luca said, "Y'all had sex."

Brantley chuckled, Trey snorted, and JJ turned an interesting shade of red.

"Sorry," Luca added with a shit-eating grin. "Not my business."

"You're right," JJ declared. "It's not."

He took her snippy remark in stride, grabbing an extra chair and pulling it over, straddling it while resting an arm on the back.

"Grab coffee if you need it," Brantley instructed. "Then pull up a chair."

"Can I put my stuff down first?" JJ muttered, heading for the stairs.

Reese took a sip from his mug, glancing at those surrounding him. He smiled to himself.

Never knew what to expect around this place, but one thing was for sure. It was never dull.

HALF AN HOUR LATER, ONCE THE TEAM had trickled in, Brantley watched as they interacted with one another.

There were some familiar responses taking place: JJ and Baz glancing at one another every so often, Trey keeping his head down, hoping no one noticed him. Charlie, smiling as she interacted with Elana, both women seemingly happy to be here. Then there were the new interactions: Slade, ever the sly one, winking at Holly and making the young woman blush, Luca talking nonstop, Becs somehow managing to keep up with him.

It was interesting to say the least, but Brantley was eager to start tackling cold cases, not sit around chatting like this was a book club.

He cleared his throat, gave everyone a moment to finish their sentences and turn their attention to him.

"I know it's gonna take some time for the newbies to settle in, but we've still got work to do. While each team will take its share of cold cases, there's one case I want everyone to pitch in on whenever you have spare time." He glanced over at Baz. "Where are we with the social media investigation?"

"Not much further than we were," Baz answered, glancing at all the faces watching him. "Back in November, we worked with a Houston detective to locate a missing teenager," he explained. "The case ended up not being related to this social media scam, but the detective thought it might be. He brought us up to speed on a group, or groups, of people who're utilizing social media to insert themselves into virtual communities by joining online forums used by neighbors, parents, teachers to get together and help each other."

JJ continued when he paused to take a breath. "A lot of people tend to overshare on social media, and these are scammers who're capitalizing on it. You've got people pretendin' to be your neighbor, offerin' to help out in any way so they can get close. Whether it's so they can steal from you or whatever. But the biggest problem lies with the ones who've set their sights on kidnappin' kids."

Becs looked like she was going to lose her breakfast. "You mean, they're gaining trust, offering to help, and then…"

"Exactly that," Baz confirmed. "There've been a couple of attempts across the nation, starting with one in Washington State. The news is spreading, but not nearly fast enough."

"And it's difficult to know who's the potential scammer and who's legit," JJ inserted. "I mean, why wouldn't you believe Cindy Smiles-a-lot isn't who she says she is? You've interacted with her for a few months, read stories about her kids, about their school, about their sports, now you're in a bind and she offers to pick up your kid. So why not?"

"That's when they take the kid," Baz added. "Luckily, the one time they knew it happened, they were able to get the boy back quickly and unharmed. However, since we've started looking into it, there've been numerous reports of failed attempts. They're getting bolder, moving faster."

"And this is somethin' we're actively pursuing?" Slade asked, looking cool and confident as he peered over at Brantley.

"Yes. Because we cover missing persons, and if we want to prevent them in this instance, we need to tackle the underlyin' problem."

"Makes sense."

"Nothin' will ever be enough as long as someone's missin' or murdered, but we'll contribute," Reese added. "If a specialized unit comes in and tells us to cease our efforts, fine. We'll pass over what we have and they can deal with it. Until then, we'll do what we can."

Brantley nodded for Baz to continue.

"JJ and I have created some anonymous profiles and identified active community groups across the state," he informed everyone.

"You said this is nationwide?" Becs inquired.

"Correct. But at the moment, we're not, so we have to start somewhere. Our resources are limited, so we focus where we can."

Brantley nodded to JJ, so she picked up with, "With Luca's help, we're monitoring these groups on the back end. I'd like to add more, watch more closely—"

"I can help with that," Holly offered, her voice somber, expression, too. "Whatever way I can."

"That'd be great," Baz told her.

"It'll certainly help, but what we need are people who can follow up on them," JJ noted. "Once we've identified questionable activity, we need to be loggin' into the groups, doin' deep dives into the people who are offerin' to help." JJ was quick to add, "Yes, we might violate some privacy, but it's for the greater good. If we can verify they're real and they have a right to be engagin' in such a manner, we'll back off."

"Everyone will pitch in," Brantley decided. "JJ, you can work up a schedule so we can log some hours monitoring."

JJ nodded. "Will do."

He glanced around the room. "If you find somethin', you'll let Baz and JJ know. They can determine at that point who and how it'll be handled. Charlie, you'll work with Baz to help with some of the footwork." Brantley looked at Baz. "If she needs someone with her, you'll go."

"Not a problem," Baz agreed.

"As for everyone else, I want us focused on the few cold cases we've kept." He looked around the room. "And if anyone needs anything, just holler. We'll do what we can to help out."

"Also, once you get settled in here"—Reese motioned around the space—"you can determine what setup works best. Rearrange as needed."

Brantley watched the new hires' reactions, attempting to gauge them.

He liked that they had a diverse group of people, and he was curious to see how it played out.

Later that afternoon, Brantley found himself back at HQ. Not because he particularly cared to be but because all those diverse people he'd hired? Well, they were now in a tizzy—Reese's word—over how they were going to set up the barn.

He got the feeling it had occurred because Allison Bogart had surprised them today, coming in shortly after their morning meeting to let them know she was ready and able to work, having been released from her temporary position she'd been in. While he got the feeling Allison was going to be a tremendous asset to the team in the long run, he realized she was going to be the point of contention in the beginning. Starting with the layout of the barn.

Truth was, Brantley didn't give two shits what they did, where they sat, but he did not want to hear bitching and moaning about furniture placement when they had far more important things to deal with.

He stood beside Baz, both of them hovering near the exit while Reese, brave and foolish man that he was, decided to step forward.

Across the room, Slade looked up, watched with what appeared to be curious amusement as Reese headed into the fray.

"There's a reason I never wanted to work in an office," Baz muttered at his side.

Brantley knew the feeling.

When Baz's phone rang, he cursed but did what any smart man would do. He stepped outside to answer, leaving Brantley to fend for himself.

Brantley ventured over to Slade's desk, perched on the edge, and watched along with the other man. "You ever see anything like it?"

"My office has been my car for most of my adult life," Slade noted, glancing up at him.

"Fair enough."

Slade laughed. "But no, I haven't."

For some reason—God only knew what—Becs and Allison were snipping at one another, arms flailing in an animated fashion. Something about a desk, a corner, not enough light.

Brantley watched as Reese walked right up to the group, barked a couple of commands for them to shut up, and managed to get every single person's attention without having to raise his voice too much.

No reason to deny it, the man was fucking hot, and Brantley's body stirred at the sight. He'd known from the beginning that Reese was a complex man. While he appeared to be laid-back, non-confrontational, and all that, beneath was a steely reserve most would never see.

He watched, fascinated as Reese took control, laid out options, and waited for the others to get on board.

They did.

"It might be wise to keep him here for a while," Slade muttered with a chuckle.

"Or better yet, wiser if all of us were out in the field."

"Good point."

The ruckus started to build again, drawing Brantley's attention. While he didn't mind watching Reese work, there was only so much he could handle. Rather than wait for Reese to rein it in again, he raised his fingers to his lips and whistled. The high-pitched noise cut right through the arguments and debates, all eyes shifting to him.

"When I come back in tomorrow mornin'," he told them as he stood tall, "I expect this shit to be worked out. If it's not, I'll make the seating arrangements, and trust me, you won't like it."

He heard Slade chuckling behind him as he headed for the door.

CHAPTER FIVE

Tuesday, September 7, 2021

WHEN BRANTLEY OPENED HIS EYES ON TUESDAY morning, he didn't immediately get out of bed. He remained just as he was, on his back, listening to the sounds of the house. Reese was breathing heavily beside him, the ceiling fan turning overhead. Other than that, he didn't hear much of anything, and he realized he'd gotten used to the quiet, to the calm.

He liked it, actually.

He honest-to-God liked where he was at in his life. Reese living with him, sharing his bed every night. Them working together.

Sure, he missed his days in the Teams, but he suspected that would always be the case. Brantley hadn't left because he wanted to, but he was adapting to the curveball life had thrown him.

Of course, his brain instantly replayed the argument in the barn yesterday...

Okay, so he wouldn't be able to take the quiet for granted since it wasn't a guarantee, but at least he could enjoy it at home. Work would always be a different story.

"What's on your mind?" a soft, rumbling voice sounded beside him.

"Just enjoyin' the solitude for a minute."

"Mmm." Reese moved closer, his hand sliding down Brantley's stomach, inching lower.

Oh, yeah. This was something else he was coming to enjoy immensely, too.

Brantley gave a growl of encouragement, urging Reese to keep going even as Brantley tossed the comforter away.

When Reese's long fingers circled his cock, Brantley groaned softly, relaxing into the mattress as a sensual heat replaced the quiet comfort of the morning.

"Fuck, that feels good," he whispered, pumping his hips, gently fucking Reese's hand, creating more friction.

Admittedly, he loved when Reese woke up like this, although these encounters had lessened in recent months. As of late, Reese seemed distracted, secretive almost. There were times Brantley would catch him looking at his phone only to hurriedly tuck it away if Brantley came near. He figured it was his own insecurities getting the best of him, so Brantley had opted not to bring it up. The last thing he wanted to do was to jinx what they had, especially since the rough edges seemed to be smoothing out the longer they were together.

Reese's hand tightened on his shaft, stroking firmly.

Brantley focused his full attention on the hand job, letting the sensations build within him, the electrical energy that ignited in his spine growing brighter, hotter until he couldn't refrain any longer. He jerked his hips, meeting the urgent grip of Reese's palm until the release barreled through him, dragging a ragged growl from his chest.

When he was replete, he grinned over at Reese. "That's one helluva way to wake up."

"It is, isn't it?"

"Maybe if you're good, I'll repay the favor in the shower."

"On your knees," Reese added with a grunt.

Brantley grinned.

Oh, yeah. He definitely liked Reese like this in the morning.

Two hours later, after a ten-mile run, an equally energetic encounter in the shower, and a breakfast of oatmeal and fruit—during which Brantley bitched the entire time—they joined the team in the barn.

Baz and JJ were already there, seemingly cozy in the kitchen, making coffee.

When they saw there were others there, they pulled apart quickly, as though they'd been caught doing something they shouldn't.

"Got a secret to share?" Brantley probed, curious as to what was going on.

"What?" JJ stepped back. "No secrets. Why would you say that?"

Brantley frowned, watching his best friend as she retreated completely. When he looked back at Baz, he got a shrug for an answer.

"I will never understand women," Brantley muttered when Baz slipped out, leaving him to pour his coffee.

When he returned to the main area, he saw Reese was walking around the new desk arrangement. Brantley had no idea what he could possibly be looking for, but he figured the man had some sort of motivation.

The door opened, and more people strolled in, filling the desks, their conversations beginning to energize the space. He decided not to intrude, so he told Reese he had things to do and headed over to his office in the house.

It was true, he did have things to do. Turned out, working for a large corporation like Sniper 1 resulted in paperwork and shit Brantley could've done without. However, he was trying to remain in RT's good graces because he knew there would come a time when his boss would frown on his decisions, so he was starting the give-and-take early.

After all, perception was key.

BY MIDMORNING, REESE WAS GRATEFUL FOR THE ten-mile run and the endorphins that heated round in the shower produced. It had gone a long way to ensuring he didn't lose his temper, something that would've surely happened when he walked into the barn to find Allison and Becs still bitching about their seating arrangement.

Funny thing was, they both wanted the same thing, but they couldn't stop talking long enough to realize it. Instead, they were snapping back and forth, both attempting to make their point at the top of their lungs, neither of them backing down.

Since they'd aligned the teams so that Allison and Becs would be working together, he figured now was a good time to switch things up. At least until they got the lay of the land and learned to deal with one another rather than shout and scold, something that was disrupting the workflow for everyone.

He noticed Trey and Holly had their heads together in the corner, reviewing the cold case Trey had been working on for the past few weeks. Charlie had taken to hiding out upstairs with JJ and Elana, reviewing the details of some report JJ was building for their weekly meeting. Baz and Luca had escaped completely, settling into Reese's office over in the house to discuss the social media investigation. And Slade was doing his best to be invisible while working in the conference room with the door shut.

That left Allison and Becs and this stupid fucking argument. Rather than let it go on all damn day, which no doubt it would, Reese walked over to the women, cleared his throat.

Allison and Becs immediately shut up, heads jerking toward him.

He waited patiently, cocking an eyebrow to see if they wanted to explain.

"It's not what it looks like," Allison said quickly.

Becs's eyebrows lifted, her disbelief evident.

It was exactly what it looked like, Reese knew.

"I'm sorry," Becs said. "We're—"

"I'm switchin' up the teams," Reese announced. "Becs, you'll move to work with Trey and Evan startin' next week when Evan comes on board. I'll have Darius work with Charlie and Deck." He looked at the conference room, then back to Allison. "Jay will work with you and Slade."

"You don't have——"

He cut Allison off. "Already done. Trust me when I say, Brantley won't hesitate to fire every last damn one of you." He pinned a hard stare at Allison before she opened her mouth. "And he can, I assure you. He's got the full support of his management team."

She clamped her mouth shut, but he could tell she still wanted to argue.

"So what do you say we get on with it?"

When he looked at Becs, she nodded. "Yes, sir. Of course."

Grateful no one had anything more to add, Reese headed for the door. He caught sight of JJ out of the corner of his eye. She was standing at the top of the stairs. When their eyes met, she gave one slight nod, clearly in agreement.

He only hoped Brantley didn't hear about this. Otherwise…

Later that afternoon, after Reese had convinced Brantley to go with him to pick up some office supplies JJ had ordered, Reese considered talking Brantley into a late lunch/early dinner just so they could avoid going back to the barn for a while. He had no idea how things were going now, but he had no desire to find out. As much as he wanted this task force to succeed, he had to admit it was significantly easier when it was smaller.

"What's on your mind, Tavoularis?"

Reese grinned. Why he found it amusing that Brantley called him that, he had no idea.

"Nothin'."

"I heard about the showdown at the OK Corral this mornin'."

Of course he had.

"It's all under control."

"I heard that, too."

"Let me guess, you've got a mole in there? Already?"

"I wouldn't call JJ a mole, but…" Brantley shot a smile his direction. "If it's any consolation, she was impressed with how you handled it."

Yeah, well. This was just the beginning. Only time would tell how it all played out.

CHAPTER SIX

One week later
Tuesday, September 14, 2021

THE PAST WEEK HAD BEEN A BLUR for Reese. Too much to do, so little time to do it seemed to be the sum of his entire existence these days.

Along with taking Tesha to two training sessions and having Magnus stop in for another, Reese had spent a vast majority of his weekend, as well as all day yesterday, working with Baz and JJ to outline a process for those coming on board. Since they seemed to have conflicting personalities in their ranks, Reese was bound and determined to align things in a manner that reduced the friction. Sure, he'd made an impromptu change already, but who was to say that would work out in the long run?

So he'd opted to work on plan B. While he knew Brantley would follow their lead, proceed however they chose, Reese wanted to ensure their plan had merit. The tasks they assigned the new members needed to add, not detract; therefore, he'd wrangled JJ and Baz to help him.

Now that the entire team was in the office, with the exception of Deck, who wouldn't be starting for a couple more weeks, Reese wanted to implement their plan.

"Mornin'," JJ greeted, strolling into the barn just shy of eight.

"Mornin'," he replied from where he stood in front of the expensive electronic board that took the place of their just-as-functional whiteboard, drinking his coffee and reviewing the list.

"Hidin' out from Brantley this mornin'?" she asked, setting her laptop bag down on an empty desk and sauntering over.

"Just wanted to get a final look before they get here."

"You have any concerns?"

"Not a one," he admitted. "Which is probably my biggest concern."

JJ chuckled. "Just keep in mind, they've got a vast skill set among them. I'm sure we'll start knockin' these cases out left and right."

Reese wasn't sure that was the case, although he wished it were true. The one thing he knew about cold cases: they were cold for a reason. He didn't question the skills of the original detectives who'd chased every lead they could only to come up empty. All the cases he'd reviewed had been thoroughly worked and regretfully set aside because there were no more leads to pursue. So unless they were dealing with a serial killer disguising himself as a detective in order to stall the investigations—as had been the case in Dallas—they would be putting in the work to move these along.

Movement on the screen above him caught his eye. Reese looked up to see Trey, Evan, and Charlie walking in together. As they neared the barn, he saw Brantley step out of the house, following them.

He had to force himself not to think about how he and Brantley had spent what little spare time they'd had over the past few days. It had involved very little clothing and a hell of a lot of distraction. Reese honestly hadn't thought much of it until last night, when he'd gone into Brantley's office to grab something off the printer only to see that Brantley had been doing a search on his computer. A search that involved the Adorites. The article had mentioned the Southern Boy Mafia, but most notably, it had mentioned Madison, Reese's former girlfriend.

And here he'd thought they had moved past that. He probably should've known better. Brantley could be like a dog with a bone at times.

Then again, Reese hadn't exactly been honest with Brantley these past few months. He'd engaged in a few text exchanges with Madison ever since she reached out to him back in March. Despite the fact they were innocent in nature, Reese knew better than to share that with Brantley. The last thing he wanted was to create a problem where there wasn't one.

But seeing the article had explained Brantley's odd behavior these past few months. He'd seemed oddly introspective, claiming this was their new normal and going out of his way to convince Reese, or maybe just himself, that he was content with it. Not to mention Brantley's insane ability to use sex as a distraction. The man was good like that, always coming up with something to do that didn't involve much talking.

Needless to say, it had bothered him, but Reese had proved he wasn't much better. Rather than address the issue, he'd pretended he hadn't discovered Brantley's research.

A round of good mornings sounded from the group entering the barn, allowing Reese to refocus his attention on the team.

"I'm happy to say, we are fully staffed as of this mornin'," JJ announced. "Well, with the exception of Deck, of course."

Reese's attention shifted to Brantley, saw the way his eyes instantly searched the room until they found him. It relaxed some of the tension that had been building since he saw that article. In fact, that simple move—the seeking him out—was what made Reese feel connected to the man. Had since that first day their eyes met when he'd been overwhelmed by a sensation that had been both foreign and unexpected.

"I was just tellin' everybody that we'll have a full house today," JJ told Brantley.

"Good."

"Why good?" Reese asked, hearing something foreboding in his tone.

"Because we've got a case."

All conversation died instantly, all eyes shifting to Brantley.

"I don't have much yet," Brantley said, nodding toward the conference room.

Reese followed the others into the space JJ had converted into a room big enough they would all fit, along with a conference table and some fancy computer system.

Brantley passed his phone to Reese. "I need you to set up the call so we can get audio and video in here."

"Who're we callin'?" Reese asked, glancing at the phone screen.

"The governor."

Well, hell.

Reese connected the phone's Bluetooth to the audio/video system then showed Brantley what he needed to do. While he worked on that, Elana delivered coffee to everyone as they began taking seats at the table. Because he was already finding it difficult to breathe in the confined space, Reese chose to stand near the door, a few feet behind Brantley.

Brantley remained standing when the phone started to ring. A second later, the governor's face appeared on the television screen, his voice coming in stereo on the fancy phone system.

"Good morning," Governor Gerard Greenwood said, looking grim.

"Mornin', Governor. We're all here," Brantley told him.

Reese noticed his tone held a hint of frustration. Probably residual runoff after being disbanded by the man who now needed their assistance.

"First, let me say thank you for making your team available to assist with this," the governor said politely.

"What've you got for us, Governor?" Brantley replied, his tone curt.

No doubt about it. Brantley still held a grudge.

"This is not the way I like to start my day," the governor said, his eyes shifting, as though he was looking at each face on his screen. "I received a call this morning from a very concerned friend of my wife's. Evidently, their top-level executives are being picked off—two of them found last week, their deaths ruled as suspicious. The third did not show up for work today."

"Sir, bein' that it's just after oh-eight-hundred, how late to work is this person?" Reese inquired when no one else spoke up.

"According to his secretary, he comes in promptly at six every day."

"But not today?"

"No." The governor's expression remained bleak. "And because his partners' deaths were ruled suspicious, I have a bad feeling about this one. Hence the reason I'm calling. I need you to look into this. ASAP."

"Of course. Do you have any information you can send us?"

"Rhonda's working on that," the governor confirmed. "JJ should have it shortly. At this time, we've got two different departments looking into both the deaths and the missing person. I want your team to take point."

"You understand our services aren't free, Governor?" Brantley countered, still hot.

"I understand. At this point, I don't give a damn. I just want him found. And I want him found alive."

"We'll do our best," Reese said when Brantley didn't speak up.

"Keep me updated, Brantley."

Brantley nodded, and the call disconnected.

"Still bitter, boss?" JJ muttered as she got up from her chair.

"I'll get my computer," Reese announced, grateful Brantley didn't take the bait. The last thing they needed was a heated discussion about how the governor had used them only to abuse them later.

As far as Reese was concerned, they needed to let bygones be bygones. Under the umbrella of Sniper 1 Security, the new setup was something that would work for them. It gave them more leeway, albeit without the immunity and means.

"You bringin' that back in here?" JJ called from the conference room.

Reese shook his head but didn't look back.

While he understood JJ's reasons behind creating a room that would allow them to work as a team, he couldn't bring himself to stay in there, and he doubted he'd ever be able to. He'd had a similar reaction to the small office used by Walker Demolition. He knew his behavior was attributed to being confined to a six-by-six concrete cell with no way out and only a sliver of a window that was too high up for him to see out of easily. Eighteen months in that hellhole, believing he'd been left for dead by his own country, Reese had damn near lost all hope. And to this day, confined spaces caused his heart to race.

"You all right?" Brantley asked, placing a hand on his shoulder when he joined Reese at the spare desk Reese had commandeered as his own.

"Fine."

Based on the way Brantley was watching him, Reese didn't think he believed him, but for now, he accepted it. Probably because they had more important things to deal with.

After all, they were now working alongside a ticking clock, and time, no matter how endless it seemed, was quickly running out.

BRANTLEY DIDN'T HOVER, BUT HE KEPT AN eye on Reese as the team got situated at their desks while Holly got the computer hooked up to the wall monitor. Although Reese hadn't out and out told him about his claustrophobia, Brantley had picked up on it. He knew it was difficult for Reese to be in confined spaces, and the smaller the space, the worse it was for him.

"I just got the information from Rhonda," JJ was saying as she came down the stairs, her attention on the iPad in her hand.

He shot one more look at Reese, saw he was pulling himself together, so he opted to move forward.

"I hope everyone's ready to work today because this is what we do," Brantley informed them as he waited for the information to be projected on the monitor.

Elana was already at the project screen, pulling up a whiteboard page so she could start taking notes.

Brantley glanced at JJ when she looked up after skimming her iPad. "What do we have?"

"Very little," she said. "But I do have a phone number for the detective assigned to the homicides."

"Call him," Brantley commanded, grabbing his coffee mug.

Elana shifted gears, removing the whiteboard from the screen and pulling up the phone system.

While JJ and Elana prepped for the video call, Brantley scanned the room, taking in his current team. He liked the size of this crew, he decided. Four teams in total, with Baz being an extra to move around as they needed, while JJ and Luca formed a fifth, handling their share of tasks from behind a computer screen. In times like this, it would allow them to span out, divide and conquer, if you would.

"Detective Mathis," JJ said into the phone receiver, "I'm going to engage video conferencing. I've got Brantley Walker, along with his task force, here with me."

He couldn't hear what the detective said to that, but a minute later, a stout redhead with unruly hair, skeptical green eyes, and a beard that hadn't seen a razor in quite some time appeared on the large monitor hanging on the wall. He did not seem impressed by the interruption to his morning.

"Detective," Brantley greeted. "I'm Brantley Walker with the Off the Books Task Force."

Detective Mathis's gaze scanned the faces behind Brantley, but he didn't respond.

Brantley continued. "We received a call from Governor Greenwood this mornin' regardin' a missin' person who may or may not be connected to two homicides you're currently workin'."

Although the detective's pale face remained passive, Brantley noticed something shift in his eyes. He didn't appreciate someone stepping on his toes, as Brantley was no doubt doing now. Brantley understood the feeling all too well, and if he had it in him to care about someone else's feelings, he might've apologized. Unfortunately, that would get them no closer to finding the missing person; therefore, he would refrain from doing so.

"Can you bring us up to speed?" Brantley requested, doing his best to phrase it as a question rather than a demand.

The man on the screen didn't say anything, nor did it appear he was going to, so Brantley decided to nudge him along.

All social niceties escaped him as frustration filled him. "Mathis, the governor's hired my team to look into this case; therefore, I expect your cooperation. I'm not here to step on your toes, but I will if I have to. Give me details, Detective. Start with who and when."

"Has this been run past my chief?" Mathis asked, pinning Brantley with a hard stare.

"Your politics are not my concern," he admitted, just as a picture of another man appeared to the right of the video screen. Name, age, and address appeared beneath. "Right now, my only objective is to find Cedric Hawkins. From the details I've got, he's a fifty-seven-year-old male who lives in Lakeway. I assume you've been notified that he's missin' since he's associated with your dead bodies?"

Detective Mathis's eyes shifted, a look of frustrated resignation coming over him. "Yes. We were notified a short time ago by Austin police."

Brantley glanced over at JJ, nodded, urging her to start digging into Cedric Hawkins's life.

Before he turned back to the screen, Reese stepped over to join him, taking over the conversation.

"Why do you believe Cedric Hawkins is missin', Detective?"

"And you are?"

"Reese Tavoularis. Brantley's partner. Why do you believe he's missin'?"

Mathis's gaze bounced between them before finally settling on Reese as though it was a shun to Brantley.

"Personally, I don't, but his secretary seems to," Mathis stated. "Like I said, APD notified me that they received a call saying Hawkins did not come into his place of employment this morning, and they are unable to locate him. Since I've got two open cases for partners at his firm, they thought it might be connected."

"I doubt it's coincidence," Brantley told him.

"I'm sure it's not, no."

"But you don't believe he's missin'?" Brantley asked. "So what? You think he's dead?"

"I can't make that assumption at this time," the detective responded with the hint of a snarl.

From the screen, Mathis continued to watch him, and Brantley waited patiently.

"Fine," the detective finally said. "You want to take these cases, you take 'em."

"I'm not lookin' to take your cases, Detective. I don't work homicides, nor do I care to. I'm interested in findin' Mr. Hawkins, if he is in fact missin', and right now, I'm goin' on the assumption he is. However, if you're not interested in being a contributing member of this team, I'll certainly do what's necessary to solve it."

That didn't go over well, sparks seeming to ignite in Mathis's gaze.

Reese took over. "Detective, if you don't mind, we do need to focus our efforts right now. The clock is tickin'."

More information about Cedric Hawkins appeared on the screen, fed from JJ's computer.

Reese didn't even pause to read, continuing to address the detective. "Based on what little we have, this does not sound like a random or even run-of-the-mill missing person. If it was, we're certain you and APD could handle it on your own. However, you're already workin' two homicides that are possibly related. We're here to help with Cedric Hawkins's disappearance so you can focus your energies where they're needed most."

"And," Brantley added, "as we all know, time is of the essence. So stop wastin' ours and give us the lowdown so we can help."

"I think it'd be best if you come here," the detective stated.

Brantley saw JJ shaking her head. She mouthed, "An hour away," as her reasoning.

"We're an hour from you, and from what I understand, Mr. Hawkins was reported missing in Austin. I'm not interested in loggin' miles unless it's necessary." He stood tall, hardened his expression. "Stop with the excuses, Mathis. I've got a team behind me who'll start diggin' into the information as soon as you provide it, and I assure you, we've got more resources than you do."

The detective exhaled heavily, and Brantley saw the moment he decided to give in, albeit reluctantly based on the gritted teeth.

"Cedric Hawkins. Fifty-seven years old, married, three grown children. His secretary reported him missing as of seven o'clock, one hour past the time he was supposed to show up for work."

"An hour isn't a long time," Reese stated. "Could it be he had a meetin' somewhere? Maybe stopped off for breakfast?"

"Anything's possible, Mr.... uh..."

"Just call me Reese. Please."

"It's possible Mr. Hawkins is otherwise engaged, but there's a big possibility this could be related to two homicides we're working on, and until we can rule that out, we're treating it as a high priority, as we've informed APD."

"How do they connect?" Brantley asked.

"Like our two dead guys, Mr. Hawkins is a partner in HJW Investments. They're a private investment group, officed in downtown Austin."

Information about HJW Investments appeared on the other half of the screen, with an address in Austin.

"If HJW's located in Austin, how'd these cases come to you?"

"The vics are residents here, as well as members of the Lone Star Country Club."

JJ's fingers flew over the keys, likely looking for details on the country club.

"Were their bodies found at their residences?"

"One was, yes. The other at the country club."

"And HJW Investments?" Reese asked. "You believe their deaths are related to the company?"

"Considering their recent dealings, it's a good possibility," the detective stated.

Now they were getting somewhere.

"I've heard of 'em," Reese said, glancing over at Brantley. "Big company buyin' up a lot of real estate and flippin' it to commercial." Reese turned to the monitor again. "And the dead guys? Who're they?"

"Brian Wright and Seth Jacobs, the *other* partners."

Brantley spoke up. "When were they killed?"

"Last week. Our medical examiner puts Brian Wright's death around eight thirty p.m. on September seventh at his home. Call came in from Annie Hawkins from Wright's residence. And Seth Jacobs"—the pause was followed by the sound of rustling paper as Mathis glanced down—"was found on Friday the tenth in the locker room at the country club, but the time of death is determined to be two days prior."

Killed on consecutive days?

Curious as to why he was reading this information, Brantley asked, "Were you the detective assigned to these cases?"

"Initially, no. I just took over today."

"So you weren't at the crime scenes."

"I was not, no."

Brantley wanted to know more, wanted to know why they'd passed the buck on two hot cases so quickly, but he didn't get a chance before Reese pushed forward.

"There were no witnesses in either case?"

"None. Mrs. Wright had been out with friends when she came home to find her husband on the kitchen floor. I'll get you the crime scene photos."

"And Seth Jacobs?"

"I'll provide what I have on him as well."

"Any suspects?"

"Oh, you know, just a few ... hundred."

"Hundred?" Brantley grunted.

"HJW Investments recently purchased roughly two hundred seventy-five acres here in Lakeway to, as they claimed at the time, build a small master-planned community. However, once the sale was final, they revealed they had plans to develop a high-density office, retail, and residential center."

"Like the Domain?" Reese asked.

"Exactly like it," Baz said from behind them. "One of those fancy shoppin' venues that has both residential and office space built above the retail stores. They've got the details on their website."

"Problem is," Mathis continued, "the area's made up of multimillion-dollar homes and a private country club."

"Same club they belong to?" Reese asked.

"Correct."

"I take it those members weren't too happy about office and retail space encroachin' on their fancy digs?" Brantley glanced at Reese. "Can't say I blame 'em."

"Not only the country club members," the detective replied. "Also the residents, as well as the former owners of the land. They feel like they were duped."

"When did the deal close?" Reese asked while JJ's fingers flew over the keys on her laptop, clearly taking notes.

"June fourth. They're set to break ground early next year."

"Three and a half months ago?" Brantley wasn't sure that tied well enough. Quite a lag. If someone wanted the partners dead because they were upset by the deal, probably would've made a move sooner. Back when tensions were highest. "Why do you think their deaths are related to the sale?"

"It's only one of the things that tie them together," Mathis said. "We're pursuing other leads, but nothing's popped yet."

"It makes sense in a way," Reese mused. "What better way to stop the project than kill off the men who now own the property?"

"That's definitely motive," Detective Mathis said, agreeing with Reese.

Brantley shot a look at Baz. "I want more about this company. Who'll take control if all partners are eliminated?"

Baz nodded, turned toward his computer.

"Did you speak to Cedric Hawkins after his partners turned up dead?" Reese asked.

Mathis nodded. "Based on the notes, we did, yes."

We, not *I*. Brantley wasn't sure what help Mathis would be since he didn't seem to be up to speed on the case.

"Did he think it was related to the sale?"

"No, he didn't. He said they'd had some communications with the country club and some of the other local businesses. They were smoothing things out."

"Doesn't mean someone wasn't still pissed," Brantley told him.

"True. We haven't ruled anyone out completely."

"Any suspects? I mean, specific ones? Not the general public," Reese inquired.

"Have you looked into those closest to them?" Brantley asked. "Spouses?"

"As usual, we look at the spouse first. The wives have solid alibis, as do Seth Jacobs's grown children. Now we're looking into those who've made threats, but that's taking time."

"There were a lot?"

"Dozens. Emails, letters, phone calls. Like I said, there were quite a few people upset by the reveal."

"And Hawkins?" Brantley asked. "Were you lookin' into him for the deaths of his partners?"

"Again, based on the notes, yes. Seemed logical since he was the last man standing. Couldn't find anything to tie him. Not on the surface, anyway."

"Was he worried he'd be next?"

Mathis was still skimming whatever was in front of him. "He didn't seem to be, no."

"You said his secretary called it in," Reese stated. "Have you spoken to his wife yet?"

"I've got a patrol unit heading to her house now."

"A patrol unit?" Brantley frowned. "Any reason you're not out poundin' pavement?"

"As I told you, Mr. Walker, I just took over these cases this morning. And right now, we can't say for sure he's missing."

"You said you're treatin' this as high priority. Since when do you get a pass on doin' the legwork?"

Reese stepped forward. "Detective, we'll keep you looped in, and we expect the same in return. If you learn anything, contact Brantley or me."

The detective's eyes were narrowed, his anger evident. Brantley didn't much care that he'd pissed the guy off. He didn't believe in passing the buck, and this was one Mathis should've been dealing with personally.

He left Reese and JJ to end the call, turning to face the rest of the team.

"Our priority is to find Cedric Hawkins," he informed them. "And we will not stop until we do."

CHAPTER SEVEN

REESE KNEW BY BRANTLEY'S TONE THAT HE was serious. They would be focused on this case until Cedric Hawkins was located. And while he fully understood Brantley's frustration with the detective, he knew they couldn't risk stepping on toes when it came to working with law enforcement. Which was why he would make an effort to smooth things over with Detective Mathis by keeping him in the loop.

"We're gonna need all investigators in the field for this," Brantley added. "If you're not up to it now, I need to know."

A chorus of agreements came from everyone, with the exception of Allison Bogart. She seemed to be the holdout, but Reese watched until she finally nodded, giving in.

Reese wasn't sure what to make of her yet, but he was doing his best to be impartial. Having been in the military, he was intimately familiar with the chain of command, and it wasn't always easy to deal with those who believed it should be set up differently. For him, it wasn't negotiable, but he didn't think Allison was completely on board with that method. Despite the fact she'd been in law enforcement, which had its own rigorous chain of command, she seemed to enjoy going up against ... well, everyone, really. Unfortunately, there'd only be so many times she could do that before Brantley snapped.

Reese didn't want to be around when that happened.

"How do you want the teams set up since we're still down one?" Brantley asked him.

Reese was surprised by the question, but he'd already given it some thought, so he answered easily. "Trey, you'll team up with Evan. Baz, I want you to work with Allison, and Charlie, you'll take Slade."

Brantley turned to JJ. "JJ, you and Luca will be at the controls. We'll look to you for additional information as you get it. I want to know everything there is to know about the company, the partners, their wives, kids. Plus, I want to know why the Lakeway PD passed these cases from one detective to another so quickly. There's a reason there."

"Will do."

Reese picked up as though they'd planned it when Brantley looked at him. He wasn't sure how it was they worked so well together, but it did seem to be the case.

"Our focus is finding Cedric Hawkins, but I believe, to do that, it'll help to get some background on the two suspicious deaths. Trey, you and Evan reach out to Detective Mathis. Find out where the dead bodies are, then head to the morgue, talk to the medical examiner."

Trey's eyes were wide when he said, "The … ah … morgue?"

"You can handle it," Brantley told him, his tone both mocking and assuring at the same time.

Trey looked a bit green at the idea but nodded in agreement.

"Give us two minutes," JJ told Trey. "We'll have that information so you can let the detective brood for a bit before we piss him off more."

Reese continued. "Baz, you and Allison need to go to the investment company, talk to the secretary and anyone else who last saw Hawkins. I also want you talkin' to secretaries or assistants to the other two partners. See if you can talk to any chatty employees. I'm sure someone's got some input on the matter. We need as much information as we can get."

Baz nodded.

"Charlie, you and Slade can head to the country club. I'm not sure how far you'll get, but question anyone who's there. Find out who saw Hawkins last, what he was doin', and if they know where he might be. Also, Mathis mentioned Jacobs's body was found in the locker room. Sweet-talk 'em into showin' you around, get a feel for what might've happened there."

"And if they refuse?" Charlie asked.

"We're not law enforcement," Brantley noted. "We don't have any jurisdiction. However, you can let 'em know the family hired us, see if that'll get you through the doors."

"Sounds like a plan," Charlie said.

Reese scanned the room. "Brantley and I will go to Hawkins's house, talk to the wife."

Brantley took over. "JJ, start by findin' out where Hawkins's vehicle is. Get contact information for his kids; the detective said he has three. Scan his social media, see if he's interactin' with anyone we should talk to. Friends, girlfriends, whatever."

"You're assuming he's having an affair?" Allison asked, her tone accusatory.

Reese considered commenting, but he left it to Brantley.

"I'm not assumin' anything. Right now, I'm tryin' to find a missin' man. *Someone* knows where he is."

"What if he just wanted to get away? Took a vacation?"

"Is that what you want us to go on?" Brantley countered. "That he's hidin' out by himself? Thought to tell no one? Not his wife, not his employees?"

"It's possible," she argued. "I don't think it's wise to automatically assume he's havin' an affair."

Reese was stunned. Why was she so tripped up by this?

Whatever the reason, he was grateful he wasn't the one facing off with Brantley right now.

Allison continued as though she was the sole defense for the victim. "For all we know, he's a pillar of the community. I don't think it's fair to doubt his fidelity."

To his surprise, Brantley didn't say anything more on the subject. Whether it was because he was at a loss for words the way Reese was or because he was trying to temper his response. Either way, Reese was happy the debate was coming to a close.

"I'll loop everyone in as I get information," JJ announced, drawing all attention to her.

"Let's get out there and find this guy," Brantley barked. "We're wastin' time."

Reese whistled for Tesha to follow, then headed out behind Brantley, doing his best to be optimistic.

STILL TRYING TO PROCESS THE ARGUMENT THAT had just transpired, Baz waited for Allison to gather her things before leading the way out to his truck.

She didn't speak for the first few minutes of the drive and for that he was grateful. Especially since she seemed to be fuming, breathing through her nose as though attempting to rein herself in. For the life of him, he couldn't figure out why she'd gotten so heated by the subject, and he'd seen the same bewildered looks on Brantley's and Reese's faces.

They'd just hit the open highway, heading to meet with the employees of HJW Investments, when she sighed heavily, said, "Is Brantley always like that?"

Baz cut a quick look her way, turned back to the road. "Like what?"

"So ... I don't know..." She sighed again. "I'm not even sure what the word is."

He opted to fill in for her. "Assertive? Determined? Blunt?"

She looked over at him, her blue eyes glittering with what looked like frustration.

Baz didn't know the first thing about Allison Bogart, aside from what he'd learned during the interview process. She had been assigned to the special victims unit out of Dallas for the past decade, didn't have a problem talking herself up, and from what she'd told him, she deserved all the credit she'd been given and then some. To put it simply, she was proud of her accomplishments and wanted everyone to know it.

That was the extent of it, though. He wasn't sure if a personal entanglement spurred her response to this situation or if she merely enjoyed playing devil's advocate.

"Those weren't the words I was thinking," she said with a huff. "More along the lines of ... angry and mean."

Wow. He hadn't picked that up from Brantley at all.

While Baz thought Allison could be successful in this unit if she gave it a chance, he still wondered what Brantley saw in her that everyone else hadn't. The consensus for her had been she was too confrontational, too eager to be in charge, yet Brantley had wanted to give her a chance, and Reese had backed him up. Baz didn't have anything against her, but he would admit he hadn't been all that keen on partnering with her today.

"I still can't believe the way he talked to that detective," Allison bitched. "It was like he was railroading him. Doesn't he know this man has cases to handle? Real cases. Homicides. I'm sure he's got more than two, but to hear Brantley talk to him, the guy sits on his thumbs all day."

Baz didn't see it that way, but he'd also had the pleasure of working with Brantley for nearly a year now. The man was blunt, straightforward, and he got the job done. It was that simple.

"And did you hear Reese? He's going on the assumption this guy's got a girlfriend."

"He doesn't?" Baz asked, cutting his gaze to her briefly.

"I have no idea."

"But you're going on the assumption he doesn't."

"I am not."

He cocked an eyebrow, looked back to the road.

"Fine. I might've jumped the gun on that one, but he did, too. He reminds me of a drill sergeant."

"You were in the military?"

Allison exhaled heavily. "No. But I've——"

"Brantley's a Navy SEAL," he told her, interrupting. "He's been a leader long enough to know there's no time to waste when it comes to this. And Reese was in the Air Force. They're used to a certain structure, and they lean on that to get things done."

"I understand that."

"Do you?"

Allison frowned. "What does that mean?"

Baz shrugged. "I'm just askin'. From what I've read about you, you're used to playing the waiting game."

"It's not necessarily waiting," she countered. "More like strategic planning. Because that's how you draw out predators."

"Understood. But we're not waiting for a predator to make a move here. We're hoping to find a man while he's still breathing."

"How do you know he's not dead already?"

"We don't. But if you were relying on someone to find you, would you want us to think along those lines?"

She didn't respond, but Baz had meant it in the rhetorical sense, anyway. He wasn't sure why this woman had a chip on her shoulder, nor was he even sure what had put it there, but based on what he'd seen thus far, Allison Bogart moved through life on the defense.

"So what should I have said?" she asked after a few moments of silence.

"Well, I've learned that *yes, boss* works wonders."

Her eyebrows darted down. "That's not how I operate. When I have something to say, I say it."

"Which isn't necessarily a bad thing, Allison. No one's saying it is. But think back on what you said. More importantly, think back on *why* you said it. Where did it get the case? If it's not constructive, is it worth speaking aloud? We're not here to prove whether Cedric Hawkins is having an affair or not. In the grand scheme of things, it doesn't matter. What does is that we figure out who saw him last and where he might be now."

"He's gonna fire me, isn't he?"

"One thing I know about Brantley, he doesn't make rash decisions. And he doesn't mind opposition, so no, I don't think he'll fire you."

Not yet, at least.

She exhaled heavily, and Baz wondered if that was relief he heard.

Allison peered over at him. "What did you do before you came to work for the task force?"

"I was a detective with APD. I met him and Reese when a case I was working intersected with theirs."

"Let me guess, Brantley took over."

"He did."

"Doesn't surprise me."

Her haughty tone had him going on the defense. "Why? Because it was personal for Brantley? Because the governor's daughter was missing, and Greenwood personally called him to help out?"

Her eyes were wide when she peered over at him. "I didn't know that."

"And again, you assumed." Baz sighed, turned his attention back to the road. "I'm not sure what it is you hope to gain from working on this task force, but might I suggest you think on it long and hard before you get in too deep?"

While he didn't want to pass judgment, Baz couldn't help but think Allison was in this for the wrong reasons. He only hoped she figured it out before she did something they might all regret.

THE DRIVE FROM HQ WAS QUIET.

Too quiet as far as Trey was concerned, but he hadn't known what, if anything, he should say to Evan, so he'd kept his mouth shut.

Not an easy feat considering the drive from Coyote Ridge to Lakeway was mapped to be close to an hour.

Thankfully, with the toll road, Trey had made good time, shortening it by ten minutes. He figured that was because of the mind-bending silence and the fact he'd kept his foot on the gas the entire way.

"You ever been out this way?" Evan prompted when the scenery shifted, Mansfield Dam denoting their location, a sign they were nearing their destination.

"Nope," Trey admitted. "Never had a reason to."

"Lake Travis might be a good enough reason," Evan said, staring out the window at the expansive blue water.

"Never been much of a fisherman," he admitted.

"Me, neither." Evan looked over at him. "I settled in Round Rock because it wasn't Austin, but it seemed central to a lot of things."

"It is now. It's all grown up over the years. Coyote Ridge used to be in the middle of nowhere."

There was a small chuckle from Evan as he leaned back in his seat, stared out the window again. "How do you want to handle this? I figured you could take point, and I'll follow your lead."

Trey shook his head. "I wouldn't suggest doin' that. Half the time, I don't know where I'm goin' or what I'm doin'."

"You're obviously doing something right," Evan noted. "You've closed the most cold cases of the entire task force. That's no small feat."

"Who told you that?"

Evan grinned. "Charlie did. The day I interviewed with her. She seems quite impressed by you."

"Nothing else to do," he said, not wanting the praise.

"I looked into one of them. Your cold cases, that is."

Trey's head jerked, eyes shifting to his passenger as he pulled to a stop at a red light.

Evan shrugged. "I was curious. Charlie mentioned a case out of Round Rock. I wanted to know what it was."

Great. He was one of those nosy cops who couldn't leave well enough alone.

"Husband reported his wife missing," Evan explained. "Said she went out with friends one night, never came home."

Oh, hell. He knew exactly which one Evan was referring to.

"Ex-husband," Trey corrected. "But yeah."

Trey remembered it well. When he'd come across it, something about it had struck him as odd. He had pored over it for nearly two weeks when Baz urged him to follow up with the ex-husband.

He glanced at Evan, saw he was waiting for more, so Trey told him. "Because they'd recently gone through a bitter divorce, the police chalked it up to her wanting to get away from him."

"I saw the report. Ex said their marriage had been good right up until she started cheating."

"That's what he claimed," Trey stated. "I didn't buy it."

"No?" Evan shifted, facing him more fully. "Why's that?"

"Just a feelin'." He shook his head, kept his foot on the gas as he weaved between thicker traffic. "I know that's not proof, but…"

"Sometimes it's all you have," Evan said. "Tell me. What's the feeling you got?"

"I couldn't get past the ex-husband's statement. According to him, he'd had a fight with her the night before she disappeared. Said they were arguin' because she was becomin' a recluse, missin' out on life. He suggested she meet new people, urged her to go out with some friends. Conveniently she does what he asks but never comes home."

"Sounds relatively straightforward."

"Yep. All tied up in a perfect little bow. Plus, he covered his tracks pretty well," Trey admitted. "Her credit card was used at a gas station leadin' outta town, another at a fast-food restaurant off the highway a couple of hours away. Meshed with his story that one of her lovers lived in Florida."

"It didn't jibe for you?"

"Not after I read the statement of a couple of her co-workers. Said she was workin' hard to move on, gettin' on with her life, goin' out more."

"The opposite of reclusive?"

"Exactly." Trey focused on the road. "She had just joined an online datin' site when she went missin'. Had been chattin' with a couple of guys."

"Did you talk to either of them?" Evan asked.

"I did. Both said she was friendly online, but she was cautious, so they hadn't yet met in person." Trey sighed. "One said they were plannin' to have coffee the next Sunday."

"I didn't make it that far in the case files," Evan said. "Sorry. She never made it to the coffee date?"

"No." Trey still remembered talking to the ex-husband, seeing that bastard's smug face. The woman hadn't changed her will at the time of her death, so everything she'd had was left to him. The house, the cars. All of it.

Since Evan had read the file, he knew that Trey had tugged on a line leading all the way back to a construction site the ex had been working at when the woman went missing, which just so happened to still be under construction. A construction site that ended up being the burial ground of the ex-wife. The police were able to tie it back to him because of DNA. The fucker had been careless, believing no one would ever find the body because he'd done his due diligence to show she was missing, not dead.

"Sounds to me like you've got some damn good instincts," Evan said now.

Trey wasn't sure about that. Half the time, he felt as though he had no idea which way was up.

"So, CHARLIE ... THIS THING WITH YOU AND my cousin ... it serious?"

Charlotte Miller glanced over at the man in the passenger seat, smiled as she turned her attention back to the road. "You realize we're on the job, right?"

"Technically, we're drivin'," Slade countered in that slow drawl that she suspected the ladies swooned for.

"You're relentless, you know that?"

Slade chuckled, and Charlie decided she liked his laugh as much as she liked his laid-back, country-boy demeanor. It hadn't been until Kylie Walker's death earlier in the year that Charlie had been introduced to many of her girlfriend's family members, including Autumn's cousin Slade. One of Aunt Rose's six kids, she'd been told.

Having come from a small family—an only child with only two cousins—it had taken Charlie a little while to get used to being around so many people. More so to be immersed in a small town that was just as meddlesome as it was welcoming, but Coyote Ridge was growing on her.

As was Autumn's family. The one thing she'd noticed about them, they were very similar in manner: strong, smart, resilient, determined. Much like Autumn herself. They were traits Charlie admired in a person. But what always caught her off guard was their innate ability to poke their nose into her personal business. Worse, because of that country charm, she found herself telling far more than she ever intended.

"So that's a yes?" Slade teased.

"I like her all right," she teased back.

"She's smitten with you, you know?"

Yeah, she knew. And she was equally smitten with the woman. Had been from the very moment they met, which in itself was something Charlie had never experienced before. She'd dated plenty of women over the years, enjoyed their company just fine, but never had she met one who made her heart flutter the way Autumn did.

Unfortunately, their fast and furious beginning had slowed significantly in recent months. First because of Kylie Walker's tragic death and the impact it had on the entire community, then because of Charlie's personal responsibilities. With her mother's deteriorating mental health, Charlie found she didn't have much time to dedicate to anyone else. Thankfully, Autumn seemed to understand, and their relationship was proving to be strong enough to weather the storms.

"Fine," Slade said with another gruff chuckle. "I'll leave it be."

"Thank you."

"While we're at work," he clarified. "When I see you at family get-togethers, I'll be givin' you shit."

Of that she had no doubt. The Jameson clan was a close bunch, very similar to the Walkers from what she could tell. It only made sense that the two families had merged at one point when Autumn's aunt Lorrie had married Curtis Walker.

"Tell me, Slade, what made you want to apply for this job?" she asked as she pulled off the toll road and continued on toward the country club.

"Kylie Walker," he said simply. "Her death and the actions surrounding it made me want to get involved."

Charlie understood that. Being that the task force had spent six months searching for Juliet Prince with no luck, Charlie knew that, had anything gone differently, Kylie might've still been there with them. Instead, she'd been taken from this world far too soon, leaving behind five young children and two husbands. Every member of the task force felt responsible, still beating themselves up over the what-ifs.

"How long've you been a bounty hunter?" Charlie still remembered being surprised when she'd seen that on the resume she'd been given. "And is it a lucrative job?"

"Six years now," he said, his gaze on the buildings they passed. "Got into it because a buddy of mine asked for some help. Figured what the hell, why not?" He barked a laugh. "And no, I don't do it for the money."

"But you like it?"

"I love it."

"So why do this?"

"A change, I guess." His tone shifted, going darker than before. "I think it's just time for a change."

Because they'd agreed to keep things business at work, Charlie decided against pressing him for details. No doubt there was something that had him rethinking his life. From what she knew, he was only thirty-one, just a year older than she was. He was also single, having been married and divorced when he was in his early twenties. She didn't know the story behind it, but Autumn had mentioned it when they were talking about their family and friends who'd married and then divorced. Charlie still didn't know how they'd gotten on that topic. Then again, they talked about pretty much anything and everything, something she adored about the woman. There was nothing off-limits for Autumn, and Charlie appreciated that.

"How do you wanna handle this?" Slade asked when Charlie stopped at one of the many red lights that dotted this stretch of road.

"Honestly?"

He peered over at her. "Yeah."

"Well, I think you should use that good-ol'-boy charm."

His eyebrows popped. "That right?"

"Yes. I think it'll put people at ease. You're easy to talk to; maybe it'll get them to open up."

"And while I'm doin' that, what'll you be doin'?"

"I figure I'll talk to the club's manager, see if I can get a feel for how well he knew Mr. Hawkins. I have to believe this is a tight-knit community, one that considers itself a class of its own. I'd like to find out whether or not Mr. Hawkins was in a relationship with someone other than his wife."

"Without makin' a harsh accusation, right?"

Charlie grinned. "Of course."

"All right then. Now that we've got a plan, let's get'r done."

She couldn't help it, she laughed.

And yes, Slade Elliott definitely had a way of putting people at ease. After all, he'd done exactly that with her. Those nerves she'd had when she first left HQ ... nowhere to be found.

CHAPTER EIGHT

WHEN BRANTLEY SET OUT FROM HQ, HE'D intended to go directly to Cedric Hawkins's house but opted to make a brief detour at the last second.

"You sure this is a good idea?" Reese asked from the passenger seat.

"Good, bad, or otherwise, I think it's necessary."

"You're just gonna piss him off."

Sure, Brantley figured making a formal, in-person introduction to Detective Mathis might not go over well, but he didn't much give a damn how his appearance at the police station affected anyone. At the moment, his only concern was the welfare of Cedric Hawkins, and it was crucial they had all eyes on this case if there was any chance they'd find the man alive. If he wasn't dead already.

Had it not been for the shifting of detectives on the homicide cases, Brantley would've left it alone, but now he was far too curious as to why they were mixing things up at a crucial time.

"It'll just take a minute," he assured Reese, pulling up to the small building that housed Lakeway's police department.

"Just promise me you won't end up behind bars," Reese grumbled. "This case is fucked up enough already."

Brantley chuckled as he got out of the truck, waited for Reese and Tesha to join him. "I'll do my best."

When Brantley stepped inside the air-conditioned space, he couldn't help but think back to their last major case, to the detective who had turned out to be a serial killer with multiple identities. Even now, all these months later, it had him questioning everything he saw, everything he knew. It hadn't taken them long to figure it out, but at the same time, it had taken *too* long. One of the women Detective John Collins was holding prisoner had died because they hadn't figured it out quickly enough.

There hadn't been a day that passed when Brantley hadn't thought about it. About what he could've done differently, should've done differently. There were always what-ifs, and he was plagued with them, not just with that case, either. At the same time, he knew he couldn't let it skew his thoughts on the present. This was a new mission, with new players. It would have a different outcome, and if he and his team were doing their jobs correctly, they wouldn't lose anyone else.

His thoughts instantly shifted to Kylie, to the loss they were all still mourning. That tragedy forever changed the Walker family, and deep down, Brantley still blamed himself. Always would.

"We're here to see Detective Mathis," Reese told the young man sitting behind a counter, a badge pinned to his uniform.

The officer picked up the phone, called someone.

While he waited, Brantley cleared his throat and forced the thoughts of their losses back. It wasn't the time or place for reflection.

A minute later, he turned his attention to the pale-skinned redhead in the nicely tailored suit strolling toward them.

"I'm Maurice Mathis," the man offered, holding out a hand and looking at them as though he'd never seen them before. "How can I help you?"

Interesting reaction.

Brantley shook his hand. "Brantley Walker," he said easily.

Recognition dawned as the detective's chin rose slightly, perhaps an attempt to hide his delayed reaction. "Then you must be Reese," he said firmly, holding out his hand to Reese.

"This is Tesha," Reese stated when Mathis glanced down at the dog. "She's in training."

Reese had been reiterating that fact wherever they went. They'd even gotten Tesha a harness that denoted she was in training and for no one to pet her. According to Magnus, when she was on assignment, she needed to remain in the zone, which meant no one petting her. No one besides Reese, that was. That man and that dog … Brantley figured it was only a matter of time before he'd be looking for a new partner, his slot filled by a canine.

Detective Mathis nodded. "Understood. Right this way."

He led them through a maze of desks toward a conference room at the back. As he followed, Brantley took it all in, finding himself amused by the decor. It was a bit more upscale than what he would've expected for a cop shop, but then again, he knew that Lakeway was where the rich went to idly spend their days on the lake or the golf course. At least, that was the impression those who'd lived around the area were given growing up.

Detective Mathis led them into a conference room equipped with a rolling glass board that reflected several pictures categorized by victims and suspects and some chicken scratch depicting theories and questions.

The detective waved a hand at the board. "I'm in the process of outlining the cases now. Like I said, I just got them this morning, and it's clear the ball was dropped."

"Is there a reason for that?" Reese asked, looking over the details on the board.

"Above my pay grade, I'm afraid."

Which meant he wouldn't be sharing that information, even if he had it.

"Please have a seat," Detective Mathis said, motioning toward the conference table.

"Thanks, but we'd rather stand," Brantley said, not waiting for Reese to respond. "I prefer to run my investigations independently."

"What he means is, he prefers not to skew his perspective with other people's theories," Reese clarified, clearly playing the nice guy. "But we'll do our part to ensure you're kept in the loop. We just came by to formally introduce ourselves, offer our assistance if you need it."

Brantley could tell the detective wasn't exactly impressed by their assertiveness, or their desire to maintain distance. However, this method was working for them, and until it failed him, Brantley had no intention of changing.

"Were your officers able to speak to Mrs. Hawkins?"

"Unfortunately, no." The detective looked disappointed. "Mrs. Hawkins's lawyer has advised us that any questions we might have should go through him. I had them ask her to come down here, but the lawyer politely"—he used air quotes— "refused. And until I have reason to believe she might have information, I have no grounds to bring her in."

Brantley considered this, then nodded. "Then we'll go speak to Mrs. Hawkins directly."

Reese added, "We've got two investigators heading to the investment group's office to speak to the secretary who called it in."

Brantley turned to leave. As he was walking away, he heard the detective's response: "I'm not sure they'll give you much, if anything at all. We've had a couple of conversations with their public liaison, and he hasn't been helpful."

"Anyone else find it interesting that they're hidin' behind lawyers when a man's life could hang in the balance?" Brantley muttered, not caring that no one heard him.

He didn't bother waiting for Reese, knowing the man would smooth the waters with the detective. Reese was good at that, maintaining balance and not ruffling feathers. It was just one of the many things Brantley loved about him.

While Reese did that, Brantley stepped out of the building, dialed JJ's number.

"Yes, boss?"

"Got anything?"

"We're diggin' in now. Trey and Evan just got to the ME's office. Allison and Baz are at the investment company."

"Have them talk to the secretary who reported Cedric Hawkins missing," he instructed. "It looks as though the wife's erected a wall of lawyers. We're gonna have to get creative to get information."

"I like creative," she said with a soft laugh. "And I'll let them know."

"We're gonna head to the Hawkins's residence," he informed her as he walked to his truck, then stopped in front of it. "See if we can sweet-talk our way into a conversation with the wife."

"If anyone can do it, you can."

Actually, Brantley knew Reese was the sweet-talker between them. He had the softer edges where Brantley's were still rough and unrefined. They made a damn good team because of it.

"Hold on a minute, boss," JJ said.

With the phone on speaker, Brantley glanced up to see Reese and Tesha strolling out of the building. Before joining him, Reese made a detour to a grassy area, clearly giving Tesha time to do her business.

"JJ's got me on hold," he explained when Reese looked confused as to the mumbling on the other end of the phone.

They listened while JJ and Luca spoke in what sounded like a different language. Of course, he was fairly certain it was English, but perhaps it was in code. A computer hacker code of some sort. Hell, they were using words he'd never heard before, all pertaining to information they were digging for online.

"You understand a word they're sayin'?"

"Not a one," Reese said with an amused grunt.

"Maybe you could loop us laypeople in, JJ. Translate, please," Brantley suggested, hating to break up their little party.

Okay, he didn't hate it.

Not even a little.

"Basically," Luca began, "we've learned that the only things the members of the country club have more of than money are secrets." He laughed. "And maybe exes. Let's just say, the sanctity of marriage is lost on these people. And I'm only halfway through the membership roster."

Brantley rolled his eyes. "Anyone hidin' their second job as murder-for-hire? Or maybe have a hobby of kidnappin'?"

"Not yet. But it's still early."

Technically, it was no longer early, but Brantley didn't bother to relay that detail. He had missed breakfast, and they were quickly moving toward lunchtime, and he was beginning to feel it. Food was definitely on the agenda for the very near future.

"I've been lookin' into some of the hate mail we ... uh ... *found* on the HJW servers," JJ informed him, "and there are definitely some people who're pissed off about the retail/office space."

"Anyone more so than others?"

"I was lookin' at that initially, but I've shifted directions." She took a breath. "I know Trey and Evan are gonna do more diggin', but we got the ME's findings from the autopsies on the dead guys. I'm not an expert on medical coding, but it doesn't sound like a passionate crime to me. One was suffocated, the other poisoned."

"What does passion have to do with anything?" Luca asked.

"If someone's driven to kill because of a retail store goin' in, and they were angry about it, you'd think it would show some sort of emotion behind it," Brantley informed him. "Gun, knife. In the moment. Not premeditated."

"Ah. Got it. Crime of passion."

"And it makes more sense to assume that the more I read," JJ went on. "These people aren't writin' love notes, that's for sure. Their frustration comes off the page."

Luca's voice came through the speaker. "You don't think suffocation's a crime of passion? Seems a little up close and personal to me."

"Agree," JJ stated. "But it's also intimate."

That had Brantley curious. "Intimate?"

"Yes. Whoever's gonna resort to that has to come face-to-face with the person, right? If you're pissed at someone you don't know, do you really want to look them in the eye right before you shut off their lights forever?"

She had an interesting way of seeing things, he had to admit.

"So not your first choice when planning a murder?" Luca asked.

"I like the poison better," she told him. "It's cold and calculated."

"And cleaner," Brantley noted.

"Yes, definitely cleaner. That's what this feels like to me. Not the spur-of-the-moment, I'm-so-pissed-at-you-I-take-you-out but more planning. Intentional. Someone close to them." JJ paused to take another breath. "I'm gonna have to call Detective Mathis. See who else they've talked to. Who they might've marked off their list."

"That doesn't mean we can cross off the offended residents' angle," Brantley told her.

"Of course not, but I'd like to expand our options."

"Just out of curiosity," Luca said, "I thought we were lookin' for the missin' guy. That not the case?"

"It is," JJ confirmed. "But I think in this case, if we narrow down who's responsible for the murders, we'll find our kidnapper."

"Good work, JJ. Keep us updated," Brantley told her. "We'll talk to you in a bit."

"Will do," she said.

Brantley hooked the phone back on his belt, looked at Reese. "You good?"

"I don't think we learned much there, but I think talkin' to the wife's still the right way to go."

"Agree."

They were back in the truck a few minutes later, pulling out of the parking lot.

"Mathis gonna give us any problems?" Brantley asked.

"No. I told him we'd keep him looped in and asked him to do the same."

"You think he will?"

"I do. I think it's fair to say we blindsided him this mornin', so he reacted accordingly. He wants these cases closed, and he knows the more eyes the better."

"True." Brantley glanced at Reese. "Which way am I goin'?"

"They live on the golf course."

"Of course they do." Brantley took a right at the next light. "You know anything more about Cedric Hawkins?"

"Luca sent me some details. Let's just say, money doesn't buy happiness."

"No, but it buys you a fuckin' nice house," he muttered as they weaved their way through the land of the wealthy.

"That it does. It also gets you a wife, two ex-wives, three kids, three vacation houses, six cars, and a couple of girlfriends."

The last part had Brantley glancing his way again. "Girlfriends?"

"Yep."

"The wife know about them?"

"Don't know, but I've got the team lookin' into his and the wife's email accounts and phone records."

"That was fast."

"Maybe. But I'm with you," Reese stated. "The wife instantly puts up a wall of lawyers. People only do that if they've got somethin' to hide."

"Or somethin' to protect," Brantley added.

REESE WASN'T EXACTLY SURE WHAT TO THINK about Annie Hawkins, the wife of the missing Cedric Hawkins, but he knew one thing for sure: the woman could stand to lose a good twenty pounds.

Of fucking diamonds.

For the past ten minutes he'd been standing here, doing his best to figure out how she managed to walk around with all that sparkly shit weighing her down. Rings, earrings, necklaces, bracelets. Hell, she even had some on her shoes. Her *shoes*, for fuck's sake.

He'd bet money she had back problems. If not from the diamonds, surely the needle-thin heels were causing her discomfort. Granted, the five-inch spiked stilettos did make her legs look fantastic. A fact she was well aware of as she did her best impression of Sharon Stone in *Basic Instinct* from her perch in what could only be described as a throne. In her foyer.

Probably would've been sexy if it weren't for the distraction of all that damn glittering shit on her fingers, wrists, and ears.

"Mrs. Hawkins, when was the last time you saw your husband?" Brantley asked.

The bottle-blonde batted her fake lashes at Brantley, her bright white teeth looking all the brighter thanks to the fire-engine-red lipstick.

And fine, Reese would go so far as to say Annie Hawkins was a beautiful woman, if not a little too skinny. Her makeup was flawless, and he wouldn't be the least bit surprised if she said it was air-brushed on. And her hair… Reese wondered how much money she spent monthly to get it to shine the way it did.

He also wondered if she owned stock in a jewelry store because … diamonds.

"My client has already spoken to the police once today," the well-dressed man at her side said.

Peter Singleton was his name, and evidently he was Mrs. Hawkins's legal counsel. Or personal gigolo, maybe. It could go either way.

"We're not with the police," Brantley told him.

Reese looked around, checking out the grand foyer, which was as far as they'd made it into the house. Then again, this was as far as he needed to go to figure out the Hawkinses were loaded. And if anyone ever said money could buy taste, they obviously hadn't met these people. He'd never seen anyone attempt a modern version of Old-World chic mixed with a little bit of Renaissance before, and seeing it now, he knew why.

"Like she told them, my client does not know where her husband is or who might've taken him."

"So you're tellin' me, your husband's not only missin', he's been kidnapped?" Brantley asked, his drawl growing thicker with his frustration.

"No, of course not," the lawyer answered for her. "She's not saying that."

"But you are?"

"No. Not at all." The gigolo lawyer sighed. "I'm simply saying, my client does not know where her husband is."

"Does *your client* not have a voice?" Brantley said, that familiar edge getting more intense.

Reese had to give him credit. He'd made it this far before losing his cool.

Ten minutes here and the wife hadn't uttered a single word. Of course, she was doing a hell of a lot of talking with her eyes as she openly ogled Brantley, something Reese found himself more than a little bothered by although he knew Brantley hadn't given her a passing glance.

"Of course she does," Lawyer Pete said, his tone flat, clearly uninterested in being helpful.

One thing Reese knew the snappy dresser *was* interested in: banging the sparkly Mrs. Hawkins. And Reese didn't even need to be a detective to figure that out. Those two had knocked boots in the last hour, if he had to guess.

Which had him wondering whether the diamond queen of Lakeway bothered to take off the bling or if they somehow managed to maneuver around it.

Brantley glanced between Mrs. Hawkins and her gigolo lawyer. "Exactly *why* is he here?" he asked the wife.

Yeah. Reese could tell Brantley was growing more and more irritated, and it was only a matter of time before they were tossed out on their asses.

"I'm here at the request of my client," Peter said, motioning to the woman still planted in that throne thing.

"For legal representation or comfort? Because I don't quite understand why you'd be needed unless Mrs. Hawkins is responsible for her husband's disappearance?" Brantley turned his stern gaze on the wife. "Is that the case, Mrs. Hawkins?"

"She's been here all morning," the lawyer stated.

"I'm assumin' you're her alibi?"

"My client doesn't need an alibi. She's not responsible for her husband's disappearance."

This douche was a lawyer? Really? Did he not know the definition of alibi because, *yeah*, she did need one.

Brantley chuckled, but there was no amusement in the sound. "Is she at least worried that he's suddenly vanished? Because I'm gettin' the feelin' that's not the case."

Reese knew if he let Brantley continue, they were going to be booted out of the house, and that was the last thing they needed if they hoped to find Cedric Hawkins.

Passing Tesha's leash off to Brantley, he smiled. "Would you mind takin' her out for a minute?"

Brantley's blue-gray eyes narrowed on his face, and Reese did his best to mask his expression.

With a heavy sigh, Brantley turned and strolled out, the door being opened by the older gentleman who could've passed for a stone statue if it weren't for the fact he blinked on occasion.

Reese turned his attention to Mrs. Hawkins, ignoring the stick-in-the-ass lawyer. "Mrs. Hawkins, your husband's secretary called the police this mornin' when he didn't show up for work. Considering what's happened with his business partners, she's worried, as I'm sure you are."

Finally, there was a spark of ... *something* ... in the woman as she waved a glittering hand in a dismissive manner. "My husband didn't come home last night."

"Is that usual for him?"

"Yes. He prefers his office to"—she pulled a Vanna White, motioning down her own body like it was a brand new car—"*this.*"

"Did he let you know he wasn't comin' home?"

She slowly pushed to her feet, balancing on those stilts, then stepped toward him, her gaze appreciative as it ran down his full length and then back up. "He did not. We don't have that sort of marriage."

"What sort *do* you have?"

"The open kind," she said, her smile widening as she stepped even closer.

The lawyer had the decency to clear his throat, something the statuesque blonde ignored.

"Do you know if he's seein' someone else?"

"Many someones, I'm sure." Her smile widened and her eyelashes fluttered. "That's why they call it an open marriage."

Reese took a step back, hoping to get some fresh air rather than continuing to inhale the toxic fumes she called perfume.

"Has your husband received any threats recently?"

The question seemed to surprise her because she took a step back, and suddenly her throat had dried up along with her words.

"My client has already provided all she knows to the police," Peter stated. "I'm sure they've got a record of her statement."

"Actually," Reese raised his voice slightly, "the statement they have on file is you sayin' she has nothin' to say. Perhaps we should have her go down to the station so we can do this legit and on record."

His eyes narrowed, but before he could say something stupid, Reese directed his next question at the wife. "Did you know the other partners well?"

"Of course she did," Peter stated, stepping forward and blocking Mrs. Hawkins from view. "They were in business with her husband." He motioned toward the door. "Now, if you wouldn't mind, my client needs time to grieve."

Reese's eyebrows locked down as he pinned his gaze on the lawyer's face. "Grieve what? As far as we know, her husband's missin', not dead. Or does she know somethin' we don't?"

"Please see yourself out, Detective."

Reese didn't bother clarifying that he wasn't a detective. He knew when to back off and now was certainly the time.

Without another word, he walked out of the house, giving the butler a quick scan on the way. Perhaps they should try talking to the staff. Maybe they had some insight into what the hell was going on here.

"Anything?" Brantley asked when Reese joined him at the truck.

"Mrs. Hawkins needs time to grieve," he relayed. "The lawyer's words."

Brantley's gaze swung back to the house. "She's hidin' somethin'."

Yes, she most certainly was.

"I'd like to talk to the wives of the partners," Reese told him.

"Great minds," Brantley stated. "I've got addresses."

CHAPTER NINE

BAZ LET ALLISON LEAD THE CHARGE WITH the investment company. Not necessarily because he wanted to, but Allison seemed determined to be in front, and the last thing he needed was a public confrontation when they were hoping to identify people who would willingly open up to them.

He had worked with aggressive go-getters before, both men and women. But there was something about Allison that set his nerves on edge. Baz figured it was better to observe than get in the way.

At least for now.

"Mr. Alexander, could you please tell us when the last time you spoke to Mr. Hawkins was?" Allison prompted.

Mr. Alexander, a.k.a. Joel, was HJW Investments' PR representative who'd been shoved at them the minute they walked in the door asking to speak with Cedric Hawkins's secretary, the woman who'd called the police regarding his absence. Why this guy was acting as a brick wall between them and real information, Baz didn't know. However, he did know Joel could tell them nothing about Mr. Hawkins's whereabouts as of late. Hell, maybe not ever.

"Mr. Hawkins was in the office yesterday," Joel told them.

"And you spoke to him then?" Allison asked.

"I did not, no."

"When did you speak to him last?" she questioned.

"I do not work directly alongside Mr. Hawkins, so our paths don't cross day to day."

"But you saw him?" Baz asked, growing irritated by the second.

"I did not, no."

Allison's tone remained syrupy sweet. "As you can understand, we're in the process of tracing Mr. Hawkins's movements for the past twenty-four hours, hoping it'll lead us to where he might've gone. I'm sure someone here interacted with him yesterday, so it'd be in everyone's best interest if we can speak with them."

"I'm sorry, no. At the moment, no one here knows where Mr. Hawkins might be, but we will notify the police as soon as we hear from him."

"So you're expecting to hear from him?" Allison asked, head tilting, frustration settling on her expression.

"I am not, no."

Well, at least he'd gotten the canned response down pat.

They were getting nowhere, and honestly, Baz didn't have time for the runaround. They were under the gun, and the fact this company was putting up a wall between them and their employees was concerning.

"Do you have a restroom?" Baz asked, interrupting. "Little too much coffee this morning."

"I ... uh..." Joel motioned to the door behind him. "Through there, but I don't—"

"Thank you." Baz nodded at Allison, then strolled through the closed door that led to the offices.

He didn't have to use the restroom, but he did want to talk to someone who actually knew what was going on here. Someone who might've worked with Cedric Hawkins and could attest to his demeanor the last time they saw him. It wouldn't give them much, but shit, at this point, they had nothing.

Just beyond the doors was proof this was a company that had held up well through struggling economic times. The decor was modern and fresh, with opaque glass walls separating the reception area from the rest of the space. Light-colored lacquered wood and bright LEDs in the ceiling woke things up nicely. The furniture looked high-end and was spread out, offering that open, airy feel for anyone who might be forced to chill in the waiting room.

He noticed the receptionist sitting at the main desk was dabbing a tissue at her eyes. Clearly she was upset, and Baz doubted her tears and Cedric Hawkins's disappearance were a coincidence.

"Excuse me," he said softly. "I'm with the OTB Task Force, and we're lookin' into Mr. Hawkins's disappearance. Could you help me? Or maybe direct me to someone who can?"

The woman looked up as she sniffled, her gaze sliding past him toward the doors he'd come through.

"It's all right," he assured her, relaxing his shoulders, going for the laid-back vibe. "My partner's out there talkin' to Joel. I'm not trying to cause problems, just need to figure out where Mr. Hawkins is."

He could tell she was hesitant, had probably been told she wasn't allowed to speak to anyone. But in those deep brown eyes of hers, he saw pain.

"Did you know Mr. Hawkins?" he asked, aiming for casual.

She nodded.

Glancing down, he found the sign on the desk with her name on it. Crystal Smith.

"Crystal, do you know where Mr. Hawkins might go if he doesn't come into the office? Besides his house? Maybe a restaurant? A favorite coffee shop?"

"No," she said softly. "He's always here. *Always.*"

"And he was here yesterday?"

Crystal nodded again.

"Do you know what time he left?"

"Right at six. We were supposed to go——"

She cut herself off, but not before Baz got the gist. He had a feeling Crystal was closer to Cedric than anyone else in this building. A little too close for a married man, perhaps.

"Crystal, I want to find Cedric, but I can't do that without your help. I'm not here to judge, but I need to know where to start looking for him."

Once again, her gaze shifted beyond him but came back quickly. "He stayed with me last night," she said in a voice barely above a whisper. "He stays with me several nights a week. We were supposed to go out to dinner, but he changed his mind, wanted to eat in, so we did."

"And after that?"

"We watched some TV, then went to bed."

"What time was that?"

She gave a slight shrug. "Ten? Maybe eleven. But he wasn't there when I woke up this morning."

"Is that normal?"

Crystal shook her head vigorously. "No. He's usually there in the morning."

"So he didn't tell you he was leaving?"

"No. When I woke up and found him gone, I figured he had come into the office early. He does that sometimes. When he can't sleep, he'll come here, but he always tells me first." Tears glistened in her eyes. "But he wasn't here when I got here."

"Are you the one who called the police?"

She shook her head. "No. Abby did. His secretary. She was expecting him for a six o'clock conference call. He never showed."

"Is it unusual for him to miss a call or a meeting?"

Crystal's eyes widened as she nodded vehemently. "Oh, definitely. Mr. Hawkins is meticulous about work. It's his life. He's always early. For everything."

Baz was afraid she would say that.

"Is there anywhere he might go? Somewhere he likes to frequent if he needs to clear his head?"

"No. This is his safe haven. He loves it here. Cedric ... I mean, Mr. Hawkins, he loves what he does."

Baz nodded as though understanding.

He heard Allison's voice getting louder, and he recognized it as a warning.

"Did Mr. Hawkins get any phone calls last night? Did he seem off in any way?"

Crystal stared back at him as though thinking, and then her eyes widened. "I think he got a phone call last night. I don't know for sure, but now that you mention it, I had a dream that he was talking on the phone. Maybe it wasn't a dream?" Her eyes glittered with renewed hope. "Maybe he got a call and answered it while I was sleeping?"

That was a very good possibility. And it would explain why he left when he didn't usually.

Baz pulled out his card, passed it to her. "Call me if you think of anything else. And if there's anyone here who has information, I'd appreciate if you'd urge them to call me, too."

She nodded, her eyes glistening once again. "Please find him."

"We're gonna do our absolute best," he promised.

"Mr. Buchanan!" Joel called from behind him. "I asked that you not speak to anyone without my permission."

Baz shot Crystal a small smile.

Yep. Busted.

"YOU SURE YOU'RE UP FOR THIS?" EVAN asked as Trey led the way down the sterile white corridor, heading toward the morgue.

He peered over at his new partner. "Are you sayin' I look bad?"

Trey wouldn't be surprised if he did. He was feeling a little green around the gills.

The smirk on Evan's face didn't have an ounce of embarrassment. "I imagine you've looked better."

Trey snorted. "You've seen me how many times?"

"Enough to know green's not your color."

"Whatever." He forced a smile. "I'm fine. I'll *be* fine."

"You've never done this before, have you?"

"Go to the morgue?" Trey shook his head. "Not on my bucket list."

Evan chuckled. "Brace yourself."

Taking Evan's advice, Trey tried to shore up his nerves as they walked into the room where dead people were prepped and autopsied. Only two seconds in, he decided one thing was for absolute sure: he did not care for the morgue at all. There was a pungent antiseptic smell, the temperature was a little too cool, the room a little too dark, and there was a morbid aura that seemed to surround the place.

"Are you with the task force?" the man sporting wire-rimmed glasses and a blue lab coat asked as they approached.

This guy looked right at home in the death room. He was as pale as the dead bodies he worked on, proof he probably didn't see a lot of sun. However, his eyes were bright, glittering with knowledge.

"Trey Walker and Evan Vaughn," Trey introduced, stopping a few feet from the metal table that was covered with a sheet. Based on the lumps beneath, he knew there was a cold, dead body.

"I'm Dr. Jason Davis, the medical examiner."

Trey would've said it was nice to meet him, but he wasn't sure it was. This guy was a doctor for the dead, and while he had never considered himself squeamish, he'd never been in here before. Needless to say, it wasn't high on his list of things to do ever again.

However, he couldn't say the same for his new partner. Evan was handling it like a man who visited dead bodies as a hobby, walking right up to the doc and offering a hand.

"Who would you prefer to see first?" the medical examiner asked, turning to face the two body-covered tables.

Neither. Trey kept the thought to himself.

"We can start with Seth Jacobs," Evan said, his tone decisive.

Trey was grateful, hoping the man would lead from here on out. At least until they were outside where it didn't smell like … like a mixture of hospital and dead people.

When the ME pulled the drape back, revealing a naked man with a gruesome Y incision on his chest, Trey realized it could get worse. His stomach twisted unpleasantly, and he had to turn his attention to the far wall. Evan, on the other hand, moved right up to Seth, taking the chart that Dr. Davis passed to him.

"Doesn't look like a crime of passion was what took Seth Jacobs out," Evan noted, still observing the body.

"I would have to agree," the medical examiner said. "No broken bones, no signs of torture or even a struggle."

"Cause of death?" Evan asked.

"Suffocation. I'd say someone held something over his face. A pillow is my assumption based on the particulates I found in the lungs, but I won't know for sure until I get the test results back from the lab."

Trey dared a peek at the body, looked away quickly. "Up close and personal, then."

"I'd say so," Evan stated. "Was he drugged?"

"His blood alcohol level was well above the legal limit, but other than that, I found no drugs. I did, however, determine that he had sexual intercourse shortly before his TOD. I identified spermicide."

"He wore a condom?" Evan inquired.

"Yes, that's my finding."

"And Brian Wright? Was he also suffocated?" Evan asked.

"He was not." The medical examiner strolled to the other body, pulled back the sheet. "Mr. Wright ingested a lethal dose of nitroglycerin."

Trey peeked at the body. Nope. Seeing another one didn't make it any easier.

"Was it his prescription?" Evan asked.

The doctor shook his head. "Not that I found based on his medical history, nor did I find any reason to believe he should be during my autopsy. His heart was healthy. His liver, however, had seen better days. I'd say he's been a heavy drinker for quite a number of years."

Trey continued to listen to the questions Evan asked, the answers the ME gave him. It was obvious this wasn't Evan's first rodeo. Based on what Trey knew of the man, he'd been doing this for quite some time, which explained how he knew the right questions to ask, the professional way to respond. No doubt about it, he made Trey feel a bit inept.

"No foreign DNA found on either of them?"

"Found a couple of hairs, sent those off to the lab. Should have information back by the end of the week."

Knowing Brantley and Reese wouldn't be happy with that response, Trey spoke up. "We'll need to push that through. We believe these deaths are directly related to a missing person."

"The lab's usually—"

"Just give me the details," Trey told him. "I'll get it pushed."

The ME didn't look as though he believed him, but he nodded. "Sure. I'm sorry I couldn't be of more help."

"Thank you for your time," Evan replied.

The death doctor dug in his pocket, produced a small card. "If you have any other questions, feel free to contact me."

Evan took the man's card then led the way back toward fresh air.

"It's not somethin' you ever get used to," Evan said now as they stepped outside.

Trey took a deep breath, prayed the stench of death would be washed away quickly. "No?"

"No. If you can get in the mindset that you work for them now, your only job to find who's responsible for their deaths, it helps."

"I'm not sure anything'll help," Trey admitted, grateful he hadn't lost his breakfast, which had been a real possibility when they first stepped inside.

Of course, he wasn't about to tell Evan that he had no desire to investigate homicides. Although he was getting better at the missing persons angle, he was figuring out he didn't much care for that either. Granted, he wasn't going to tell Brantley. Trey had no choice but to fight through. He figured eventually he would grow to like it.

He hoped.

Evan chuckled. "It takes time. But you did better than I did my first time in the morgue."

"Yeah?"

"The first dozen times, if I'm being honest. I learned not to eat before I knew what the plan was for the day."

Great.

Trey wasn't sure he wanted to endure even one more, much less a dozen.

CHARLIE PULLED UP TO THE COUNTRY CLUB, grinning as she noticed the men and women wearing their fancy gear. White skirts or pants, sweater vests. Those little visors to keep the sun out of their eyes.

Honestly, she'd figured that was all stuff set up for television. Evidently, there was a store that sold clothes just for golfers.

"What's funny?" Slade asked.

She looked over. "Nothing. Just checking out the wardrobe requirements."

Slade ran a hand over his chest. "I think I'd look good in a pink shirt and a plaid vest, don't you?"

Charlie opened the door, climbed out, laughing as she pictured Slade trading his Wranglers in for white pants. Just the thought made her laugh again.

"Have you ever been to a country club?" he asked when Charlie joined him at the front of the SUV.

"No. You?" She watched as a golf cart carrying two people and bags of golf clubs cruised down the path to the course.

"Hell no," he muttered under his breath, his disdain for the notion making her laugh.

"You have somethin' against golf?"

"Not the game, no. But bein' around all this"—he waved a hand to encompass the people in the cart—"makes me itchy."

"I don't think all courses are quite this ... pretentious," she said when she earned a side-eye from an older man in a cart.

"Nice hat," Slade called out to him. "I can buy one of those inside?"

The man ignored him but continued to stare.

Slade motioned toward the building. "That way? Awesome. Goin' to buy me a hat."

Charlie was laughing when Slade opened the door to the building, stepped back, and waited for her to go in first.

She stepped inside, felt as though she'd walked into another era. The walls were lined with dark wood, the floor with patterned carpet. There were leather sofas and chairs scattered about, short tables alongside, providing the perfect spot to sit down and share a drink.

"Might I help you?" a man asked as they approached what looked to be a reception area complete with a fancy mahogany desk and an antique banker's lamp sitting on top.

"You might, yeah," Slade said, almost as though it was instinct to respond.

"My name's Charlie Miller. This is my partner, Slade Elliott. We're with the OTB Task Force," she explained. "And we're looking for Cedric Hawkins. He was reported missing this morning, and we're hoping someone might be able to assist us."

The man walked around the desk, adjusting his fancy suit coat as he did. Although he was a few inches shorter than her, Charlie felt as though he was still looking down his nose.

"I'm Anthony Grandley the Third. I manage this club. I'm sorry to say, Mr. Hawkins is not here at the moment."

"That's because he's missin'," Slade muttered under his breath.

Charlie ignored him, addressed the club's manager. "Could you tell us when the last time you saw him was?"

Anthony seemed to think on that, his eyes closing dramatically as he took a deep breath.

Charlie cast a quick look at Slade, saw he was staring wide-eyed at the man. Thankfully, he kept his mouth shut.

"I do believe I last saw him on Saturday. He stopped in for lunch." His eyes opened slowly. "Yes. Lunch."

Having lunch at the club just a few days after his partners were murdered? Sounded a bit odd to Charlie.

"Was he with anyone?"

Once again, Anthony did the dramatic thing, this time a shocked sigh, before answering with, "My sincerest apologies. I do believe I was wrong in the timing. It must've been the weekend prior. He was here with Brian Wright and Seth Jacobs, God rest their souls."

That made more sense. "Did anything seem off with them when they were here?"

"Not that I recall. They stopped in quite frequently to have lunch or dinner, play a round of golf, or even to have a drink in the gentlemen's room."

Charlie wasn't going to touch that one.

"Do you know if there's anyone here who might know Mr. Hawkins? Perhaps they've seen him recently? Outside of the club, I mean."

"It's a bit early in the day," Anthony said, his head tilting back in that haughty manner that had her molars clamping together. "Perhaps you'd like to come back this afternoon."

"Actually," Slade interrupted, "we'd like to find Mr. Hawkins before then. And for us to do so, we could really use your help. He's currently missing. Two of his partners were murdered. We'd very much prefer he didn't meet the same fate."

Anthony didn't seem at all bothered by the curtness in Slade's tone. "I understand, sir. However, it's unfortunate that I cannot help you at this time."

Before Slade could say something more, Charlie intervened. "Thank you for your time. Would it be all right if we got a look at the locker room where Mr. Jacobs's body was found?"

That seemed to catch him off guard. "I'm sorry?"

"Mr. Jacobs's body was found here," she relayed, recalling the updated information she had. "It was an active crime scene."

The snooty man looked sincerely confused, shaking his head. "No, that's not correct. Mr. Jacobs's body was never here."

"Perhaps he was and you weren't told?" she inquired.

He was shaking his head in earnest now. "No. No, that's not correct. I truly don't know where he was found, but it certainly was not here."

Charlie could've continued to argue because the police report reflected as much, but she got the impression this man was telling the truth. Which meant there was something fishy going on, and she got the distinct feeling he would not appreciate them snooping around, interrupting their clients by chatting them up, so Charlie opted to refrain from asking.

"Well, we appreciate your time, Mr. Grandley." Charlie produced her card, held it out. "If you happen to come across any information you might believe helpful in finding Mr. Hawkins, don't hesitate."

"Of course." He nodded once, took the card, holding it as though it might possibly contaminate him.

She cast a quick glance at Slade, nodded toward the door.

Once outside, she breathed a sigh of relief.

"That was … odd," Slade stated.

"More than a little," she acknowledged.

"Where to now?"

Before she could answer, her cell phone buzzed with an incoming text.

It was Reese letting her know they were stopping to talk to Mallory Jacobs, the wife of one of the partners. After that, they would be grabbing some lunch and requested them to join.

Charlie quickly typed a response, confirming they would. At the last second, she added on what they'd learned from Anthony Grandley the Third. Figured knowing that Seth Jacobs wasn't found here at the club was rather pertinent information. Especially since it appeared someone had tampered with the police report.

CHAPTER TEN

BRANTLEY HADN'T BEEN AT ALL IMPRESSED WITH Annie Hawkins, the wife who coated herself in diamonds and let her boy toy with the law degree do all the talking.

He was even less impressed with Mallory Jacobs.

And it had nothing to do with her outward appearance. Compared to the first wife they'd interviewed, Mrs. Jacobs was what he would consider tame. They were similar in the fact it looked like Mrs. Jacobs spent a vast majority of her time in a spa. Her glowing skin was flawless, her fiery red hair glossy and straight, emerald-green eyes highlighted with makeup that probably cost as much as Brantley's Sig.

No, she didn't have diamonds dripping from everywhere, nor was she sporting ankle-breaking heels, but there was something about this woman that set off red flags.

For fuck's sake, the woman's husband had been dead for barely a week, and already she was moving his things out of the house because, according to her, it was just too painful. Might've sounded more believable if she wasn't whistling while she worked, tossing things into boxes without a care.

If that wasn't suspicious, he didn't know what was.

Now, as he watched Mrs. Jacobs move around the six-car garage, shifting piles of clothes and checking pockets, he was only grateful her lawyer wasn't there. At least he stood a chance at getting information, anything that might lead them to where Cedric Hawkins might be.

"Mrs. Jacobs, do you know of anyone who would've wanted to hurt your husband or his partners?" Reese asked kindly.

Good cop, bad cop, Brantley thought. Although neither of them was a cop, the roles had been mapped out prior to their arrival. Hell, maybe those roles were simply the rule because Brantley couldn't see himself being the good guy. Not when some woman seemed almost relieved her husband wouldn't be coming back again. Luca was right; the sanctity of marriage was lost on these people.

Mrs. Jacobs looked up. It was then she must've realized her expression was one of relief, not sorrow, because she quickly schooled it, shifting into grieving-widow mode.

"It's just so horrible," she said with a sniffle.

Again, might've been believable if she didn't flip open a small jewelry box, skim a pair of cuff links before tossing them into a box marked CONSIGNMENT.

"Ma'am, how long were you and Mr. Jacobs married?" Brantley probed, hoping to put her at ease with some personal questions.

"Four years in May," she said quickly.

He waited to see if she would break down from the realization that there wouldn't be any more anniversary dinners in her future.

She didn't. Instead, she retrieved what looked to be a twenty-dollar bill from a pants pocket, smiling as she tucked it into her own pocket.

Nope. Nothing suspicious here.

"Was he married before?" Brantley asked.

"Oh, yes. Twice," Mrs. Jacobs said with a wave of her hand. "But the third time's the charm, right?"

Evidently not.

"Do you think one of his ex-wives would've wanted to hurt him?"

Reese's cell phone buzzed, distracting her for a moment. When he looked down to check it, Brantley repeated the question.

"Seriously doubtful." She was so matter-of-fact, her eyes darting back to the box she was looking in. "Considering the alimony they receive."

A fact Brantley realized took some suspicion off the ex-wives. Jacobs had been worth far more to them alive than dead. Unless, of course, there was some sort of post-nuptial agreement. After all, you had to protect the money, right?

"Does that continue upon his death?" Reese asked.

She looked up, seemed to think on it a minute. "You know, I don't think it does." A smile formed. "I will have to look into that."

Mrs. Jacobs tossed a pair of loafers into another box.

"Can you tell us how long your husband was missing before they found him?" Brantley asked, suddenly fed up with the bullshit.

She clearly sensed his mood going south because Mrs. Wright looked up, her green eyes narrowing before she once again masked her expression.

"He was on a business trip," she said. "Or that's what he told me. Hard to believe it now since they found him here."

"Here? As in your house?" Reese asked, although they both knew that wasn't the case.

Her hand went to her chest, rubbing over her heart. "Oh, heavens no. I couldn't stay here if his ... body..." She shivered. "If his dead body had been here."

Funny. That sounded more like it was intentional. Heaven forbid she not be able to live in this mansion of a house.

"Where did they find your husband?" Brantley probed.

"At the country club." Her tone softened, her eyes glassy with unshed tears, but Brantley noticed a steely determination behind them. "Which doesn't surprise me, really. He loved that place. Spent more time there than he did at home."

Bitter much?

"Did he go with his partners to the club? Were they friends outside of the office?"

"Good friends," she confirmed. "They played golf every Monday morning, said it helped to clear their minds for the week ahead. It's just"—she looked down into a box—"so sad. He won't get to go to the club again."

Brantley wondered if it was difficult for her to do that. To pretend she gave a shit, because he knew without a doubt, this woman was not a fan of her dead husband. That didn't mean she'd killed him, but she certainly wasn't losing sleep now that he wasn't coming home.

"They found him..." She sobbed, sniffled. "They found him in the locker room at the club."

"Did you actually see him there?" Reese inquired.

"What?" Mallory Jacobs's eyes bounced back and forth between them.

"Were you a witness to his death, Mrs. Jacobs?"

"No. I just ... I heard from ... the ... um ... the police. They told me they found him there. In the locker room. He was suffocated."

Brantley looked at Reese, waited to see if he had more questions. When he shook his head slightly, Brantley asked, "And you weren't aware he was in town?"

Her answer was quick and curt. "No."

"Where were you the night he died?" Reese asked.

"I was out with friends. We had dinner, then went to a movie. I've got the receipt and the ticket stub."

Really fucking convenient.

"And Brian Wright? Where was his body found?"

Something passed in her eyes. "I ... I don't remember."

"You don't remember?" Reese frowned over at him. "But I thought you and his wife are friends."

"We are. Best friends. I went over there that night but..." Her hand went to her chest again, rubbed lightly. "But only because Nancy called me." She straightened. "Yes. I'm sorry. It was such a traumatic event. Nancy called me when she found him. I rushed over to console her. Annie was already there. She called the police because Nancy was too distraught."

"She was too distraught to call the police but not to call you?"

"What?" Her hand rubbed over her heart and a bead of sweat formed on her upper lip.

"Never mind." He peered down at her hand still lingering over her heart. "Do you know if Mrs. Wright has a heart condition?"

Mallory frowned, this time pressing more firmly on her chest. "No. No, she doesn't. Why does that matter?"

"Because Mr. Wright died from a lethal dose of nitroglycerin," Brantley said flatly, relaying the information he'd received from JJ a short while ago.

Her eyes widened briefly. "I wasn't aware. I... We hadn't heard that."

Brantley nodded, as though confirming. "That's what the autopsy report reads."

"That's terrible. Who do you think could've done that?" she asked, her gaze swinging back and forth between them.

He was tempted to say she was more concerned about Mr. Wright's death than her own husband's.

"We don't know, ma'am, but we intend to find out," Reese informed her.

Brantley saw a flash of something in her eyes. Something cold.

"When was the last time you saw Cedric Hawkins?"

"Saturday night," she said quickly. "He and Annie came over. I didn't want to be alone after..."

"Mrs. Hawkins told us that she and her husband have an open marriage. Do you know if that's true?"

Her eyebrows lowered. "Why? Do you think his girlfriend killed him?"

"Is he dead?" Brantley countered.

Mrs. Jacobs's gaze bounced back and forth between them. "I ... I ... No. I mean, I hope not. He's—"

Her cell phone rang, and Brantley was positive she exhaled in relief, snatching the phone from a nearby table.

"Hello?" Her voice shook only slightly. "Yes. Yes, I am."

Brantley looked at Reese, knew this conversation was now over. More than likely that was Annie Hawkins or the gigolo lawyer telling her she should not speak to them.

Probably a good idea, he figured, since Mallory Jacobs was definitely hiding something.

MALLORY JACOBS HELD THE PHONE PRESSED TO her ear while her heart pounded unnaturally in her chest. She watched the two tall men as they strolled toward their vehicle, the guns on their hips not helping her panic. She'd done her best to play off their presence, but from the moment they stepped up to her garage, her heart had started pounding so hard she could hear the blood rushing in her ears.

Was that pain she felt? Was she having an anxiety attack? Or was this a heart attack?

"Oh, God," she muttered under her breath.

"You need to keep it together, Mallory," Annie insisted when Mallory began rambling incessantly on the phone, doing her best to relay what they'd asked her. "Are they still there?"

"No," she confirmed as she glanced out through the open garage door to see a black Chevrolet truck pulling away from the curb. "No, they're leaving now."

"Good. I'll be there in five minutes. Do not move."

Like she had anywhere to go. Mallory couldn't even think about getting behind the wheel of a car. She'd probably drive into someone's yard with how shaky her hands were. Plus her chest felt tight, like she was having an episode.

An episode.

Hurrying into the house, Mallory raced to her bathroom, rummaged in the medicine cabinet for the nitroglycerin she'd been prescribed for her angina. She stared at the bottle for a moment, remembering what the two detectives had told her. How had they figured out Brian had overdosed? Annie had told her there was no way to trace it.

"Oh, God," she whimpered. Should she throw it out? What if they traced it back to her? What if they found out she was the one who'd given it to Brian?

This was not going the way Annie had said it would. Brian, Seth, and Cedric should've all been dead by now. And there shouldn't have been any way to trace it back to them. It was supposed to look like the real estate deal had gone bad and one of those crazies out to get them had snapped. That was supposed to draw the attention away from them. Plus, their alibis were solid. For their own husbands' deaths, anyway.

Only now Cedric was missing and Nancy was nowhere to be found, either. Mallory should've known Nancy would be the weak link. She'd doubted the woman had the guts to roofie someone, much less do what was necessary to get rid of them completely. And now Nancy's incompetency was bringing suspicion on all of them.

Setting the pill bottle down, Mallory took a deep breath.

Annie would know what to do. She always knew what to do, which was why Mallory had agreed to this plan in the first place. Ever since Annie told her Seth was cheating … Mallory's heart thumped painfully. How could her husband have done that to her? How could he have been with other women? She'd been livid when Annie told her she'd seen him at the club, drinking with some blond bimbo.

Mallory took a deep, cleansing breath. Seth had deserved what he got. So had Brian.

Yes, she would stay calm, keep it together. They could still get out of this and if not…

Well, she had enough money to buy the best lawyer.

CHAPTER ELEVEN

REESE STARED OUT THE WINDOW, PROCESSING EVERYTHING they'd learned while he waited for Brantley to advise where they would be stopping for lunch.

After leaving the Jacobs residence, they'd gone over to have a chat with Brian Wright's wife, but no one answered the door, and there hadn't been any signs of life at the house. At that point, Brantley suggested they go back to Cedric Hawkins's neighborhood and chat up the neighbors. Unfortunately, they weren't all that chatty, a couple of them even refusing to talk at all. Reese didn't think it was because they were hiding anything, more like they didn't want to get involved in anything that didn't exist in their own orbit.

"What are my options for food?" Brantley asked as he steered them out of the neighborhood.

Reese rattled off the list he'd pulled up of nearby places.

"Mexican food," Brantley said quickly.

Reese smiled to himself. The man was a bit predictable when it came to food.

"Be sure to text Trey and Charlie, tell 'em where we're goin'. I told 'em we'd meet up when we were done."

Reese typed a message to both of them, hit send. When he was done, he tucked his phone away and stared out the window, once again recalling how nonchalant both Annie Hawkins and Mallory Jacobs had been about their husbands' deaths.

"Did it sound to you like Mrs. Jacobs was rehearsin' lines she'd forgotten to memorize?"

Brantley laughed. "She did sound guilty, huh?"

"If not guilty, she definitely knows somethin'. And I wouldn't say she's all too worried that her husband's dead."

"You think?" Brantley snorted. "She couldn't seem to get rid of that shit fast enough."

No, she didn't seem to have a problem tossing it out, Reese had noticed.

In fact, neither wife they'd spoken to had been all that concerned with their husband, and it took effort to keep his inner conspiracy theorist down. Had they participated somehow in their deaths? Or had their relationships simply been unfulfilling, and this was more of a relief? Perhaps just a happy accident, one that happened to benefit them in the long run. He could see it going either way, honestly. While money provided a lavish lifestyle, it didn't always equate to happy.

And while it looked as though they were guilty, Reese was doing his best not to jump to conclusions. He didn't want to taint their search for Cedric Hawkins by going down this rabbit hole, so he stuck to what he knew.

"You think the wives were threatened, too?" he asked, looking at it from a different angle. "Maybe they weren't brought in the loop about the real estate deal beforehand. I couldn't imagine their friends were too happy with that revelation."

"It's possible." Brantley pulled into the restaurant's parking lot. "I guess that could explain their relief."

"Yeah. They don't seem like the type of women who'd do well under scrutiny from others." Especially Mallory Jacobs. She didn't appear to have as thick of skin as Annie Hawkins and her diamonds.

When Brantley parked, Reese got out, took Tesha's leash in hand, then followed Brantley into the restaurant. His mind continued to churn through all the information they'd gotten, the women, the lawyer, what JJ had uncovered about the men's deaths, what Trey had confirmed after his visit to the ME, and Charlie's revelation about the country club. It was a lot to process at one time, and he was still hung up on how tight-lipped Annie Hawkins had been considering her husband was missing.

"Law enforcement animal," Brantley informed the hostess when she looked at Tesha sideways.

Once they were seated, Brantley ordered iced tea for both of them, then dug into the chips while Reese continued to mull over what they'd learned while they waited for the others. He wanted Trey and Charlie to be there so they could bounce the information off them, get their first impressions. Plus, he was hoping to see Evan and Slade in action, where their thoughts were on what they'd learned so far.

"What about Wright's wife?" Brantley asked. "She wasn't home, but has anyone been able to locate her?"

"According to JJ, Detective Mathis said he's still trying to get in touch with her, too. He has notes from a brief conversation with her but wanted to talk more in depth."

Brantley crunched a chip. "Have we traced her phone?"

"Yes. JJ said it's turned off." Which Reese thought sounded a bit suspect, but it could be she didn't like to be disturbed, and with her husband's death, she was likely dealing with an overwhelming amount of family and friends concerned for her.

"What's the word on her?"

Reese shrugged. "JJ doesn't have much yet, but that's where she's now focused."

Brantley looked up, smiled at someone over Reese's head, so he looked back, saw Trey and Evan weaving their way through the scattering of tables. The place was filling up with the lunch rush.

"We haven't ordered yet," Brantley informed them, shoving the menus in their direction.

"I think I'll pass," Trey said.

Reese looked at him, noticed he was a tad green.

Evan smiled down at his menu. "Morgue."

"Enough said." Brantley chuckled. "First time to see a dead body?"

Trey didn't respond, but the glare he shot his brother was hot enough to make sparks.

"I told him it doesn't get easier."

No, it didn't. Reese had firsthand experience from his time in the Air Force. It hadn't been a common occurrence for him, thank God, but there'd been a few instances he would prefer to never relive.

"Make room," Brantley commanded. "We've got two more."

Reese looked up, saw Charlie and Slade strolling through the restaurant, speaking as they walked.

"Glad y'all could make it," Brantley greeted, motioning for them to take a seat.

They took a few minutes to peruse the menu, snacking on chips and salsa. When the friendly waitress stopped by, they managed to rattle off what they wanted while she scribbled it down on a pad. She promised to bring drinks and more chips, then rushed off to another table.

"All right, what's the lowdown?" Evan asked, surprising Reese with how easily he jumped into things.

"I'll go first," Brantley said, then gave a very colorful overview of his thoughts on Annie Hawkins.

"I saw their financials," Charlie said, nodding toward her phone. "JJ sent them over a short while ago."

"Not hurtin'?"

"*Generations* won't be hurting," she confirmed. "For any of them."

Reese didn't mention the diamonds, although he figured those things might just suck up a good chunk of that money if the woman didn't chill.

"The business?" Brantley inquired.

"The investment group is doing well," Charlie confirmed. "In the black. This recent purchase is predicted to make them quite a chunk of change based on their reported analysis."

"I didn't think they wanted that kinda retail out here," Reese said.

"Based on the threats, you'd think not," Charlie answered. "However, they've done their homework, and it looks like the overwhelming response is positive."

"If that's the case, do we still think Hawkins's disappearance is related to that land purchase?" Slade asked, looking at all the faces at the table.

"I'm not leanin' that direction," Brantley admitted. "I don't see how someone benefits by kidnappin' him after two of the partners turned up dead. To me, he'd be dead like the other two."

Reese was in agreement.

Brantley grabbed his iced tea. "Personally, I think it's somehow tied to the wives."

Reese stared at Brantley, not surprised he was going down the same path. It was hard not to think that, considering the conversations they'd just had.

"And Nancy Wright's nowhere to be found," Brantley continued.

"Speaking of Nancy," Evan said. "There's something I noticed that stands out in JJ's notes, not sure if you've had time to see it."

Reese shook his head. He hadn't realized she'd been sending them already.

"Go on," Brantley urged, dragging another chip through salsa.

"Nancy Wright filed a restraining order against her husband six years ago."

Reese pulled out his phone, too curious not to look for himself.

"She never followed through with it," Evan continued, "claiming it was at the urging of the hospital when she came in for treatment."

"Treatment for?" Reese asked, still skimming his phone.

"A broken arm and a laceration to the head. She later stated she fell down the stairs."

"Any hospital incidents since then?" Charlie asked.

"None." Evan's disbelief was evident.

"Not a *single* one," Reese reiterated, reading the details. "In fact, she hasn't seen a medical professional of any sort since then."

"Sounds off," Brantley said. "Have JJ dig deeper."

Reese typed up a note to JJ requesting more details.

"Do we know how long they've all been members of the country club?" Evan asked.

"Hawkins and Jacobs were members first," Charlie answered, clearly having memorized the details. "Wright not until a few years ago, when they brought him on as a partner. From what I read, he came into a financial windfall and wanted to pursue the investment angle."

"What was the windfall from?" Slade asked.

"JJ didn't know," Charlie answered. "Not sure it's relevant."

Maybe, maybe not, Reese thought.

"Which is when the wives met?"

Reese knew no one would have the answer, so he typed it up, shot it to JJ, told her to follow up on details along those lines, looking into Brian Wright's history and more on Nancy.

"We learned something interesting," Charlie added, her dark eyes bouncing between everyone at the table. "When I asked to see the scene where Wright's body was found, the manager informed us he'd never been there."

Brantley leaned back. "What do you mean?"

"Exactly that. Seth Jacobs did not die at the country club, nor was his body ever there," Slade commented. "The manager was rather convincing, too."

"The police report states he was discovered there," Reese argued, glancing back at his phone and reading up on the details, wondering if they'd gotten it wrong and, if so, how the fuck they could've gotten it *so* wrong.

"It actually makes sense that he wasn't there based on what I learned from the medical examiner," Evan said. "His COD was suffocation. He found particulates in the lungs, said it would've likely come from a pillow. The country club doesn't tie in with that. I mean, sure, maybe they've got pillows, but it specifically states the locker room."

"Was he drugged?" Charlie asked.

"His blood alcohol level was well above the legal limit, but other than that, he found no drugs."

"What about the other guy? Was he also suffocated?" Slade asked, eyes darting at every person at the table.

"Brian Wright," Evan clarified. "No, he wasn't. ME said he ingested a lethal dose of nitroglycerin."

"Was it his prescription?" Charlie asked.

"ME said it wasn't in his medical history, nor did he find any reason to believe he should be on it based on the autopsy."

"I've got JJ digging into Mrs. Jacobs's medical history," Reese told them. "To see if she's been prescribed nitroglycerin."

Reese felt Brantley's eyes boring into him.

"What?"

"You caught that, too?"

"Caught what?" Trey asked, looking intrigued.

"When we were talkin' to Mrs. Jacobs, she kept clutching her chest," Reese explained. "I thought it was worth lookin' into."

"I don't believe in coincidence," Brantley muttered.

Neither did Reese.

Charlie leaned in. "You think she drugged him?"

"At this point, anything's possible. The only thing I know for certain is that Annie Hawkins and Mallory Jacobs are both hidin' something."

"And Mrs. Wright is MIA," Slade offered.

Reese glanced at Brantley.

"The ME did say Wright's liver had seen better days," Evan added.

"Heavy drinker," Slade commented.

"For quite a number of years," Evan agreed.

"No foreign DNA found on either of them?" Brantley asked.

Evan's eyes lit up. "He found a couple of hairs, sent those off to the lab. Said he should have information back by the end of next week."

"We can get that pushed through," Brantley informed him.

"One step ahead of you," Trey answered with a smile. "I called JJ, figured she'd be the one to make things happen. She said she'd get it taken care of. Somethin' about callin' Rhonda to get the governor to make a call."

"I'm still hung up on why the police report says Jacobs's body was found at the club. Something's off," Charlie said. "Did someone tamper with the report? Or was it deliberate?"

"Damn good question," Evan replied.

Reese didn't like the direction this was heading. It was all getting turned around and quickly, and they were focusing their efforts on the deaths rather than the missing person. It was easy to do, but he knew it wasn't going to help Cedric Hawkins.

He typed up another message for JJ, requesting she create a timeline for when they got back to the office. They needed to see this mapped out because there were too many inconsistencies.

He was just finishing typing when his phone rang.

"It's Detective Mathis," he informed Brantley before answering.

"We were able to get in contact with Mrs. Wright," Mathis said curtly. "She agreed to come down to the station to speak to you."

"Perfect. What time?"

"Forty-five minutes."

"We'll be there," he told the detective. "Thanks."

The call disconnected, so he relayed the news to the team.

"Charlie, why don't you take this one," Brantley suggested.

Reese watched the exchange, curious as to why Brantley was passing it off.

"If Mrs. Wright was abused, she'll probably feel safer speaking to a woman."

"I can do that," she said with a nod.

Considering how well their interviews had gone thus far, Reese didn't figure it would give them much to go on. However, she was a key component in this, so setting eyes on Nancy Wright might be enough.

THE CONVERSATION SHIFTED FROM THE CASE TO casual chitchat while they attempted to enjoy their lunch.

Brantley didn't contribute all that much. He wished he could say it was because he was so hung up on the case. Unfortunately, that wasn't it. No, his distraction was with Reese and the fact the man seemed to be focused on his cell phone more than usual.

And fine, maybe that was some paranoia shit since they were actively working a case, and most likely Reese was messaging with JJ or Luca. Still, Brantley's brain was conjuring up other ideas. Like Reese was texting Madison Adorite since the man hadn't bothered to cop to the fact he'd done so in recent months. At least once, Brantley knew.

He hadn't intentionally gone snooping in Reese's phone to find that out. In his defense, it had been an accident. When the message had come through, Reese's phone had been sitting on the breakfast bar, and Brantley'd been sitting there. He'd only seen the alert portion of the message, so he didn't actually know what they'd discussed, but he figured that was inconsequential. The fact of the matter was, Reese was texting with his ex.

Now as they sat there and Reese continued to look at his phone, Brantley knew he should've let it go but found he couldn't, so he inquired as to whether it was JJ with more details. Reese's answer was a curt head shake, but he didn't elaborate, didn't tell him who it was.

Despite the evidence, Brantley knew it was stupid to worry about something going on between Reese and that woman. He knew deep down that Reese wasn't doing something he shouldn't. Hell, when did the man have time? They were always together.

Brantley's phone rang, dragging him from his thoughts.

"Hey, boss, we found Hawkins's car," Baz said when Brantley answered.

Brantley glanced at the faces around the table, made a quick decision based on the information he had and perhaps a bit of that lingering paranoia. After instructing Baz to send him the details and meet him there, he disconnected the call.

"Charlie, I still want you to talk to Mrs. Wright. Take Trey with you," he commanded, not surprised by the looks he received since he was mixing up the teams. "If you're right and there's a possibility she was abused by her husband and hid it for so long, I don't think I'm the person she needs to be interviewed by."

"Good call." Trey held up his truck keys. "Who's takin' my ride?"

"Reese will," he decided. "Reese, you and Evan can head back to HQ, see what JJ needs. Slade, you and I will go meet Baz. They found Hawkins's car."

Brantley saw the curious look Reese gave him. As of now, they'd remained a team throughout all the cases they'd worked. And though he preferred it that way, he also knew it wouldn't always be the way things were. Especially not when they were getting the new members of the team ramped up. This would allow them both to see the others in action, which would help him decide how to proceed.

It certainly wasn't because Brantley was pissed about Reese's secrecy.

Or so he told himself.

"After," he told the team, "we'll meet back at HQ."

While the team began to disperse, Brantley motioned for Slade to give him a minute and asked Reese to stay behind. When they were alone, he signaled the waitress for the bill.

While he waited for her to return with his credit card, Brantley turned to Reese.

"You cool?"

"Why wouldn't I be?"

And that right there, the bitterness in his tone, told Brantley that Reese wasn't as cool as he wanted him to believe.

"I just want to see Slade in action," Brantley said in defense of his decision.

Reese looked him in the eye, held his gaze. "You don't have to explain yourself to me."

The waitress returned, passed over his card and the receipt. Brantley was scribbling his name when Reese got up and headed for the door, Tesha in tow. He gritted his teeth at the fact Reese would just walk out without so much as a goodbye.

He managed to catch up just outside. "Hey."

Reese stopped, turned. "What?"

Brantley, not caring who might see them, stepped right up to Reese. "Yes, I do have to explain myself."

To his shock, Reese didn't step back, didn't shift away. He remained right where he was, nearly toe to toe with him.

"It's important the new team members see us all in action."

Reese nodded, but Brantley could tell he wasn't in agreement.

Knowing his explanation wasn't going to penetrate Reese's thick skull, he told Reese he'd meet them back at HQ. He'd made the decision and he was not going to change it now. Not for himself and not for Reese.

Brantley forced a smile, tried to lighten the mood. "And when I get there, I'm gonna be in the mood for a break."

"We'll see," Reese retorted, his tone flat.

"Reese." Christ Almighty, did he really need to explain this now?

Before he even had the chance, Reese stepped back, calling for Tesha to follow. "We'll see you at HQ later."

Brantley watched as Reese headed to Trey's truck, got himself and the dog inside. Not once did Reese look back at him, and Brantley felt that same insecurity he'd felt before shift through him.

He had to remind himself that this was his call, not Reese's. He was the one who'd decided to split the teams, so he had no right to worry about Reese's reaction. And as he walked to his own truck, he did his best not to think about the information he'd dug up on the woman Reese had, at one time, wanted to marry.

Brantley clicked the button to unlock the truck, schooled his expression, and got behind the wheel. Slade slid into the passenger seat, silent for a moment.

He had a sort of tunnel vision as he started the truck, put it in gear, headed for the exit out of the parking lot.

"Where's the car?"

Brantley glanced over at Slade. "What?"

"Hawkins's car?"

Right. Car.

Pushing his personal life out of his thoughts, Brantley steered the truck onto the main road heading to the toll road that would take them to Austin.

"They found it at a convenience store just a few blocks from his office."

"He what? Just left it there? Took a walk?"

"At this point, we have no idea, but it's worth a look."

Brantley was grateful when Slade left it at that, the two of them riding in silence for the thirty-minute trip. Every single minute of that Brantley spent thinking about Reese, about the things he didn't know about that man.

It was stupid to ponder such nonsense, but he couldn't help it. Maybe it was the case that had his thoughts going awry. Having met the wife of a man who'd gone missing, and another wife of a dead man, both of whom didn't seem at all bothered by the fact their husbands weren't coming home, Brantley had begun second-guessing relationships. More specifically marriage.

Then again, if he thought about his family, his parents having been married for as long as they had, aunts and uncles the same, he knew it wasn't all bad. It worked for some. Others it was a means of getting what they wanted, whatever that might be.

Had he actually thought about marrying Reese? Simple answer was yes. He'd thought about it.

Hell, when it came to Reese, Brantley'd even dared a peek at what the future might hold for them. That wasn't something he'd ever done before. Day to day was his motto, and until he met Reese, it had worked for him. Now, going to bed and waking up with the man he loved every morning ... he found he didn't want it any other way.

The problem was, he wasn't sure Reese felt the same.

And that was the blasted insecurity eating him from the inside out.

CHAPTER TWELVE

"So, how long've you and Brantley been together?"

Doing his best to keep his expression bland, Reese peered over at his passenger, considered his answer. Not because he would deny the fact he and Brantley were together. These past few months, he'd come to terms with what he wanted, and he didn't feel the need to pretend otherwise. No, it wasn't exactly easy to open up about it, but that had more to do with the fact he was a private man than because he was in love with a man.

Or so he wanted to believe, anyway.

At the same time, Evan Vaughn was technically a stranger, and Reese wasn't sure how much detail he wanted to get into with him.

"Never mind," Evan said with a rough chuckle. "Not my business."

"Almost a year," he told him.

It wasn't like he could hide it, *especially* since Evan worked for them. Hell, Reese lived on the same property where he worked, with the man they all called boss. If they didn't know already, they'd figure it out sooner or later.

"How is it?" Evan asked. "Partnering with the same person you're in a relationship with?"

"It's got its challenges," he admitted.

"I can imagine. But the two of you seem to work well together."

Reese had thought they did, sure. But as of late, they'd been having their fair share of bumps in the road. In fact, he was wondering if that was what this was. Brantley pushing him away, keeping him at a distance. He knew the man was researching Madison Adorite, likely trying to figure out just how serious things had been between Reese and her.

And Reese wasn't entirely innocent either. He'd been communicating with Madison. Innocuously, yes, but that didn't mean his thoughts had remained virtuous. There were times when he revisited his relationship with Madison in his mind, trying to remember who he was before he'd met Brantley Walker, before he'd learned something about himself he never would've expected. Bottom line was, Reese wasn't sure he even knew who he'd been before Brantley, and he wasn't sure he liked that, so yeah, he would reminisce from time to time, try to decide when, where, and why things had changed so drastically.

Didn't seem to matter how much he thought about it though, Reese never came up with the answers to his many questions.

"What about you?" Reese asked, not wanting to get stuck in that mental rut. "You ever date one of your partners?"

"No." Evan was very matter-of-fact. "I … uh … I haven't dated anyone since my wife died, and she was my high school sweetheart."

Reese cast a glance over, nodded. "I'm sorry."

He knew the story behind Evan's wife dying, expected it was a sore subject for the homicide detective.

"I'm in therapy," Evan said gruffly. "It's helping."

"Yeah?"

"Yeah. I didn't think it would help, you know. Not me. Why the hell would I need someone to pick through my brain and try to fix what can't be fixed?" Evan shrugged. "I was wrong. Grief takes time, and he's helping me to see that."

Because Evan felt the need to open up, Reese took advantage of it. "And wanting to do this? Will that help?"

Evan was silent for a moment, and Reese figured he'd overstepped. Before he could offer his own apology for intruding, Evan exhaled.

"If you're asking me whether it's personal, yeah, it's personal. I've got an ulterior motive for wanting to join this task force, sure. I won't deny it."

Reese had figured as much. But who could blame the guy? His wife was murdered six years ago. Kidnapped, raped, and murdered by a man they still hadn't found. A man authorities suspected of being responsible for at least a dozen other similar crimes in the past ten years.

"Will that be a problem?" Evan asked.

Reese answered immediately. "No. It's motivation. I understand that." He glanced over. "You just can't let it make you lose focus."

Neither of them spoke for a couple of minutes, the silence in the truck settling around them comfortably.

It wasn't until they were nearing Coyote Ridge that Evan spoke up again. "What about this case? You don't think this is related to the real estate deal."

Reese was surprised it was a statement rather than a question, but he answered anyway. "No. I don't. This is personal."

"I can see it, too."

Reese could feel Evan watching him as he drove.

"The wives you talked to? You think they have something to do with it?"

"I think it's possible," he confirmed. Although Reese hadn't quite figured out how they'd done it or even why.

Not that logical reasons were required for people to do shitty things to other people. It was the world they lived in, the one that benefited from task forces dedicated to locating missing persons. Had there not been fucked up people, there wouldn't be a need for those who wanted to help.

"If they did, they timed it right," Evan continued. "With the real estate deal, it has us looking in other directions."

"They've got solid alibis."

"Sure they do." Evan cleared his throat. "For their own husband's disappearance. But do they have alibis for the others?"

Reese shot a look at the detective as he understood what he was saying. "You think they took each other's husband out?"

"Why not? It wouldn't be the first time."

No, it wouldn't.

As he drove, Reese tossed that around in his head.

"I've only got one problem with that theory," he told Evan as they were pulling down the driveway toward the house and HQ.

"What's that?"

"I don't see Annie Hawkins getting her hands dirty."

Then again, Reese hadn't thought he'd ever come across a cop with multiple personalities who locked women in rooms and killed them for kicks, but he'd come face-to-face with exactly that.

"Did she hire someone?" Evan asked.

"I'd say that's more feasible, sure. But who?"

"Question of the day," Evan stated.

"No, the question of the day is where the hell is Cedric Hawkins?" He glanced over at Evan. "Because if you're right, if they've taken out each other's husbands, we need to find Nancy Wright."

Evan nodded. "You're right because if Annie took out Seth Jacobs, then Mallory took out Brian Wright."

"And that leaves Nancy to take out Hawkins," Reese completed for him.

Shit.

Was there even a small chance the man was still alive?

"This has netted us nothing," Allison bitched as Baz pulled his truck into the parking lot where Cedric Hawkins's Mercedes had been abandoned.

Baz shot a glance her way. "Tell me, how many times have you worked an easy case?"

"All of them," she countered.

Pulling the truck to a stop, he stared at her. "You're serious?"

"Yeah. I am. Every case I've worked involved luring someone in. There was rarely a lull because there's always someone to reach out to, to watch, to talk to."

Baz sighed. He honestly didn't know how to respond to that. He'd been a cop for far too long to know that there was rarely anything that came easily on the job. He had no idea how Allison had been sheltered, but she clearly had.

"Go in and talk to the clerk," he instructed her. "See if they've got surveillance cameras."

"Surely they do," she muttered as she climbed out.

Baz got out of the truck, pulled on a pair of latex gloves as he scanned the parking lot. He noticed a couple of cameras installed on the side of the building, but who knew if they worked or if they were merely there as a deterrent.

The sound of tires behind him had Baz turning in time to see Brantley pulling his big black Chevy into the parking lot. He was surprised to see Slade was with him and not Reese, but he figured now wasn't the time to mention it.

"Anything?" Brantley asked as he approached.

"Just got here. Allison's inside talkin' to the clerk."

Brantley nodded, walking around the fancy Mercedes, peering into the windows but not touching the doors.

"Looks clean. And unlocked," Brantley stated, dragging a pair of latex gloves out of his pocket. "You get the passenger side."

After donning his own gloves, Baz opened the front passenger door, peering down into the door, the seat, the floorboard.

The car was immaculate, not a crumb or empty cup. The leather seats looked as though they'd been maintained well, the floor mats the same. No doubt Cedric Hawkins was meticulous about his car.

Squatting down by the door, Baz gently felt beneath the seat, careful to move slowly. Brantley was mirroring his actions on the other side, lifting the floor mat, checking in the door.

The back door opened and Baz heard Slade doing the same search back there.

"I'll check the trunk," Brantley said before he stepped back out of view.

Baz leaned over, looked in the crevice between the seat and the center console. He carefully reached down, ran his fingers along the edge. When he felt something, he grabbed it.

"Hey, boss, we've got a phone here," he called out as he eased out of the car, standing tall.

"I thought we traced his phone," Brantley said when he walked around.

"We did. Secondary, maybe?"

"Why the hell's this guy got a second phone?"

"Girlfriend? Maybe this is how she reaches out to him?"

"Wife said they have an open marriage. If that's the case, why does he need to sneak around?"

Good questions. Ones Baz didn't have an answer to.

"Please tell me you found something."

Baz and Brantley looked over at the same time, watching as Allison walked toward them. She looked like a woman on a mission. A *failed* mission.

She glanced between them, her frustration evident. "The clerk knows nothing. Said their exterior cameras are just for show. Only one that works is inside, aimed at the register, and he doesn't have access to the feed. Said we'd have to wait for the manager, but she doesn't like to be interrupted during the day."

Baz glanced at Brantley, curious to see whether the man would blow a gasket, insisting the manager get her ass to the store ASAP.

His face hardened, his lips pursed. Yep, he was gearing up to—

Brantley's cell phone rang.

"Walker," he barked, his eyes narrowed on Allison before turning away quickly as he listened to the caller.

Baz didn't interrupt, just listened to the one-sided conversation.

"That's an interesting theory." *Pause.* "Have you talked to Charlie?" *Pause.* "Yeah, you do that."

When Brantley disconnected, Baz waited patiently for whatever had the man's temper cooling.

"That was Reese," Brantley said, looking from Baz to Slade and then to Allison. "Evan and Reese are now workin' on the theory that the wives conspired to kill their husbands, which means it's imperative that we find Nancy Wright."

"Holy shit," Baz muttered. "How'd they jump to that conclusion?"

"A lot of variables," Brantley said quickly as he was dialing his cell phone. "Hey, Charlie. You talk to Mrs. Wright yet?"

More silence on Baz's end, but he could tell by Brantley's expression that he didn't get the answer he wanted to that question.

"Yeah, all right. Sit tight for a few more minutes. Maybe she got hung up somewhere. If she doesn't show, y'all can head on back."

Baz could see the wheels turning in Brantley's head when he disconnected the call. His gaze shifted to the burner phone Baz held in the evidence bag.

"Why was he here?" Brantley mused, taking the phone.

"To meet someone," Baz figured. "Girlfriend said she thought she was dreaming that he got a phone call in the middle of the night. Maybe it wasn't a dream."

"You didn't tell me that," Allison said, far too much accusation in her tone.

Brantley spoke as though she hadn't said a word. "He gets a call, comes here to meet whoever it was. But if that's the case, they didn't call this phone. No incomings for the past week."

"JJ attempted to trace his main phone," Baz explained, "but it's either turned off or destroyed."

"Same with Nancy's," Brantley rumbled. "She didn't show up at the police station and we need to find her." Brantley passed the phone back to him. "Take this back to HQ. See if JJ can work her magic. I want to know what he uses that for."

"We need a lead," Allison ground out.

"We'll get one," Brantley stated, sounding far more certain than Baz felt.

"So you say," she countered. "This is a wild goose chase."

Baz wasn't sure how Brantley was being so cool about her attitude. The woman clearly had an issue with something, but for the life of him, he didn't know what it was. However, he had to wonder whether or not working for this task force was something she was actually interested in doing.

More importantly, he was starting to wonder whether or not she'd be good for the team.

CHAPTER THIRTEEN

JJ LOOKED UP FROM HER COMPUTER SCREEN when she heard the door open below.

She pretended there weren't chill bumps on her arms and that her stomach wasn't churning with anxiety. It was the same reaction she had every time she was startled, and admittedly, she'd been so wrapped up in her research, she hadn't realized she was the only one upstairs at the moment.

Without being prompted, she grabbed her laptop and headed down the stairs, knowing whoever it was would require an update. They'd spent all morning compiling information on the three couples as well as the investment company, coming up with a lot of data, but nothing that would lead them to Cedric Hawkins.

"Where's Brantley?" she asked when she saw Reese.

"He went to meet Baz."

"And you didn't go with him?"

Reese didn't answer, simply stared at her as though urging her to use deductive reasoning to answer her own question. And fine. She could obviously see he hadn't gone with Brantley, but her real question was why not?

"What've you got, JJ?"

Yep, and that was a flash of temper she heard in his voice.

"Oh, sorry." She shook off the strange vibe, shot a smile at Evan, then shifted her attention back to Reese. "Very little, to be honest. I just finished a deeper dive of Hawkins's financials."

"Lookin' for?"

"Anything and everything. I was mainly focused on property he owned, thinking perhaps he might've gone off to hide somewhere, but, like I said, I found very little. They've got several vacation homes, one in Hawaii, one in Cancun, and one in St. Maarten. All of which have twenty-four-hour video surveillance."

"What I find interesting is that you call three vacation homes 'very little,'" Evan said with a grin.

"Considering the numbers before the decimal point on his bank statement, it's actually kinda modest."

"The security?" Reese noted. "I assume you hacked it."

JJ smiled. "You know me so well. I saw nothing out of the ordinary, and there've been no glitches in the software. I'd bet money he's not off taking a vacation." When they continued to stare at her, JJ continued. "What I did find that was interesting was the money he's been squirreling away for a while. Hawkins has an offshore account that he's funneling money to through his investment firm."

"How much are we talkin' about?"

"Roughly twenty million." She glanced between them. "Money his wife clearly doesn't know about."

"But perhaps she suspects," Reese mused.

"Which speaks to motive," Evan stated. "If he's hiding that, what else is he hiding?"

"He's also payin' for his mistress's apartment, and let me tell you, her digs ain't cheap."

"Wife claims an open relationship."

"My ass." JJ set her laptop down, tapped a few keys. "I checked her out on social media, and nothin' in her posts indicates they're anything more than a happy, loving couple. However..." She paused for dramatic effect. "Somethin' else interesting. Her search history. Plus I was able to uncover a few of her messages as well as a couple of emails."

"I'm assuming you've got a warrant for that?" Evan asked, frowning as his gaze darted between them.

"Immunity and means," JJ declared, despite the fact their immunity and means had been revoked when the governor shut down the task force. "Our goal is to find him, not prosecute. However, if it does lead us to somethin', I assure you, we'll have all the backup we need."

At least, she hoped that was the case. Truth was, JJ didn't worry too much about the legal repercussions when their main focus was on finding a missing person. Her objective was to locate them before the search and rescue became a search and recovery. One day, that would probably bite her in the ass.

When the door opened, all eyes turned to see Baz strolling in.

He scanned the space, his expression shifting from somber to worried. "What's wrong?"

"Nothing," she said quickly. "Honestly. Did y'all find anything?"

Baz raised his hand to show an evidence bag that held…

"Is that the vic's cell phone?"

"*A* cell phone," Baz answered. "Found it in his car." He glanced at Reese. "Aside from that, we found nothing else that might help us."

"Where's Allison?" JJ inquired, curious to know how the woman had done out there today.

"She headed out."

Oh, crap. Baz did not sound impressed by that.

"Did she say why?" Reese asked.

And no, Reese didn't sound impressed either.

"Said she had some things to take care of."

Reese's expression went blank, and JJ could tell he was pissed. She understood the feeling. They were looking for a missing person. One whose very life could depend on when they found him. The more eyes the better, and Allison decided to take a hiatus?

Reese nodded to the cell phone, met JJ's gaze. "See what you can find on that. And pass over whatever information you've dug up to Evan. Let him have a look at it."

"Did Charlie get anything from Mrs. Wright?" JJ inquired as she headed for the stairs.

"She was a no-show, and we need to find her." Reese's gaze shot to the desk on the far side of the room. "Luca, see if you can trace her steps for the past forty-eight hours. She's somewhere."

"On it."

JJ went right to work, plugging the burner phone into the fancy equipment they'd gotten from Sniper 1 Security. It wasn't magic by any means, but it did allow them to search the history of the phone faster than if JJ had to hack into it.

It took roughly an hour, but JJ finally got some information that might help them, although it wasn't at all what she'd expected.

"This phone was purchased in Lakeway by Nancy Wright," JJ announced as she started to stand.

She instantly squealed when she turned to find Baz and Reese both standing there, obviously waiting for her to finish.

"Announce yourselves, would you?" she grumbled, pressing her hand to her heart. "You could give a girl a heart attack."

"Nitroglycerin," Reese muttered, pulling out his phone as he walked away.

"What?" JJ shook her head. "I'm not havin' a heart attack, dummy. I said I *could*."

"What'd you find?" Baz asked, his tone soft and apologetic.

She held up the phone. "This isn't our vic's phone. It was purchased by Nancy Wright. I was able to trace the number back to where it was purchased, and with that, I did a search of local cameras around the time of the sale. Mrs. Wright bought the phone a month ago."

"Before Jacobs and Wright met their untimely fate," Baz noted.

"Exactly."

"Has it been used to make any calls?"

"Just one. To another burner phone on the very first day she purchased it."

"Who bought that phone?"

JJ shook her head. "No idea. If I had to guess, that phone's been destroyed."

Okay, so maybe the information wasn't as helpful as she'd hoped.

BAZ SPENT THE NEXT COUPLE OF HOURS digging deep into Nancy and Brian Wright's life while the rest of the team divided and conquered the other couples.

While their main priority was locating Cedric Hawkins, the theory Reese and Brantley were now going off of—the wives had conspired to off each other's husbands—required that they do a deeper dive on everyone in hopes of pinpointing where he was. If he was being kept somewhere, it wouldn't be in a public place, which meant they needed to drill down on possible locations. Property owned by one of them seemed the likely answer.

He found it interesting that they'd come to this conclusion so quickly, but Baz figured that had something to do with so many people looking at the same puzzle. A diverse group was going to have the best outcome because they each saw things that the others didn't. In this case, it had been the reactions of Annie Hawkins and Mallory Jacobs that had thrown up the red flags.

Well, that and the fact that Nancy Wright was nowhere to be found despite the fact Detective Mathis assured them she had agreed to come into the station.

"Who talked to her?" Baz wondered aloud, thinking back to the police report that stated Jacobs's body had been found in the locker room.

"What?" Evan asked from his desk across the way.

"Mathis said Nancy Wright was comin' into the station. Do we know who talked to her to confirm that?"

Evan glanced down at the notes on his desk. "I don't see anything, no."

"Hey, JJ," he called up to the loft and repeated the same question.

"Mathis didn't say," she answered.

"What're you thinking?" Evan asked, turning in his chair and stretching back. "Maybe they've got help on the inside?"

Baz gave it some thought. "The original detective on the cases is no longer working them…"

"That definitely raises questions.

"And if the police report was altered ... the one about Jacobs's body being found at the country club..."

"More questions," Evan agreed.

"What I don't understand is the crime scene information. What happened to it? Altering the report is one thing, but not all of it. What did the original detective find at the crime scene?"

"Better yet, why would it benefit anyone to alter it?" Evan mused. "Who does it help if they believe Jacobs's body was found somewhere other than where he died?"

"Maybe someone's tryin' to cover up where he really died. I'm gonna call Mathis," Baz stated, pulling out his phone. He dialed the detective's number, put the phone on speaker.

"Mathis."

"Detective, this is Sebastian Buchanan with the OTB Task Force. I've got a question for you."

"Shoot."

"The police report for Seth Jacobs's death states his body was found at the country club. When we spoke to the country club manager, he said that wasn't the case. Did you work the scene?"

"I did not, no. I was out of town."

"Who did?"

"The original detective," Mathis said simply.

Too simply.

"And who was that?"

"I'm not at liberty to say."

Baz frowned at Evan. What the hell kind of police department were they running?

"Look," Mathis added, "this is being handled higher up on the food chain. I've been told to work the cases from the beginning. That's what I'm trying to do."

"Did you take a look at the crime scene after the fact?"

"I'll admit, I haven't had a chance yet," he said, sounding sincerely apologetic. "It's been a hectic day, and I'm doing my best to align all the information I've been given. Because there's too much to work for one person, I'm trying to get some help here."

Baz tried to remember that Mathis had only received these cases this morning. He knew from experience that it took time to get the information together to see what leads would shake out.

"What about Mrs. Wright?" Baz asked. "Did you talk to her?"

"I didn't speak to her directly, no. One of the other detectives took her call. I don't know why she didn't show up."

"And who was that?" he asked, hating that he sounded like a broken record.

"Phillips," Mathis answered, as though they would possibly know who that was.

"Mind if I speak to him?"

"He's … uh…" Mathis paused, his breaths coming in heavier, as though he was moving around. "I don't see him, but I'll track him down and let you know."

"All right." Baz sighed. "If you learn anything, will you give us a call?"

"As long as you do the same."

"Will do," he promised.

The call disconnected, and Baz stared blankly across the room. "What do we know so far?" he wondered aloud. "The facts."

JJ strolled up to his desk, immediately answering his question. "We know that Cedric Hawkins spent the night with his girlfriend last night and possibly got a phone call in the middle of the night. He then drove to a convenience store where he somehow ended up with a burner phone purchased by Nancy Wright in his vehicle."

Elana hurried over to the electronic board and began jotting down the notes so they had them in one place.

"Is it safe to say that Nancy Wright met up with him?" JJ asked, glancing between him and Evan.

"I'd say it's highly probable," he agreed. "How else did her burner phone get in the car?" He looked up at JJ. "You think she planted it so she could track it?"

"Untraceable." JJ smirked. "Unless she's got some mad skills."

Baz doubted cyber-hacking was one of Nancy Wright's hobbies, but he didn't know the woman.

"We know that Brian Wright died of an overdose of nitroglycerin, found by his wife in his home," Evan added.

"The reports are all in sync for that," JJ chimed in. "According to the report, his wife was out to dinner with friends that night. Annie Hawkins called the police when Nancy got home to find her husband dead. From what Reese said, Mallory confessed to going over to the house after the fact when Nancy called her."

"So Annie was out with Nancy on the night her husband overdosed on nitroglycerin," Baz said, watching as Reese came over to join them.

"But Mallory wasn't with them?" Evan asked.

Baz frowned. "Where was Mallory when *her* husband's body was found?"

"When it was found, I don't know," Reese said. "However, she had an alibi for the time of death, which was supposedly two days prior to finding the body. She told us she was at dinner and a movie, had the receipt and ticket stub to prove it."

"Do we know who she was with?"

JJ held up a finger as she skimmed her iPad screen. "She was"—her head lifted, eyes widening—"with Nancy."

"So they alibi each other out," Evan noted. "Nancy is out with Annie when her husband dies. And Mallory is out with Nancy when *her* husband dies. And now, when Annie's husband goes missing, she's safely at home, and Mallory is alibied because of our investigation. That leaves Nancy."

"So, what? Mallory kills Nancy's husband, Annie kills Mallory's, and Nancy is slated to kill Annie's?" Baz mused.

"It seems logical," Reese stated.

"There was one more thing," Evan noted. "According to the ME, there was evidence Seth Jacobs had sex prior to his death."

"Could that be why the report was falsified?" Baz asked, looking at Evan, then Reese, then JJ. "To shift the attention off of whoever he had sex with?"

"Do we know it wasn't the wife?" Evan asked.

"Her alibi was verified," JJ stated. "She was at dinner and a movie at the time of his death, so it's safe to say she was not the one having sex with him."

"We need to relay this information to Detective Mathis," Reese said firmly. "Let him take the lead from here. The deaths aren't our main focus."

"Agree," Baz said, nodding to JJ.

"Elana and I will compile what we have and send it over to him."

Reese sat on the edge of Baz's desk. "If our assumptions are accurate, Mallory Jacobs was involved in Brian Wright's death."

"Do you think that's true?"

Reese's eyebrows rose slowly. "It doesn't help that I confirmed Mallory Jacobs *does* have a prescription for nitroglycerin."

"What made you look that up?" Evan asked, leaning forward, showing his interest.

"When we were talkin' to her earlier today, she kept clutchin' her chest. At first, I thought she was being overdramatic, but the more she did it, the more I wondered if she has a heart problem."

"Talk about missin' your calling," Baz said with a smile. "You should've been a detective."

Reese rolled his eyes.

"What about Seth Jacobs?" Evan asked. "If it plays out the way we're showing it, that means he would've been with Annie Hawkins the night he died. Did he have sex with her?"

"That's a damn good question," Baz said, looking up to see what Reese had to say.

"As much as I'd like to tie these women to the deaths, it's not the best use of our time right now. We know that Nancy Wright is currently MIA, as is our victim. We need to figure out where they are."

Baz nodded, turning back to his computer. "Good point. I'll get with Luca, see if he was able to look at traffic cams in the area. We need to see if we can track where Cedric Hawkins went after he stopped at the convenience store."

"Do the same for Nancy Wright's home," Reese instructed. "If she was the one to call him, maybe she asked him to meet her."

When Reese walked off, Baz turned his attention to his computer. He always enjoyed this part of a case. That moment when things seemed to come together, when there was hope of figuring it out on the horizon.

If they were on the right track, now it was just a matter of finding Cedric Hawkins before Nancy Wright did something stupid.

CHAPTER FOURTEEN

REESE LEFT THE TEAM IN THE BARN so they could do what they did best while he took Tesha out to meet with Magnus.

Although it would've been easy to push Magnus off, to reschedule the training session, he refused to do so. As far as he was concerned, Tesha deserved his full attention, and because he was focused on getting her the proper training that would keep her safe as long as she was working alongside him, he had dedicated his time to these sessions.

He found Magnus sitting on the back porch stairs, his phone in his hand and a smile on his face.

"There she is," Magnus said by way of greeting when Tesha trotted over to him. He held up one finger. "Sit."

Tesha instantly sat in front of him.

"Good girl," he praised, getting to his feet. "Stay."

This was one she was still working on, but Reese watched as she remained where she was as Magnus approached slowly.

"Stay," he repeated when her butt bounced to get up.

She plopped back down.

Magnus's grin was wide. "Good girl." He offered a treat he produced from his pocket, then gave her a pat on the head. "Go play," he said before turning his attention to Reese. "How's she doin'?"

"Great with the basics. Well, except *stay*." Reese grinned down at Tesha. "It seems to be the most difficult for her."

"Considerin' all she's learned this year, I'd say she's doin' remarkably well."

Reese would have to agree. Tesha had come a long way from the malnourished, trembling dog she'd been when he found her chained in someone's backyard. Now she was well-fed, well-loved, and on her way to well-trained.

"As soon as you're ready, I'd like to move into the tracking phase. It'll take a lot more focus, though, so I think we'll want to increase her sessions."

Reese had known it would come to that, and he fully understood. Problem was, he never knew what his schedule would be, so he figured he would be leaning more and more on Trey to help out.

"What did you have in mind for today?" Reese asked, calling Tesha to his side, where she heeled at his feet.

"Actually, I was gonna see if I could borrow her for a few hours. I'm workin' on a dog who's hesitant around other dogs. Tesha's proven to be good in those cases. Thought she might be able to help out. If you don't mind, of course."

"Not at all." Reese knew the importance of socializing Tesha with other dogs. "Just holler later because we might not be here."

"Closin' a case?"

"If we're lucky." He motioned to the house. "Lemme grab her leash."

Reese went inside to grab Tesha's leash from the hook on the door. He was about to step outside when he heard Brantley's voice. He was obviously talking to someone, but there was no response, so he figured he was on the phone.

"I understand that." Brantley's words were spoken softly. "I still want to know." There was a brief pause, followed by, "Yeah, all right. Get back to me once you find out."

Not wanting Brantley to know he was eavesdropping, Reese hurried back outside, passed the leash off to Magnus, said goodbye to Tesha.

When he came back inside, Brantley was in the kitchen, his eyes glued to his phone.

"Who were you talkin' to?" Reese asked, closing the sliding door behind him.

Brantley looked up. "What?" He shook his head. "No one. Just waitin' on Trey. They said they were on the way back." Brantley tucked his phone in one of the pockets of his cargo pants. "How's it goin'? Any luck on the case?"

Reese explained the theory they were working on while he grabbed a bottle of water from the refrigerator.

"Where would Nancy Wright go?" Brantley asked, pondering the same question Reese had.

Reese didn't answer because that was the million-dollar question. Unlike the other two men, the Wright's didn't have any other property. No vacation homes or apartments. But Brantley already knew that, and clearly, the man was distracted. Enough he was not making eye contact as Reese eyed him carefully.

Something was going on, but he didn't know what it was. Sure, he had a few ideas, but Reese refused to believe that a chasm was developing between them because of someone from his past.

Then again, Madison wasn't exactly in his past, now was she? Just a little while ago he'd gotten a friendly text from her, telling him she hoped to see him when he was in Dallas this coming weekend for training with Sniper 1 Security. What was worse was the fact that, rather than brush her off the way he had for months, he'd told her he would see what his schedule was like.

Yeah, he blamed it on the fact that Brantley had pushed him away this afternoon, sending him off to work with Evan rather than maintaining their partnership as they had thus far. He'd been hurt and angry, and, yes, texting Madison back had been a form of punishment. One Brantley wasn't even aware of.

When he glanced over, he saw Brantley was watching him. There was so much skepticism in his gaze it made Reese feel guiltier than he already did.

"Tesha went with Magnus," Reese informed Brantley. "I'll … uh … just go back and help the team."

Brantley stared and nodded, neither broaching the subject that was quickly growing between them.

MAGNUS LED TESHA AROUND THE SIDE OF the house, intending to get in his SUV and head back to Camp K-9.

As he neared the parking area, he saw a car coming up the drive. He didn't recognize it, but he waited anyway, curious as to who else was part of this elite task force. As it approached, he noticed the small Uber sign in the front window, and a smile pulled at his mouth when he realized it was Trey getting out of the backseat.

"You think we should sneak out or say hello?" he asked Tesha, patting her head when she nudged his hand. "Yeah, I agree. Never pass up an opportunity to say hello."

Magnus opened the rear door of his SUV, pretended to be rummaging around for something while he gave Trey time to move closer. It wouldn't surprise him if the man chased down his ride and disappeared the same way he came. They hadn't had much interaction this past week, aside from Magnus stopping by in the middle of the night for their usual booty call.

He turned when he heard the crunch of gravel beneath Trey's boots, wondering if the man would even bother to say hello if Magnus didn't get his attention first.

He got his answer in the form of Trey's back as Trey headed toward the backyard, passing right on by without a word.

"Trey!"

The man pulled up short but didn't turn around.

"The least you owe me is a conversation," he said, ensuring Trey heard his disappointment.

No, maybe they didn't have a relationship in the traditional sense, but they did have something. Magnus refused to be brushed aside and ignored as though he never existed.

Trey slowly turned, his eyes hidden behind the dark lenses of his sunglasses. "Last I checked, I owed you nothing."

Magnus lifted his chin, stared the man down, waited.

He didn't have to wait long before Trey was stalking toward him, his anger apparent in the square of his shoulders and the tense line of his neck.

Because Magnus knew there was a camera monitoring the driveway, he waited until Trey stepped behind the SUV, giving them a modicum of privacy, before he stepped up to the bigger man.

"Actually," Magnus lowered his voice, "you owe me an orgasm."

He felt Trey's body harden, knew if he dropped his hand between Trey's legs, he'd find a rock-hard ridge hidden behind the zipper of those jeans.

Magnus kept his hands to himself. He knew better than to push too hard, and here, at Trey's brother's house, the place where Trey worked, Magnus did not want to push his luck. While he felt no need for them to hide what was transpiring between them, he still respected Trey's need for discretion.

"I hope you close your case soon," Magnus told him. "Because when you do, I'm comin' to collect."

To his surprise Trey didn't say a word, he simply stared, eyes still hidden by the mirrored lenses.

Taking a chance, Magnus leaned in, putting his mouth close to Trey's. "In fact, I think I'll collect tonight, regardless."

This time when Trey's body hardened, Magnus wondered if he was getting ready to snap.

BRANTLEY CONSIDERED CALLING REESE BACK BEFORE HE headed over to the barn, but he was at a loss for words. Reese had surprised him by coming inside, and Brantley had felt guilty about the conversation he'd been having before the man showed up.

Not that he had anything to feel guilty about. He knew Reese would not fault him for looking into Dante Greenwood's current status. Brantley had been keeping track of the man ever since he went into rehab shortly after he was caught earlier this year when he had staged his own kidnapping. His partner in crime had died during the attempted apprehension, and because of the whole *his word against mine* bullshit, Dante had gotten off scot-free, convincing everyone that he had been kidnapped and held against his will. It had helped that he'd lost a finger in the ordeal, which had garnered him sympathy and offered credibility to his story.

Brantley knew different. And because he hadn't been there to protect his best friend at the time, Brantley intended to keep JJ safe from Dante going forward. He would do that by ensuring Dante was watched at all times.

However, Brantley also knew that Reese was feeling guilty about something. Hell, it was written all over his face, and it had gotten infinitely worse since Brantley had split up the team earlier. What he wanted to know was what the hell was Reese hiding. Why was he keeping secrets now, after all this time?

Brantley paced to the front of the house and looked out the window, wanting to ground himself before joining the others in the barn. He paused when he saw movement in the driveway, looked over to see...

"Well, I'll be damned." He shook his head.

Standing behind the dog trainer's SUV were Trey and Magnus, looking mighty cozy as Magnus got up in Trey's face. It didn't look confrontational. Not in the hostile sense. It did look a bit heated, though.

Exhaling, Brantley shook his head again and stepped away. What Trey and Magnus did was none of his damn business. If they wanted to keep their relationship a secret, let them. They were grown men, quite capable of handling their own shit. They didn't need Brantley's warnings or his meddling.

Plus, Brantley had too much shit to deal with to worry about his brother's love life.

CHAPTER FIFTEEN

THREE HOURS LATER, AND NO CLOSER TO finding Cedric Hawkins or Nancy Wright, Brantley decided he needed a breather.

Baz, Evan, and JJ were still working while Luca, Elana, and Holly had gone to grab some food to bring back for them. Brantley had sent Becs and Jay home, assuring them he would call if something came up. He'd tried the same with Darius, but the man was determined to pitch in however he could. At the moment, he was running city-wide scans to see if they could catch Nancy Wright on a public camera. Charlie had returned from Lakeway a short time ago, disappointed that she hadn't been able to meet up with Nancy. When she attempted to stay to help out, Brantley sent her home to take care of her mother. Like he had with the others, he assured her he would call if they found something. And last but not least, Brantley had instructed Trey and Slade to head out but to stick to their phones in case they were needed. Neither had argued, and Brantley couldn't very well blame them. It had been a stressful day, and it wasn't quite over yet.

He left them to it with a promise that he would return before strolling out of the barn, wondering where Reese had disappeared to. He'd thought he was outside with Tesha, but when he looked around, he saw that man and dog were nowhere to be found.

He headed for the house, going in through the back door. He paused as soon as he stepped inside to see Reese standing at the stove.

"Hey," Reese greeted with a quick look over his shoulder. "I'll have it ready in a few."

Have what ready, Brantley didn't know, nor did he really care because his attention was on the fact that Reese was shirtless, a pair of shorts the only thing he wore. He had to swallow hard to choke back the lust that ignited. That was how it always was. No matter where he was at in his head, seeing Reese always had this effect on him.

Brantley hated where they were at right now. The tension that lingered between them was growing more intense with every passing day, and Brantley knew he was partially to blame. His own attempts to pretend everything was all right were failing him the more his insecurities increased. Worse, he didn't know how to eliminate it. They were managing to skate past their issues, but the thread keeping them from falling apart was tenuous at best. Using sex as a distraction to keep from having to broach the subject, as he had for the past few months, clearly wasn't helping. At the same time, it wasn't a surprise that he was considering doing the same thing now.

"I'm gonna..." He closed the back door. "I'm gonna shower."

Yes, that was what he would do. He would focus on getting cleaned up beneath icy spray and not think about Reese standing in the kitchen, looking like sin on a stick. It wasn't like he didn't see the guy shirtless often. Daily, in fact. However, seeing him doing something so ... *domestic*... like that. Damn.

"Christ," he muttered on his way to the bedroom, tugging his T-shirt off on the way.

"You know, we can't—"

Brantley spun around to see Reese standing in the doorway, his mouth open but no more words coming out.

"What?"

Reese's gaze slid downward, over Brantley's chest, and that damn heat spiked in his blood. He fucking loved when Reese looked at him like that. Fucking loved knowing he could turn the man on without much effort. There was no doubt about it, the physical attraction was still burning hot between them.

"I thought you were cooking," Brantley said, putting his hands on his hips, the move drawing Reese's gaze a little lower.

"I am." Reese took one step forward. "I *was.*" Another step. "I *will be.*"

Brantley waited to hear what came next, holding his breath and doing his level best to maintain eye contact. What he wanted right now was to put his arms around this man and pull him in close. He wanted to feel him everywhere because he needed that connection. Anything to keep him from feeling as though things were unraveling when in reality there was no reason they should be.

"Brantley..." Reese said softly, the single word barely a whisper of breath.

He knew in that moment that Reese felt the same, wanted the same thing. *Needed* it.

If he were a stronger man, Brantley would've resisted. He would've backed away until he felt settled, until he knew which direction they were headed. Perhaps even until they'd had a conversation. Unfortunately, he wasn't that man, the one who talked about feelings and nonsense. And he had no intention of starting today.

He stepped toward Reese, but it wasn't hesitant. It was more like a lunge as he reached for him, jerking him closer, their mouths crushing together. He drove his tongue into Reese's mouth even as he backed the man up a step, shoving him against the wall. All sense of decorum was gone, overridden by this insane passion, this driving need.

"We should talk," Reese muttered against his mouth, although he never stopped participating in the kiss.

Brantley made a noncommittal sound as he nipped Reese's lower lip, then sucked it gently. When Reese groaned, Brantley slid his tongue inside his mouth once more and licked urgently.

"Brantley ... we really..."

Brantley forced himself to pull back, gripping Reese's head with both hands and meeting his stare. "Is that what you want?" he rasped roughly. "To fuckin' talk right now?"

Reese didn't speak for long seconds, but finally, his answer came in the form of a head shake.

Brantley was on him then, pinning Reese to the wall with his entire body. Chest to chest, hip to hip. He kissed him forcefully, tilting Reese's head for a better angle as well as to signal where he was going next. When he managed to break away from the bliss of Reese's kiss, Brantley's lips trailed along Reese's hard jaw then down the warm column of his neck. He couldn't resist touching Reese in the process, his hands roughly caressing what he could as he worked to rid Reese of those damn shorts.

Once he had the man naked, he'd intended to move things to the bed, but clearly Reese had other plans because he took over, ripping at Brantley's clothing, discarding every piece in a fury of movement as their hands continued to roam and caress.

Finally naked, they made it to the bed. Brantley didn't pretend to be courting Reese when he shoved him down on his back. He didn't follow him down, instead taking a moment to observe all that bare skin and those deliciously sculpted muscles while Reese lay out before him, cock in his fist.

Oh, yeah, he definitely enjoyed seeing Reese jerking himself slowly, as though the tease would be more than Brantley could resist.

Fair enough, he decided. He couldn't resist the man if he tried.

Brantley moved around to the other side of the bed, where Reese's head was. *Then* he joined him, crawling over him and straddling his face so that he could work Reese's cock with his mouth while the man he loved returned the favor.

"Fuck," he hissed when Reese engulfed his dick, taking him in deep. Brantley's hands fisted as the sensation blasted through him. It was intense as always, but there was something else. A uniqueness, he would say. As though this was their first time together.

Leaning down, he took Reese in his mouth. He bobbed and sucked, not waiting for Reese to give him permission or to guide him along.

Maybe that was what was different about this time. It was the first time that Brantley wasn't holding back. He wasn't seeking permission, wasn't looking for reassurances. He wanted Reese the way Reese wanted him. Hard, fast. Now.

Unable to resist the mouth drawing on his cock, Brantley rolled his hips, fucking Reese's face while he sucked the man's cock in return. The fact that he was giving as much as he was receiving was likely the only reason he didn't come down Reese's throat within minutes. He was that worked up, that on edge.

Thankfully, Brantley kept his sanity because he did not intend for this to be a quick oral session. Oh, no. He intended to fuck Reese within an inch of his life, to remind the man who he was and that what they had between them was not something either of them could find elsewhere.

Pausing his oral ministrations, Brantley hooked his arms behind Reese's thighs and pulled him so that his feet lifted from the bed and his knees bent toward his chest. Yep, he liked Reese just like this. Vulnerable and open to whatever Brantley had in mind. He heard Reese grunt seconds before Brantley thrust his tongue into Reese's asshole. He wasn't slow and gentle, no teasing rim job, just a good ol' fashion tongue-fuck.

"Oh, fuck," Reese cried out, his body hardening beneath Brantley.

The sixty-nine position wasn't the same when he had Reese nearly bent in half, but it was exactly how Brantley wanted him. Unable to move, pinned beneath him. For the first time in their relationship, Brantley wanted to dominate him, to show Reese precisely the man he was getting.

Reese surprised him when he began rocking beneath him, clearly attempting to take Brantley's tongue deeper. To help him along, Brantley pulled back and pushed a single finger inside Reese's ass.

"Oh, God, yes," Reese grunted from beneath him. "Feels good."

Brantley used his own saliva to ease the way, adding another finger, fucking him harder. "Like that?"

"Yes … yes … just like that. Fuck me," he groaned harshly.

"You wanna be fucked?" Brantley taunted, stopping what he was doing so he could turn around.

"Yes."

Although he considered fucking the man dry, Brantley had a last-minute change of heart and grabbed the bottle of lube from the nightstand.

When he was kneeling between Reese's thighs, he gripped his knees, forced them back and wide so he had a better view of that tempting hole.

"You sure about that?" Brantley met Reese's gaze briefly. "Because I won't hold back anymore."

Reese's gaze narrowed, his expression hardening. "I didn't realize you were."

"Oh, you have no idea," Brantley rumbled, dripping lubricant on Reese's hole before tossing the bottle away and rubbing it in with a finger, then two.

Reese was writhing beneath him within seconds, and Brantley was too on edge to torment him for long. With another shift of his body, he had his cock pressed against Reese's hole and his eyes pinned on Reese's.

"You ready?"

Reese's chin tilted up slightly, and the rough command was unlike anything he'd heard from him before. "Fuck me, Brantley."

He did.

Brantley pushed into Reese's body, and he wasn't gentle about it. He thrust his hips forward, driving past the tight ring of muscles, gritting his teeth as the blessed heat of Reese's body consumed him. With his hands once again on Reese's knees, he held him open as he retreated, then slammed in again. He didn't hold back, fucking Reese the way he'd wanted to since the very beginning.

No holds barred.

REESE HAD NEVER SEEN THIS SIDE OF Brantley before. Not when it came to sex, anyway.

Had it been a year ago, Reese probably would've panicked. But here and now ... he felt an intensity between them that he'd never felt before. Another first that Brantley was giving him. There was nothing gentle about the pounding of Brantley's hips against his ass, the way he was driving his cock down into him and retreating, the friction making every nerve ending in Reese's body spark. The pleasure was unbearable, making sweat dot his temples. He was at Brantley's mercy, pinned beneath him, and he loved every second.

"This how you want me?" Brantley growled, slamming home. "Rough? You need this, Reese? Need this to remember what you wanted from me?"

All the air in his lungs burst out as those words sank in.

"Stop," he gritted out, reaching for Brantley.

Brantley met his gaze, but he didn't stop. He continued to impale him, driving in harder, deeper, faster.

Reese knew they needed to stop, they needed to talk about this, but it was useless to fight it. There was so much emotion behind Brantley's movements, the way he fucked him, the way he held his stare. They were connected in a way they'd never been, but Reese feared there was an underlying emotion neither of them would accept: insecurity.

"Shit..." Brantley hissed. "I'm ... gonna ... fuck."

Reese did the only thing he could think of. He gripped Brantley's wrist and held on, rolling his hips in an attempt to take more of him. He closed his eyes and let the sensations batter him until his own release was inevitable. Gripping his cock, he jerked himself firmly until he saw lights flash behind his eyes, the pleasure overwhelming him.

"Oh, Jesus ... Reese ... fuck..."

"Come for me," Reese demanded, digging his fingertips into Brantley's wrist as though his only job was to hold them together.

Brantley slammed into him one final time. Reese let go as Brantley roared his release, the two of them coming apart at the same time.

An hour later, after they'd cleaned up, after Reese had finished cooking and they'd scarfed it down, Brantley left him at the house so he could return to the barn. Reese figured he could've followed, helped out in whatever way the team needed him, but something held him back.

Despite the fact they'd had what was likely the best sex Reese had ever experienced with anyone—man or woman—he had the suspicious feeling that something had fractured between him and Brantley. Something significant.

Rather than chase Brantley down, he used their brief separation to attempt to get some clarity. He headed for his office upstairs and closed himself inside. He stared at his laptop, wondering if he could replicate the queries that Brantley had done when looking into Madison, figure out what might've triggered this chasm between them.

Not that he didn't have some idea. The media's view of the Southern Boy Mafia hadn't changed over the years. At some point, they had decided to glorify Maximillian Adorite as a gangster, using that in their headlines, coming up with the stories that would keep people coming back for more. And Max's family wasn't off-limits either. There were stories about Ashlynn, Victor, Brent, Madison, and Aidan all the time. They were the Kardashians of the underworld.

At this point, Brantley probably knew the same about Madison and the Adorite family as Reese did. His relationship with Madison hadn't been one based on shared secrets or intimacy. Sure, there'd been sex involved, but even Reese had known there'd been a detachment to it. A means to an end. On both their parts.

And yes, somewhere down the line, Reese had gotten comfortable enough with Madison to consider a future with her. The problem had been in that comfort level. It wasn't that he'd been in love with her, certainly not to the point he didn't think he couldn't live without her. No, more like he'd felt the need to settle down. So many people in his life had been getting married and having kids at the time that Reese had felt as though they were leaving him behind.

Reaching for his phone, Reese pulled up the chat thread he had going with Madison. He started back at the beginning:

March 8, 2021

In case you don't recognize this number, it's Madison. I hope you don't get upset, but I still have your number in my phone. Thought I'd check in.

Not upset. Good to hear from you.

I heard you just finished working a case that had something to do with my brother.

Doesn't everything somehow come back around to involving your brother?

I guess in a way that's true. How are you doing?

I'm getting by pretty well. A lot going on. New job and all.

One day you'll have to tell me about it. I'd love to know how things are going, what you're up to.

March 10, 2021

I heard you were gonna be in my neck of the woods. Thought maybe you'd want to grab some dinner while you're in Dallas. It would be nice to catch up. I've missed you, Reese.

March 13, 2021

Are you really going to ghost me, Reese?

Not ghosting you. Been really busy lately.

Too busy to type back a simple acknowledgment? :) So, is it true? Are you working in Dallas from time to time?

Training with Sniper 1 Security. Every few weeks we make it up that way.

Who's we?

Me and my team.

Ah. So not a girlfriend? That's good to know.

No girlfriend, no.

I wish I could tell you that didn't make me happy to hear that. I've been doing a lot of thinking about the past lately and you're a big part of those thoughts.

March 16, 2021

I just looked back at my last message, noticed how it probably sounded to you. I promise, I'm not hinting at anything. I would really like to see you though. Catch up in person.

One of these days, I'd like to do the same.

Really? Wow. Now my heart is fluttering.

Don't read anything into that, Reese Tavoularis. I'm not coming on to you. I promise.

Ok, maybe I am. A little. Can you blame a girl?

April 21, 2021

Well, it's been a month and I just learned you and your team were in town this past weekend. No calls? No texts? I don't bite, Reese.

Sorry. I meant to. Just have a lot going on right now. Transitioning to a new company and all. I promise when I have time, I'll let you know.

So does that mean you'd like to see me, too?

Yes, Madison. I would like to see you.

Reese continued to stare at the screen, skimming the messages for the months following. There weren't all that many, and, yes, that was mostly his fault because he'd come up with one excuse or another as to why he couldn't meet up with Madison while they were in Dallas.

If he was honest with himself, he wasn't sure he wanted to. Not because he worried what he might do. He would be faithful to Brantley for as long as they were together. That wasn't something he questioned. However, he wasn't sure he wanted to risk what might happen when he saw her again. The feelings that she might evoke.

Again, it wasn't that he'd been in love with her, but Reese had loved her. More importantly, he'd been attracted to her. Possibly more so than any other woman from his past. What happened if he saw her again, and it stirred those old feelings? Namely, lust. For a woman. Would that be enough to conjure up the insecurities he'd had when he'd first gotten together with Brantley? Would he begin to question everything again?

On the other hand, Reese wondered if that was something he needed to know. Did he still have the ability to feel something for a woman? Was this thing with Brantley temporary? A curiosity that needed to be sated?

He glanced back down at the phone, found the start of the last thread they had between them.

September 8, 2021

I think I've got it figured out. Looks like you come to Dallas on the third Friday of every month. That means you'll be here in a couple of weeks, right?

Yes, I'll be up there on the seventeenth.

Oh, wow. Barely over a week. Does that mean you'll have some free time while you're here?

I expect I can, sure. Why? What did you have in mind?

Dinner. My treat. A chance for the two of us to catch up.

Where?

You really are committing to this, huh?

I'd like to see you, too, Madison. And I can't say no
to dinner. Where did you have in mind?

Jason's Deli.

Why did I know you were gonna pick that place?

*Because it's my favorite and we used to have a good time just
sitting around and talking while we were there.*

We did have a good time.

So that's a confirmation you'll meet me? What time?

I'll let you know when my schedule's clear.

Don't you dare ghost me again, Reese.

I won't. I promise.

Reese had no intention of ghosting her this time. Although
he knew it was wrong that he was going to meet with her, he knew
it was important.

If for nothing else than the future of his relationship with
Brantley.

He needed to clear up the uncertainty, and until then, he
wasn't sure he was even capable of moving forward.

CHAPTER SIXTEEN

Thursday, September 16, 2021

FOR THE FIRST TIME IN A LONG time, Brantley didn't lead the charge on the case. Rather, he allowed his personal thoughts and his mood to get in the way of progress, so he kept a safe distance and let the team work their magic. They'd spent the entire day yesterday outlining everything they knew and searching various places they determined might be a good hiding place for Nancy Wright, to no avail. After two full days on this case, nothing had turned up and he knew the team was growing more frustrated by the second.

Brantley didn't blame them. He'd been keeping the governor apprised of the situation, so he was feeling the heat from all angles. Their case had gone from one missing person to two and though Brantley believed they were related—find one, you'd find the other—it pissed him off that they couldn't catch a break.

While they hadn't been able to pinpoint Nancy Wright's location yet, they'd made some progress on tracking her recent activity, which just so happened to coincide with Annie Hawkins's and Mallory Jacobs's activity. Although there was still the chance they wouldn't find Cedric Hawkins alive, they had compiled quite a bit of evidence that would help Detective Mathis with an arrest. Or three, as would be the case here.

When he woke up a couple of hours ago, he'd gone on a solo run, leaving Reese and Tesha behind, although he knew they would've both joined him if he'd asked. Ever since their encounter on Wednesday night, Brantley had felt off. That good mood from last Friday, the one he'd thought was a precursor to upcoming events, was nowhere to be found. In its place, a shitload of insecurity and doubt. Oh, sure, the intimacy they'd shared had been beyond anything Brantley'd experienced in his life, but there'd been something missing. Something he was sure had been there in the beginning.

Now as he ventured out after a quick shower in the guest bath, he found Reese in the kitchen, cutting up cantaloupe. Neither of them spoke although their eyes met briefly. Between them was a boatload of shit that needed to be discussed, but neither one of them was going to be the first to bring it up. Work was a much safer subject.

"Anything new on the case?" he asked in an effort to make small talk.

"Not that I've heard. Darius and Trey have been at it all night. No luck. JJ and Baz got in half an hour ago. They went home for a quick nap and showers sometime last night."

"Anyone else here?"

"Luca was asleep on the couch in the loft when I looked in on them a little while ago. Elana, Slade, and Holly got in early. Evan and Jay weren't far behind. Darius arrived with kolaches and donuts, so I'm sure JJ's wired for sound."

"Anything from Charlie or Becs?"

"Becs called, said she was on her way. I haven't heard from Charlie yet."

Brantley nodded. He was about to head over to the barn when his cell phone rang. He snatched it from his belt, glanced at the screen. He saw that it was Detective Mathis and prepared himself for an ass chewing when he answered with a barked, "Walker."

"We've got a situation."

"What's that?" he asked, stepping out the back door.

"We found Nancy Wright."

"Being that was our goal, I would've thought it was a good thing," he said, taking the steps down the back porch.

"It would be, but she's taken a couple of hostages."

Brantley pulled up short. "Wait. What? Where is she?"

"At the Hawkins's residence."

"Why're you callin' me? Don't you have a negotiator who can handle this sort of thing?"

"We do, but I figured you'd like to know since Charlotte Miller is your employee."

Brantley glanced at the driveway to see if her car was there. It wasn't.

"Charlie? What does she have to do with this?"

"She's a hostage, Walker."

"Are you sure about that?"

"Considering she's the one who called, I think I'm positive it's her."

"What the fuck?" Brantley took off toward the barn at a run. "Tell me everything."

Five minutes later, Brantley was behind the wheel, Reese riding shotgun and Trey in the backseat. Behind them, Evan, Slade, Baz, and Luca were in Evan's Ford Expedition. The rest stayed back at the barn to assist on their end if possible, with JJ at the helm.

"Does anyone know why the fuck Charlie went to Annie's house alone?" Brantley barked as he pressed his foot to the floor, heading for the toll road that would deliver them to Lakeway.

"She didn't say anything to me," Reese said firmly.

"Yesterday she mentioned talking to the vic's wife again," Trey contributed.

"That was yesterday."

Trey shrugged. "Don't fuckin' ask me. I told her I'd go with her if she decided to go. She never brought it up again."

"Do we know how this happened? How Nancy ended up with hostages, one of them being Charlie?" Reese asked, shifting the subject.

Brantley glanced over, shook his head. "Detective Mathis doesn't really know. He said Charlie left him a voicemail this morning, asked if he would try reaching out to Nancy Wright again. Said she was heading that way to talk to Annie Hawkins. Next call he got was from Charlie tellin' him there was a hostage situation at the Hawkins's home."

"Who all's there?" Reese asked as he keyed something into the laptop that was installed in the truck thanks to Sniper 1's tech analysts.

"That's a question I'm hopin' you'll get the answer for while I drive."

IF SHE HAD PREDICTED SHE WOULD BE held hostage by a terrified woman and her bitchy friends today, Charlie would've never gotten out of bed.

Hell, she was questioning her motives now, wondering why she'd gotten the big idea that she was going to drive out to Lakeway and make another attempt at getting a face-to-face with Nancy Wright. Since they still hadn't had any leads on where she was, Charlie had thought talking to one of her best friends might produce results.

The good news was they now knew where Nancy was.

The bad news ... well, for starters, the shit show currently taking place. The one where there were a handful of hostages—Charlie included—and a very panicked Nancy Wright.

Worse than that, Charlie hadn't bothered to tell her team, not wanting to interrupt their efforts in case nothing panned out on her end.

Teach her to want to help.

Charlie sat utterly still on the white leather sofa in the den, watching as Nancy paced back and forth, her movements short and clipped as though she wasn't sure what her next move would be.

"I can't *believe* I let you talk me into this," she muttered.

Charlie wasn't sure who she was talking to, but she suspected Annie was her prime target. Ever since her arrival, she'd been practically spitting fire in the other woman's direction.

"Nancy, I think I can help you if you'll just tell me what's goin' on," Charlie urged.

When Charlie had arrived an hour ago, she'd been greeted by Peter the Lawyer. Despite the fact he'd been dressed in a fancy suit, Charlie had instantly known there was a problem. His pale face and shaking hands had been her first clue. At that point, walking into this house had been the equivalent of stepping onto the set of the *Real Housewives*. All three women had been screaming at one another, issuing threats, feigning hurt. All while Cedric Hawkins was lying in a heap on the floor and Peter the lawyer was attempting not to crap his pants.

At first, Charlie had offered to help, trying to calm the situation and check on Cedric Hawkins, who was no longer missing and—at least for the time being—was still alive, unlike his partners. Unfortunately, based on some of the heated exchanges, it didn't appear he had a lengthy life expectancy because Nancy had other plans. During one of their many back-and-forth shouting matches, Nancy had grabbed a butcher knife from the marble block in the kitchen. The fire in her eyes as she waved it around had told Charlie she was on the verge of a breakdown.

That knife had gotten Annie's and Mallory's attention as well, both women going the overdramatic route, crying in earnest and begging Nancy not to kill them.

If Charlie hadn't witnessed it, she never would've believed it was real.

So here she was, sitting quietly on the sofa while the others whimpered and cried, and Nancy continued to track steps on her fancy watch. The calm was just a facade, she knew. At any moment, one of the terrified hostages could freak out and cause Nancy to snap, something she appeared dangerously close to doing. Charlie'd wanted to get a handle on the situation, giving the police a chance to come since she'd opened the line to Detective Mathis as soon as Nancy had grabbed that knife. She only hoped he was listening and gathering the necessary people to get them all out of this unharmed.

"Talk to me, Nancy," Charlie said again. "Help me understand what's happening."

"It's obvious," Nancy said softly, her hand trembling around the hilt of the knife.

As though it was, Charlie nodded, pretending to understand.

Nancy Wright was a slight woman. No more than five foot two, probably a good ten pounds underweight with small features and small bone structure, she wasn't an imposing figure. Had it not been for the angry expression, she probably would've blended into the wallpaper, familiar with fading into the background. Even though she had control of the room since she wielded the knife, she looked as though she wanted to disappear into the floorboards.

"Nancy, why are you doing this?" Annie asked, her voice trembling, her expression one of a terrified woman.

Charlie got the impression Annie Hawkins was good at pretending to be something she wasn't. Not for a second did Charlie believe that woman was scared of Nancy.

"Me?" Nancy's voice raised slightly, waving the knife. "This is all your doing. *You* did this."

"Me?" Annie's gaze shot to Charlie briefly, then back to Nancy. "Whatever are you talking about, honey? I think you're just traumatized. Losing your husb—"

"Don't you dare," Nancy seethed, her delicate features hardening.

Charlie watched the interaction, not moving so Nancy wouldn't feel threatened. As it was, Cedric Hawkins was currently laid out on the floor unconscious. She didn't know if he'd be breathing for much longer, but she wanted to believe he would. If only she knew the extent of his injuries, she might be able to gauge what she should do next. When she'd come into the house, he'd appeared to be conscious, surprising Charlie with his presence. He was the man they'd been looking for, and here he was, alive and well. Only he didn't look all that well anymore.

"This is *your* fault," Nancy told Annie. "This was all your idea."

"That's ridiculous," Annie declared haughtily, her gaze snapping to Charlie again. "I think he drugged her or something. She's not making any sense."

Oh, yeah. Definitely the master manipulator.

"And *you!*" Nancy bit out, glaring at Mallory Jacobs. "You went along with it. Did you even know she was sleeping with our husbands?"

Based on how Mallory's red eyebrows launched skyward, Charlie would take that as a no.

"She's insane," Annie stated, looking right at Charlie. "You know that, right? She's insane. Anything she says is a lie. She's been abused for years. That makes her crazy."

Charlie remained completely still, trying to get a read on what was going on here. She didn't know if anyone was outside preparing to breach the house, but she had to believe her team would come for her. They would get her out of this and hopefully get everyone else out of it as well. And then she could apologize profusely for jumping the gun and not bothering to clue them in when she should've.

Nancy glared at Mallory. "Did you know she was screwing Seth when she killed him? In her own bed."

Mallory's green eyes were wide as she stared over at Annie.

"It's a lie," Annie said, again sounding bored with the conversation.

"Peter told me," Nancy admitted, stabbing the air in Peter's direction. "You called him when you needed help removing his dead body. From. Your. Bed."

Annie's eyes narrowed infinitesimally before she schooled her expression. "I have no idea what you're talking about. Seth died at the club. In the locker room. You read the report yourself."

"Seth was never at the club," Charlie noted.

That appeared to be news to Mallory. "What?"

Keeping one eye on the knife-wielding Nancy, Charlie told Mallory about her visit to the club on Tuesday. No sooner were the words out than she realized she wasn't helping the situation at all.

"Peter did that, too," Nancy admitted, glaring at the lawyer. "You paid someone to falsify the report. You were protecting *her!*"

"You were sleeping with him?" Mallory asked, her voice small, almost childlike.

Charlie watched the exchange, wondering who Annie *wasn't* sleeping with.

Annie shook her head but didn't look at Mallory.

"You told me he was sleeping with someone else," Mallory accused. "And it was *you?*"

"Does it matter?" Annie retorted. "He wasn't faithful to you, Mal." Annie looked at Nancy. "And Brian. He was trash. He beat you, for chrissake, Nancy. He would've killed you if he had the chance. I had sex with him to take the edge off his frustration."

Ouch.

"He hated you," Nancy growled softly. "He called you a slutty whore."

Annie's eyebrows rose as she sucked in air, clearly taken aback by the statement.

"This was your idea," Mallory whispered, staring blankly. "It was your idea to kill them. You said they were *all* cheating."

"They *were* cheating," Annie snapped.

"With you," Nancy shouted back. "You were just pissed that Cedric was planning to leave you for his secretary."

"She's not his secretary," Annie countered hotly. "She's a brainless bimbo who answers the phones. She was screwing him for his money, that's all."

"You can't handle the fact that he loves her," Nancy whispered. "He loves her, and he was going to leave you."

"He was not," she bit out.

Charlie shifted, hoping her phone was still on and someone was listening to this.

Annie sucked in air. "You're crazy." She looked at Charlie. "She's crazy."

Yes, they were all crazy, Charlie realized. Certifiably nuts.

From his spot on the floor, Cedric groaned, clutching his chest.

Charlie looked up at Nancy. "I need to help him, Nancy. I need to make sure he's all right. You don't want to be responsible for his death, do you?"

Nancy's eyes filled with tears. "I couldn't do it. I couldn't kill him. She wanted me to. It was my turn. I was supposed to kill him because she killed Seth and Mallory killed Brian, but..."

Oh, boy.

Nancy turned to Annie. "I called him, just like you told me to. He met me at the gas station."

Well, that explained how her burner phone got into his car.

"Then I drugged him," she continued, her gaze lowering to the floor as though she might find solace there. "He was too heavy. He fell when I tried to get him in my car. Hit his head." She touched her head with her other hand. "Hit it hard. Then that guy helped me. He helped get Cedric in the car."

Charlie wasn't sure who she was speaking to, but again, she hoped someone was listening on the other end of the line.

"I was going to kill him," she muttered almost incoherently. "But I didn't want to. I don't want to hurt anyone." Her eyes were wild when they lifted to meet Charlie's. "I didn't *want* to."

"You didn't kill him," Charlie said softly, wanting to take control of the situation. "Right now, you haven't done anything wrong. But we need to make sure he's all right, Nancy. He needs to go to the hospital."

Nancy shook her head.

"My team is gonna come looking for me," she said, speaking directly to Nancy. "You don't want them to find us like this. You don't want to be holding anyone hostage when they get here. Put down the knife, Nancy. Put it down, and let me look at Cedric."

For a brief moment, Charlie thought she had a handle on the situation. Nancy turned, her hand lowering, the knife down at her side. She looked remorseful, a sob tearing free. It was coming to a close without any harm being done, and Charlie wanted to exhale a sigh of relief.

That breath didn't come out easily because the next thing she knew, Annie launched herself at Nancy, taking the woman to the ground as she screamed and railed.

Charlie didn't hesitate, shooting to her feet, grabbing Annie, and dragging her off of Nancy. It had lasted all of a few seconds, that was it. It should've been an innocent catfight. Over before it really started.

Only there was blood pooling on the floor beneath Nancy. Pooling fast.

Charlie dropped to her knees, turning Nancy over to find the wound, to see where it was coming from. The knife was wedged into her stomach, her face already turning an ashy gray.

"Call nine-one-one!" she shouted. "Now!"

TREY'S HEART LODGED SOMEWHERE IN HIS THROAT when they pulled up to Annie Hawkins's house to find it surrounded by emergency vehicles, including an ambulance.

Brantley threw the truck in Park, and the three of them bolted out, racing toward the house, bypassing the cops who were attempting to maintain a perimeter.

"What the hell happened?" Brantley barked at Detective Mathis, who was stepping out onto the porch.

Behind him, Trey saw a body being zipped into a bag, and his heart stopped beating. Charlie? Please, God, don't let that be Charlie. If it was, this was all his fault. He'd been partnered with her last, and he should've insisted she get with him before she did anything else. Instead, he'd brushed off her concerns to focus elsewhere.

"There was an … incident," Mathis said, his tone somber. "A confrontation ensued, and she took a knife to the torso. It was a fatal wound. She was dead before the ambulance arrived."

Trey swayed on his feet.

"You can go in; just stay away from the scene."

Trey followed Brantley and Reese, his heart pounding in his ears, his eyes glued to the gurney being rolled out, the body bag closed, hiding the death it held inside. Flashes of memory took root, at the hospital the day Kylie had been hit by the car. He could still smell the sickly sweet mix of antiseptic and death, the loss of a member of his own family so great it had choked him.

"Hey."

The voice barely registered because Trey was still staring at the bag, and he briefly wondered if it came from inside. Was Charlie talking to him? Was she—

"It was an accident."

Trey spun around as more words registered. He saw Charlie standing there, alive and breathing, not covered in black plastic and being carted off.

For a second, he thought his knees would give out, his relief was so potent. She wasn't dead. He hadn't lost another person he knew.

"She was calming down," Charlie explained. "Lowered the knife and Annie Hawkins jumped on her. Nancy landed on the knife."

"You all right?" Brantley asked her, his gaze sweeping over Trey momentarily.

"I will be," she answered.

Trey took a deep breath, let it out slowly. He stood taller, wanting the eliminate the concern in his brother's eyes.

"Cedric Hawkins?" Reese prompted.

"He's fine," Charlie told him. "Doped up on whatever Nancy drugged him with, but the EMT said he'd be fine. They're taking him to the hospital."

"And Annie and Mallory?" Reese asked.

"Arrested for murder. It was just as you suspected; they conspired to kill each other's husbands."

Trey looked around at all the fancy furnishings in the fancy house in the fancy neighborhood. Not for the first time, he was content with his humble life.

His thoughts drifted to Magnus, to the way the man had taunted him in the driveway, promising to come over to collect on the debt he claimed Trey owed him. Trey had spent that night alone because Magnus had come over, but Trey hadn't bothered to answer the door. And last night ... well, last night Trey had avoided his house altogether, staying at the barn simply because he wasn't man enough to own up to the feelings he was developing for Magnus.

Later he would blame it on the adrenaline coursing through him and the overwhelming relief that Charlie was all right, but at the moment, he knew he would be seeking Magnus out. It was time they had a conversation.

CHAPTER SEVENTEEN

Friday, September 17, 2021

BY THE TIME FRIDAY MORNING ROLLED AROUND, Reese had a strange twitch between his shoulder blades.

He wasn't sure what or who was spurring it.

Now, as he perched on the corner of an empty desk, listening while JJ ran through the itinerary for the upcoming training session at Sniper 1 Security, he glanced from one person to the next.

Charlie was a bit solemn after yesterday's events. She had apologized profusely about going on her own, something Brantley apparently couldn't even wrap his head around and had told her as much. Reese had sat by while she promised never to do it again and Brantley threatened to fire her if she did.

Baz was also more subdued than usual, his attention continuously going to the phone in front of him. The one that continued to buzz every so often.

Reese also noticed the way Luca was watching Baz, as though he knew a secret and desperately wanted to tell the man. However, if it looked as though he was going to say something, Holly would reach over and poke her brother in the arm, shaking her head firmly when he would look her way. Reese was curious but not enough that he was willing to interrupt Brantley to get the details.

"I want everyone on the road by nine," Brantley instructed the team. "That should put you in Dallas no later than one. Grab lunch when you can and we'll meet at the simulation building no later than two. Baz? You and JJ ridin' together?"

"That's the plan," Baz answered, hitting the button on his phone to silence it.

"I've got room," Trey announced, "if anyone wants to ride with me."

"If you don't mind the company, I'll take you up on that," Evan replied.

"Me, too," Jay added.

"I'll drive," Slade offered. "So I've got some room, too."

Luca looked over, raised a finger as though signing up. Darius also took him up on the offer.

Reese observed while Elana, Holly, Becs, and Charlie figured out their travel arrangements. They were still hashing it out when Baz's phone buzzed again.

"Take the goddamn call," Brantley snapped at him, drawing everyone's attention.

Baz looked both traumatized and furious as he grabbed the phone and stood. A second later he was marching out of the barn.

Needless to say, this was going to be an interesting weekend.

And Reese was sure it was only going to get worse from here.

BAZ STEPPED OUTSIDE THE BARN, TRADING ONE form of chaos for another.

To be honest, he would've much preferred to listen to the ruckus inside the barn than the overly emotional woman on the phone. Of course, ignoring her hadn't done any good.

"What do you need, Molly?" he ground out through clenched teeth when he finally answered.

"Where are you?" she pleaded, her voice dripping with tears. "I need to see you. Where are you?"

Baz had gotten familiar with this conversation because it now took place two to three times a day. Every. Single. Fucking. Day.

Now that she was nearing her due date, she'd become more emotional than usual, and Baz knew her to be unstable on a good day. Problem was, he didn't know how to solve the problem. At the same time, he couldn't very well ignore her since she was having his baby.

"I'm at work," he answered, keeping his tone light, easy. "Where I am every day."

"I thought you were going to come by," she said with a sob.

"I did come by. Last Saturday."

"You didn't stay."

"No. And I don't plan to stay, Molly. We've talked about this."

"No, *you've* talked about this."

There was an awkward silence that followed, and Baz paced the yard, trying to gather his thoughts, trying to come up with the best way to tell Molly that he intended to limit his time with her because this was getting them nowhere. Before he could speak, she did.

"You just don't get it. You're supposed to spend more time with me. That's how this works, Sebastian."

Baz rolled his eyes. She was the only person in the world who called him by his full name. Not even his parents called him Sebastian. He wasn't sure they ever had.

"I get it, Molly. I do. You're pregnant, I'm the father. That's relatively simple. But that doesn't—"

"There's nothing simple about this!" she shouted. "Nothing! Do you hear me? You're supposed to be here to support me. To take care of me."

To love me, he filled in because that was where she was going with this. It seemed to be her only objective. From day one, Molly had been telling him how much she loved him. She would go so far as to ask him to say the words. Once she'd even told him it was all right if he didn't mean it, she just needed to hear it.

Needless to say, Baz hadn't said them. He wouldn't because they weren't true, and the last thing he wanted was to lead Molly on.

"I can't do this without you, Sebastian. I can't have this baby without you. You did this to me. You put me in this position."

Oh, he definitely knew, because she'd told him again and again how this was all his fault. How he was the one who'd had sex with her without a condom, although for the life of him, he still could not remember the events of that night. Nothing past a few fuzzy puzzle pieces of moments that didn't quite come together.

"I'm here, Molly. Just like I said I would be. And I'll be here for the baby, too."

"No, you're not! You're there, not here."

"I have a job. I have to be here."

"No!"

Baz stopped pacing. "What?"

"No," she said more firmly, her tone going from irate to eerily calm. "That's not how this is gonna work."

"Molly, I think you need to—"

"No, Sebastian. I'm not doing this your way any longer. If you want anything to do with our baby…"

He waited when she trailed off.

Baz heard more sobbing in the background.

When she came back, her voice was smooth and even. "You need to marry me, Baz."

His entire body went ice cold. Marry her? Not a chance in hell. Baz had already started giving Molly money to take care of things. He'd bought a majority of the baby items she'd told him she would need, plus he'd promised he would start paying her rent once she went out on maternity leave and until she could return to work, something she insisted wasn't going to be possible because she believed she needed to be a stay-at-home mom. From what she'd told him, she had it all planned out. Problem was, Molly's version of the future was nothing more than a fairy tale that wasn't going to come true.

"Molly—"

"No!" she screamed. "You don't get to say no this time, Sebastian. We're getting married because that's what people do when they have a baby. I love you and I want our baby to have a father the right way. It's the only way this works."

"And if I refuse?"

"Then ... then ... then I won't have the baby! I won't! I'll get rid of it, Sebastian."

"Molly, stop," he demanded, his body tense from her threats.

"I won't have your baby! Do you hear me? Are you listening?"

Oh, he was listening, all right. His ears were open and he was listening as he made a beeline for his truck.

He would admit he knew very little about Molly Ryan, but the one thing he was certain of, she was seriously unstable. During the past nine months, ever since the one and only time they'd been intimate in any way, she had conjured up this relationship, convincing herself they were something they weren't. Not once had Baz ever placated her, never had he pretended he wanted something with her. He had insisted from the beginning he would be part of the baby's life because he was as responsible as she was. Never once had he denied that.

But he wasn't going to pretend to care for her or want to be in a relationship. What happened between them ... it had been a drunken mistake.

"I'm on my way over there, Molly," he told her as he yanked open his truck door. "We'll talk about this."

"Don't bother, Sebastian!" She was screaming at the top of her lungs now. "Unless you plan to marry me today, you and I are done. And you won't have to worry about a baby because——"

"Molly?" Fuck. The call disconnected.

Baz floored it, the truck's tires spitting gravel in his wake as he headed for the main road.

He tried to call her back, but it went right to voicemail.

He kept his foot on the floor as he commanded Siri to call JJ.

"Hey," she greeted with what sounded like a smile in her voice. "Where'd you go?"

"I'm going to Molly's," he blurted, his heart pounding in his chest. "I think she's gonna do somethin' stupid, JJ. She's actin' crazy. Said she wouldn't have the baby if I didn't marry her today."

JJ's sharp inhale made Baz's heart ache.

"I won't marry her," he assured JJ. "It's not an option."

A second of silence before JJ finally said, "Oh, jeez. Okay. Just … uh … call me if there's somethin' we can do."

"I will. Just let Brantley and Reese know."

"Of course." JJ's voice lowered. "And Baz … be careful."

"I will. I'll call you in a little while."

The drive from HQ to Molly's was only ten minutes, but it felt like ten hours.

Baz managed to find an empty spot in the apartment complex's lot. Although he tried to play it cool and calm, something told him that Molly had finally come unhinged. She'd been headed in this direction since the very beginning, but he had somehow convinced himself she would eventually settle down and realize the only way this would work was for them to be co-parents, not a couple. Baz had attributed some of her irrationality to the pregnancy hormones and the fact that she was still young. Only twenty-one and pregnant out of wedlock. Probably not how she'd seen her life unfolding.

When he reached her second-floor apartment, Baz knocked. Quietly at first, then louder.

"Molly, open the door." He glanced left and right, hoping he didn't draw the attention of her neighbors. "Open the door so we can talk."

A second later, the door opened and Molly stood there. Her face was red, her hand cradling her stomach as she folded over in obvious pain.

"What did you do?" he accused.

"Nothing," she groaned. "The baby's coming, Sebastian. Oh, God. The baby's coming."

Baz frowned, stepping inside, closing the door behind her. "Are you havin' contractions?"

"Yes! Yes. God, it hurts."

"Okay." He tried to keep his calm. "We need to get you to the hospital."

"It's too soon," she said, sobbing. "The baby's not due yet."

"Maybe not, but if he's ready, then we need to be at the hospital."

"Not until the eighth," she insisted. "That's when he can be born. Not until the eighth."

Baz ignored her ranting and went in search of the suitcase he knew she'd already packed for the hospital. He found it in her bedroom at the foot of her bed. When he turned to leave, his gaze snagged on the wall where she had a couple dozen pictures of him pinned up. They looked to be candid shots, taken when he wasn't paying attention. All here in her apartment, several from when he was getting in or out of his truck in the parking lot, taken through the window blinds.

Frowning, he stepped closer, noticed she had Photoshopped a couple of them so that they looked to be together. One shows her kissing him on the lips.

Oh, boy.

That had never happened.

There was also a framed and decorated sign with the words:

Sebastian and Molly Buchanan
married 2021
Love for eternity

Holy shit.

She really was delusional.

Pretending he hadn't seen any of that, Baz returned to find Molly holding on to the wall, her other hand curled tightly around her protruding belly.

He helped her out into the hall, closed and locked the door behind them. A few minutes later, she was in the passenger seat of his truck, her gaze scanning the interior as though she was looking for something. Her entire demeanor had shifted. Gone was the panicked, freaked-out mother-to-be, in her place a calm, assessing planner.

"We'll need to get an SUV," she said with a smile. "Something that'll be easier for me to get the car seat in and out of."

Baz cocked an eyebrow and peered over at her.

It was then he realized Molly Ryan was more than hormonal or unhinged.

She was quite possibly batshit crazy.

JJ STARED BLANKLY AT THE PHONE AS she set it on her desk.

Now that the team had solidified the travel plans, everyone had dispersed, and they'd shifted their attention back to how they wanted to rearrange now that Allison wouldn't be returning to the task force. Downstairs she could hear Holly and Becs chatting about who would sit where, which direction the desks should be facing. It all faded away as Baz's words repeated in her head: *She's actin' crazy. Said she wouldn't have the baby if I didn't marry her today.*

Marry her.

Not for the life of her had JJ considered that might be an option for Baz. Even knowing he would forever be tied to the other woman, JJ's mind had *never* considered marriage.

Of course, he'd just told her he wouldn't marry Molly, but that was now. He was a good man, one of the best she knew. He was a stand-up guy, a true gentleman. Would he change his mind one day? Be with Molly for the baby's sake?

JJ pressed her hand to her stomach. The thought of Baz marrying anyone caused an ache she couldn't ignore.

He'd never mentioned it before. From what she knew, the relationship between him and Molly was strictly platonic, had been since that one and only night they'd been together. And she believed him.

He'd said he wouldn't, she reminded herself. No sense in jumping ahead of herself.

This was all Molly. The woman who called and texted him three dozen times a day, always asking where he was, who he was with. JJ wasn't sure how Baz could stand it. He had to turn his phone off otherwise he couldn't get through a simple meal without an interruption.

"Do you want a say in what's—"

JJ looked up, her thoughts interrupted by Brantley's voice. "What?"

"Everything okay?"

She glanced down at her phone, back up to her boss. "That was Baz. He said…" JJ cleared her throat. "He has to go to Molly's. Said to let you know."

"Somethin' wrong with the baby?"

JJ shrugged. "I don't think so. I…" She shrugged again.

"Well, let me know if there's anything we can do." Brantley motioned toward the downstairs. "If he can't make it to Dallas, you can ride with us if you'd like."

JJ nodded. She hadn't even considered that Baz might not go. They were sharing a hotel room, which meant if he wasn't there, she would be sleeping alone. It would be the first time since… God, she didn't want to think about that right now.

Brantley cleared his throat, motioned toward the main floor. "You want to weigh in on this once and for all?"

Forcing her thoughts away from Baz, JJ shook her head, smiled. "Nope. That's why I'm up here and they're down there." She canted her head. "Did Allison really quit?"

"That's what her email said."

"And you're just gonna let her?"

Brantley snorted. "What people do or don't do isn't somethin' I can control. Nor do I want to."

JJ just found it strange that this woman, one no one wanted to hire in the first place—no one but Brantley—would up and quit on day one.

"I'm sure Luca's grateful for you lettin' him hide up here," Brantley said, glancing over at the desk Luca had commandeered.

Initially, JJ had been against sharing a space with Luca, but when she realized they worked well together, she'd conceded, but only if he promised to stay on his side of the loft. So far, he'd turned out to be a decent office mate. He didn't eat at his desk, didn't leave dirty cups or trash.

In a word, he was tolerable.

JJ spent the next hour pretending to work while constantly looking at her phone, waiting for Baz to call. She was on the verge of chewing her fingernails when her phone finally rang, the sound making her jump.

"Hey," she greeted, her heart suddenly in her throat. "Everything okay?"

"No."

At least his voice was calm.

"What's wrong?"

"I had to bring Molly to the hospital. She went into labor."

"So soon?" JJ sat up straight. "Isn't it too early?"

"She's thirty-seven weeks, so I don't know. We're waiting for the doctor to get here, to do an exam."

"Okay." JJ fought to draw air into her lungs. "Do you want me ... *us* ... to come up there?"

Baz's voice lowered significantly. "I can't ask you to do that, JJ."

"You didn't," she said. "I offered."

And she honest-to-God hoped he turned her down. Although she wanted to be there for Baz, JJ wasn't sure she would survive seeing him with Molly and their baby. Even thinking about it made her heart crack wide open.

"I think it's best I'm the only one here right now," he said softly. "She called her mom and dad. They're on the way. So is her sister."

"What about your parents? Are you going to tell them?"

JJ knew Baz hadn't told his parents that he was going to be a father. They'd discussed it over dinner one night, and he'd admitted he needed to tell them, but he was hesitant. Baz had surprised her when he followed by saying he would have a paternity test done once the baby was born to confirm it was his before he told his family. JJ had been strangely relieved, although she didn't understand why Molly would have a reason to lie about it.

Granted, she still wasn't sure Molly was completely on the up and up. There was a reason she hadn't allowed Baz to go to the doctor with her when she went, but JJ hadn't figured out what it could possibly be. She hadn't even let him see a sonogram, hence the reason there'd been some doubts as to whether or not she was really pregnant.

"I will. If it comes down to it." Baz sighed. "I'm not gonna be able to go to Dallas this weekend, JJ. I can't leave her right now."

Although JJ hated it, she understood. "I already told Brantley what's goin' on. He'll understand."

"Thanks, JJ. I'll call you later."

"All right."

JJ disconnected the phone, staring down at it.

Not for the first time, she wished she could go back to New Year's Eve. If she could, she would've never answered Dante's call, she would've had dinner with Baz, gone back to his place, and spent the entire night in his bed. If she'd done that, they wouldn't be where they were now.

Baz wouldn't be having a baby with another woman.

And JJ wouldn't be scared of her own shadow.

CHAPTER EIGHTEEN

WHEN JJ DISCONNECTED THE CALL, LUCA BURIED his top teeth in his bottom lip and stared at the computer monitor in front of him although he had no idea what was even on the screen.

He'd been biting his damn tongue for two fucking weeks now, and if he didn't tell her the pressing information he had, it was damn possible he was gonna spring a fucking leak in his head. If it weren't for his pain-in-the-ass sister insisting he keep his nose out of everyone else's business, he wouldn't be fidgeting with this ridiculous urge to blurt out the information he'd dug up.

And fine, maybe it hadn't been his business, and he never should've done the deep dive on Molly Ryan that he had done. But come *on*, someone had to. Hell, he'd been surprised JJ didn't know everything about the woman, right down to her credit score. Turned out, for whatever lame-ass reason, JJ was minding her own business, claiming she didn't want to know, despite the fact that this was the woman who'd hooked up with the man JJ was clearly in love with.

In his defense, Luca was looking out for JJ. That was the *only* reason he had done some online snooping, enough that he had a comprehensive breakdown of Molly Ryan's entire life. What he'd found was beyond disturbing, and Baz deserved to know. But rather than tell Baz he'd been a nosy motherfucker, Luca preferred to give the info to JJ and let her do with it what she would.

"Don't you do it."

Luca's gaze shot up, and it was then he noticed Holly standing in front of his desk.

"Do what?" he asked his sister, flopping back in his chair and regarding her with amusement.

"You shouldn't have that information, and it's not your place."

He regarded her, flipping his ball cap around on his head and cupping it into place. "Maybe not, but I *do* have it, so someone deserves to know."

"Luca," Holly warned.

He leaned forward and pressed a finger on the manila folder that contained what he'd printed out. He scooted it toward Holly. "Why don't *you* read it and decide for yourself who should know or not?"

Holly shook her head. "No way am I gettin' in the middle of that," she said in a rushed whisper.

"In the middle of what?"

Luca shot up straight in his chair when he realized JJ was looking over at them from her desk.

"Nothin'," he said too quickly, even as Holly snatched up the manila folder.

JJ's dark eyebrows lowered.

Luca had to admit, he'd always had a crush on JJ. She was one of the hottest women he'd ever met, but it was more than her striking good looks that had captured his attention all those years ago. He had a penchant for smart women, and ones with that dry sense of humor really did it for him. Fortunately, she'd never accepted his advances; otherwise, they wouldn't be here now, working together. He would be the first to admit he could burn a relationship faster than anyone else. He preferred the hit-it-and-quit-it method, and since that usually happened before he could ever develop a friendship with a woman, things always went south.

So he considered himself lucky that JJ had always shunned him. He didn't hold it against her. Like he'd said, she was a smart woman. And he was glad to call her a friend.

"What's in that folder?" JJ asked, her gaze pinned on Holly.

"Nothin'," Luca repeated.

"That's a whole lotta nothin' for one guy," she remarked, eyebrow quirking as though she didn't believe him.

He shrugged, not sure what to say. No way did he want to tell her that the man she loved was having a baby with a crazy woman. And that wasn't just him being juvenile and calling Molly Ryan names.

No, the woman was certifiably crazy, and he had the documents to prove it.

"If it's nothin', let me see it," she insisted, stepping toward them.

"JJ, no," Holly said softly, then glared at Luca.

Did he feel guilty about unearthing that information? Nah. Luca didn't feel guilty about much. However, he had no desire to hurt JJ, and he knew the information in that folder would. More accurately, the fact that he'd kept it from her would.

JJ held out her hand to Holly.

His sister glared at him again before holding it out. "Please don't read it," she said to JJ.

"Why?" JJ took the folder, stared at the outside.

"Because it's about Molly. My stupid brother is nosy."

JJ was looking at him again, and Luca could only shrug. It was true. He did stick his nose where it didn't belong, but he made no excuses for it. A higher power had given him the skills to do it. He damn sure wasn't going to pass it by. And no, he didn't feel guilty, although the way she was looking at him told him he probably should.

She waved the folder, still not looking inside. "Why do you have this?"

Luca exhaled heavily and went for the truth. "Because I got tired of Baz's phone buzzin' all the goddamn time. It's not normal. And since she's the one blowin' the damn thing up, I decided to have a look-see."

JJ was watching him, and he could tell she wanted to know more.

"It's all there, JJ. The cold, hard truth about Molly Ryan."

"Are you sayin' it's worth readin'?" she asked, glancing down at it again.

"Personally, I'd wanna know if I were you."

Her gaze snapped back to his. "Why?"

"You love him, don't you?"

Her eyebrows lowered, but she didn't answer.

"If I loved someone and they were mixed up with a woman like that…" Luca shrugged and leaned back. "I'd damn sure want to know."

Evidently his argument was convincing enough because JJ turned away … and opened the folder.

AS BAZ SAT IN MOLLY'S HOSPITAL ROOM waiting for the doctor to come in for an examination, he recalled the movies that the warped and twisted side of himself enjoyed. The ones with the stalker—friend, roommate, lover—who had a completely dark side that no one expected. Those movies never turned out well for at least one person, and he suspected this was a similar situation.

Molly was currently propped up in the bed, her hand on her belly, a beaming smile on her face.

Oh, and he couldn't forget the little tiara she'd produced from that overnight bag, as well as the silky blanket that she had laid out over the hospital blanket that was covering her legs. He honestly did not want to know what else she could pull out of that thing, but he had to assume he would need to make a run for the store before the baby came home. It appeared as though Molly's main focus was herself.

What was creepier than that was the fact that she was watching him so intently, as though if she kept her eye on him he would never leave.

"This is going to be lovely," she said, smoothing out the thin silk. "I wish they would let me wear my own gown though. This one is scratchy."

Yeah, but it was replaceable for, you know, when she gave birth.

"Could you get me some ice chips, honey?" she said sweetly.

Honey?

Oh, Jesus.

Rather than comment, Baz swallowed the frustration and pushed to his feet. Molly's contractions were evidently real, but they were spaced about thirty minutes apart. The doctor they'd seen upon arrival said it would still be a while, but because Molly's blood pressure was elevated, they wanted to keep an eye on her, so they admitted her. Baz figured her high blood pressure was from the panic attack she'd had while she was planning the wedding they would never have and realizing it wouldn't come to fruition.

"Oh, and maybe some water," Molly tacked on. "And a straw. Pretty please."

"Anything else?" he asked on his way to the door.

"I think that's all I need for now."

Baz stepped out into the hallway and glanced left then right to locate the nurses' station. He requested ice chips for Molly then pulled out his phone and shot a quick text to JJ, letting her know the status. At the moment, they were in limbo, but he figured sometime in the next seventy-two hours, there'd be a baby. Regardless, he didn't see himself making the trek to Dallas with the team this go-round. While he wasn't worried about that, he was worried about leaving JJ alone. Without a roommate at the hotel, this would be the first time since her attack that she would have to sleep by herself, and that bugged him. He didn't want JJ to be alone.

It wasn't that he didn't care about Molly and the baby. He did. Well, the baby, anyway. Molly made it really damn hard for him to care about her because her expectations were so high. She had somehow twisted and manipulated their one night into something that it wasn't. If you asked her, she would likely say they'd made love for hours on rose petals after drinking champagne and eating caviar. The way Baz remembered it … well, the truth was, he didn't remember it. Nothing past going into Moonshiners that night. Everything else was a blur.

As he was walking back toward Molly's room, a nurse was rolling a machine in. He followed close behind, but the moment Molly saw Baz and the machine in the same room, she was shaking her head.

"He can't be in here for this," she insisted.

"What's *this*?" he asked, not even sure what was going on.

"It's an ultrasound machine," the nurse replied. "The doctor wants to take a peek, just to make sure everything's all right." She smiled at Molly. "It's perfectly all right for the father to be in here."

"No," Molly demanded, her voice holding that weird edge of panic. "I don't want you in here for this, Sebastian. You need to leave. Right now."

Baz frowned, met her gaze, held it. "I'd prefer to stay if it's all the same. I'd like to see the baby, too."

Molly was visibly trembling. "No. You can't. Not until she's born. You can't."

Baz set the ice chips on the table and went stone still. "She?"

Molly's eyes bounced from him to the nurse then to the machine. "What?"

"You said not until *she's* born. You told me we were havin' a boy."

Her eyes were wide, her mouth slack. "We are. I mean, I don't know. We won't know until October eighth. That's the due date."

The nurse looked up from where she was placing a tube of gel. "I show the due date to be September nineteenth," she said kindly, reaching for the chart. "Dr. Tinder says you're right on schedule."

Baz paused. He didn't need to do the math, because he knew a healthy pregnancy was forty weeks, and since they'd only had sex the one time, there was only one day that was forty weeks out. October eighth was exactly forty weeks from January first. Meaning…

"You're wrong," Molly insisted. "Dr. Tinder's wrong. The due date is October eighth."

The nurse was looking at the chart, as though worried she'd made a mistake. "Due date is September nineteenth," she said as she read. "And the sonogram done at sixteen weeks shows to be a girl." She looked up and smiled. "Another sonogram at twenty-seven weeks shows the same thing."

Baz was staring at Molly, unable to look away. She'd lied to him. About all of it. Yes, she was most definitely pregnant, but she wasn't pregnant with his baby. Hell, she'd gone so far as to alter the baby's gender in her stories. Why the fuck would she do that? Did she think he needed to have a boy to be happy?

She was loony tunes.

His cell phone buzzed on his hip, so he grabbed it, saw JJ's name. He tapped the screen to decline the call.

"I don't need that machine," Molly insisted. "No one needs to see the baby. It's not time yet. October eighth is the due date."

The nurse looked sincerely confused and perhaps a bit concerned by Molly's agitation.

"Could you give us a minute?" Baz asked the nurse.

She looked back and forth between them. "Of course. Dr. Tinder should be here in a few minutes to do the ultrasound."

Baz nodded, waited until the door closed behind her. He remained across the room, not wanting to get anywhere near Molly.

"You shouldn't see the baby yet," she demanded, her fingers now twisted in that silky blanket. "It needs to be a surprise."

"Oh, I don't think you'll be disappointed," he mumbled. "This is definitely a surprise."

"Sebastian, I can explain."

"Can you? Can you explain why, for the past thirty-seven weeks, you've strung me along and told me you were pregnant with my child when, really, you were already pregnant the night we met?"

"But I didn't know."

He barked a mirthless laugh. "That doesn't make the baby mine, Molly."

Her eyes turned glassy. "You'll make a good father, Sebastian. And when I'm not pregnant, you'll want me. You'll want to have sex with me. I promise. We can try again. Next time I'll be better and it'll work. You just have to give us a chance. You won't drink alcohol and it'll work."

Baz wasn't sure what the hell she was rambling about. "What do you mean it'll work?"

"That night ... it was a mistake." Her face was so animated, her eyes wild. "You said so. And I agree. I was too excited and you ... well, you were drunk, which is why you couldn't ... you know. But that's okay. It means we get a do-over. The way you kissed me that night ... you wanted me. I know you did, but you just couldn't..."

Baz's eyebrows popped as he waited for her to elaborate. "Couldn't *what*, Molly? Spit it out."

"Get it inside me," she said softly, tears filling her eyes. "I know you wanted to and I tried. I got on top, put on the condom, but it wouldn't go on, so I tried again and it broke. It didn't matter though. We didn't need it. We're gonna be together forever. We're having a baby."

Baz's heart was pounding, his blood roaring in his ears. They hadn't…

"I really tried, but … we get a do-over," she said adamantly. "And the baby … the baby will only make us love each other more."

He was still hung up on one thing. "We didn't have sex?"

"We tried," she repeated. "You weren't … you know … hard. It was the alcohol. I read that it does things like that. The alcohol made it not work, but it will. Next time it will. You'll want me like that again, I know you will. And when you do, we'll try again."

Baz fought to remember that night just like he had a million times since. No matter how hard he tried, there were only brief flashes of memory. He remembered being on the couch, Molly lying on him, kissing him. He had a vague impression of her rolling on a condom. But the most he remembered was watching as she straddled his hips, riding him. Hadn't she?

"You wanted *me*," Molly stressed. "Not her. *Me*."

"Her?" Baz stared at Molly. "What are you talking about?"

"You called me Jessica by accident. But you were drunk, so you were confused."

Baz felt his stomach churn.

"But you wanted *me*," she bit out, her sweet demeanor shifting to furious. "You were there with *me*."

Baz took a deep breath. "Molly, tell me the truth. Is that baby mine?"

Her eyes were wide, tears now streaming down her face. "Is it?"

"She can be."

"Did we have sex that night?"

"We tried," she whispered, her eyes darting away.

He noticed she was looking at the chart.

That was where the truth was. That was the reason she wouldn't let him go to the appointments with her. If he had, he would've realized she was further along than she said she was. Granted, it was only by a few weeks, so it could still be his.

Unless, of course, they'd never had sex in the first fucking place.

Baz walked over, flipped open the chart, skimmed the information. She was forty weeks according to this, her due date in two days. It showed her date of conception to be in mid-December. Her first missed period was December twenty-ninth. That was before he'd ever even met her.

And according to the notes, she was having a girl.

Curious, he glanced at Molly's name to see if that was even her name. It was. Molly Elizabeth Ryan born on November twenty-ninth...

"Oh, my God," he muttered, lifting his gaze to hers. "You're"—his heart slammed into his ribs—"*nineteen?*"

Her eyes were wide.

"You told me you were twenty-one, Molly."

She was in a fucking bar when they'd met, for fuck's sake. She lived in her own goddamn apartment.

Nineteen?

Baz was going to be sick.

"Sebastian, please, I can explain everything. I can. Really. You just have to give me a chance. We can work this out. I *love* you. The baby *loves* you. Please, Sebastian. Please give us a chance. I know—"

He shook his head, seriously worried he was going to vomit. The past nine months had been a lie. One after another at that. They hadn't even had sex. The baby *couldn't* be his because they hadn't had sex. He'd lost nine fucking months with JJ because of this shit.

"Jesus, Molly. How the fuck could you do this?"

He headed for the door. It opened before he could reach it, and an older couple appeared, both of them smiling.

The man's gaze narrowed on Baz, probably wondering who he was.

"You must be Kevin," the woman greeted, her eyes skeptical as they bounced over to where Molly was still begging him to stay.

"I'm sorry?"

"Kevin? Liz's boyfriend?"

Liz? She went by Liz?

And she'd told them his name was Kevin?

Holy fuck.

Baz shook his head. "No. I'm … uh … no, I'm not Kevin. If you'll excuse me."

The last thing he heard as he headed for the exit was Molly or Liz or whoever the fuck she was calling his name.

He didn't turn around.

CHAPTER NINETEEN

JJ STARED AT THE OPEN FOLDER IN front of her, at the two sheets of ordinary white paper with the black ink on them. Funny how something so common could be so … disturbing. Then again, it wasn't the paper or the ink but rather the details. That saying … the devil is in the details … well, it was quite literal in this case.

She had tried to call Baz once, but he hadn't answered and she desperately wanted to talk to him.

Thankfully, the barn was clearing out as the team got on the road for Dallas. She had promised Brantley she would be there in time for the afternoon training when he offered Reese's truck for her to drive since they would be driving up in Brantley's. Although she wasn't keen on the idea of going alone, she would do it just to prove that she was reliable.

But first, she was hoping to talk to Baz.

Not that sharing the particulars was going to change the fact that Baz was having a baby. It didn't matter that Molly was nineteen years old or that she'd been committed to not one but three different psychiatric facilities in the past eight years, she was obviously pregnant based on what Baz had told them. Despite the fact she had been diagnosed with schizophrenia at a young age, had birthed two other children by two different men—one when she was only fourteen, the other when she was almost eighteen, both put up for adoption—it appeared Molly Ryan was still having babies with unsuspecting men.

She knew without a doubt Baz wasn't aware of any of this. In fact, he didn't even know she was a teenager. Although JJ had never cared about the personal details of the woman Baz had made a baby with, she had assumed Molly was at least legal drinking age. Safe assumption since they'd met in a bar.

Granted, that was the least of their worries.

Forty-five minutes later, after she'd attempted to call Baz two more times and the call had been sent directly to voicemail, JJ knew she needed to get on with her day. When she did get ahold of Baz, she could break the news to him then.

No sooner had she stood when she caught a flash of movement on the other monitor on her desk. She no longer simply relied on the screen downstairs to show her the camera angles. These days she was far too paranoid to not have that information at hand, so she kept them streaming on the second monitor on her desk. There, pulling into the driveway, was Baz's truck.

"You can do this," she muttered to herself, running her hand down the front of her shirt to smooth it. She could relay this information to Baz in a non-critical way. She could warn him without getting emotional.

A minute later, she heard the faint beep of the keypad outside the door, held her breath as she waited for him to come inside. She listened to his footsteps, fearing what he was there to tell her. Had the baby been born? Would he want to celebrate? Was he here to tell her she would need to find a new place because he needed to set up a nursery in the bedroom she slept in?

Her stomach cramped at the thought.

When he reached the top of the stairs, JJ turned and froze.

His eyes looked haunted.

"What's wrong?" She bolted up from her chair. "Is the baby okay?"

He shook his head as he stepped closer.

Oh, no.

"Were there..." JJ wasn't sure the right word for it, something that wouldn't sound too morose. "Complications?"

His pretty blue eyes met hers and he frowned. "No. I'm sorry. No complications." He shrugged. "Not that I know of anyway. I left."

Wait. Huh? "So she didn't have the baby?"

"The baby's not mine, JJ."

JJ was tempted to stick her fingers in her ears to clear them out. Had she heard him right? "What?"

"The baby ... she's not mine."

She? JJ was almost positive Baz was having a boy. He'd talked about it, about having a son, teaching him to play baseball, going to football games.

"I don't understand." JJ reached for his hand, pulled him toward an empty chair, and urged him to sit down. "What's goin' on?"

He eased into the chair as though he was ninety-two years old, not thirty-two.

"Molly..." He swallowed hard, looked at her when she pulled her chair over and sat in front of him. "I didn't have sex with Molly."

Her heart galloped in her chest even though she didn't understand.

Baz shook his head, his eyes lowering quickly. "I guess we tried, but I was drunk. I couldn't..." He cleared his throat. "Molly was already pregnant by then."

"Oh, my God," she muttered. "So she what? She trapped you?"

It made perfect sense considering all JJ had learned about the woman.

He nodded. "I guess. She's nineteen, JJ."

JJ sat back, inhaled deeply. "I know."

"She told me she was twenty— Wait. What do you mean, you know?"

For a second there, she'd wondered if she could get away with not telling him what she'd learned.

She took a deep breath. "Luca ... he, um, he did some *research*."

"Into Molly?"

JJ nodded, holding his gaze, wondering if he would be pissed. "What did he learn?"

That wasn't the question she had expected. Her first question would've been *why?*

Baz shook his head, held up a hand. "Never mind. I don't want to know. Hell, I don't *need* to know."

JJ didn't offer it up. If he honestly didn't want to know, she had no problem keeping the details to herself. She would warn Luca to do the same.

So that meant the next question was... "What happens now, Baz?"

He shrugged. "Nothing. I left her at the hospital with her parents." A small smile formed. "Apparently they thought I was Kevin, the baby's father."

"Kevin?"

Okay, so seriously, this girl really was whacked.

They sat there, staring at one another for what felt like an eternity. So much hope had built up in her chest that she could hardly breathe with it all. The last nine months had been brutal, mentally, emotionally. And here Baz was telling her that it was all a mistake, that he wasn't going to be a father.

"JJ?"

She kept her eyes locked with his. "I love you," she blurted.

Baz's dark eyebrows slowly rose as though he couldn't quite understand her.

"I love you, Baz," she whispered, feeling the emotion building in her sinuses. The last thing she wanted was to cry, but she was overwhelmed with relief.

As though he'd been hit with a live wire, Baz jerked forward, moving toward her. He was on his feet in an instant, pulling her up, crushing his mouth to hers. JJ went willingly, trying to get closer, letting the emotions free as she held on for dear life.

She couldn't believe this was happening. JJ couldn't count how many times she'd prayed that it was all a mistake, that the universe or God or whatever higher power there was couldn't be that cruel.

When Baz backed her against her desk, JJ hopped up on it, let him settle between her thighs as he pushed her skirt up to her hips. While his mouth moved over hers, she fumbled with the button on his jeans, working them open. She needed to feel him, needed to know that this was real, that she wasn't dreaming.

"Baz…"

"Fuck," he growled, pulling her toward the edge of the desk as his hand slipped between her legs. "I need to be inside you."

Chills danced down her spine from the promise in those words.

"Yes," she insisted. "Now."

He tugged her panties to the side and guided himself home, and for the first time in months, JJ felt pure, overwhelming relief. There was no fear of the future, no impending sense of loss. She felt like the pieces of her life had worked themselves back together.

"Baz!" JJ's arms wreathed his neck as she held on tightly, letting the sensations pull her into that erotic abyss that numbed the mind and sated the body. "Oh, God, Baz."

"Tell me again, JJ," Baz demanded, his hand on her hip as he thrust his hips forward, burying himself deep. "Tell me you love me."

"I love you," she breathed into his neck, holding on tight.

"I love you, too," he growled, fucking her roughly, as though he couldn't get enough of her.

When she came a few minutes later, it was with his name on her lips and tears falling from her eyes.

Never in her life had she felt this content, this … whole.

She would hold on to the feeling for as long as possible, she decided. After all, whenever something good happened in her life, it was usually followed by something epically bad.

BRANTLEY'S EYES WERE ON THE ROAD, HIS attention on anything other than the man sitting in the passenger seat of the truck.

They'd made it to Dallas in good time, managed to check in to the hotel, and were on their way to the training facility to meet up with RT and the rest of the team. This weekend they were undergoing simulation training regarding hostage situations. Considering he and Reese had already encountered one during their short tenure with the task force, there was a good chance they'd come face-to-face with one again, and he wanted to ensure the entire team had the know-how to deal.

For the first time, he considered calling off the mission, such that it was. He got the feeling these efforts were not going to calm the waters between them. Adding tension to an already stressful situation never worked out well.

Brantley's phone buzzed in the cupholder.

"It's JJ," Reese noted, as though it was completely natural for him to be reading the text alerts.

Funny considering the text messages he suspected Reese was hiding from him. He'd only seen the one from Madison that one time, but he couldn't help think there were more.

"What does it say?" he asked, curious but not enough to take his eyes off the road.

Reese picked up the phone, typed in Brantley's password, and it was then Brantley realized how much of an open book he was to this man, but the same could not be said in reverse. Somewhere along the way, Brantley had invited Reese into his life in every way, but somehow, Reese had managed to keep Brantley on the periphery of his own.

"Baz and I are on the way," Reese read. "Big news! Baby isn't Baz's. I'll let him tell you about it when we see you later. We're running a little behind but we'll be there. Promise."

"Text back a ten-four," Brantley told him.

"You're not curious that the baby isn't Baz's?" Reese asked as he typed.

"Not my business." Although there were a few other topics he would've gladly discussed if Reese would've simply brought them up.

Thankfully, a minute later they were pulling into the parking lot of the Sniper 1 Security training facility, and the risk of hashing this out once and for all was in the rearview.

CHAPTER TWENTY

Three hours later…

"Go!"

Reese motioned with two fingers and advanced with purpose.

Keeping low, he walked down the dark path created by the large shipping containers stacked three high on either side of him. Beneath his feet was smooth concrete, which allowed him to tread silently, while at his back, Trey and Baz watched his six.

There wasn't any light to guide the way, so he relied on the night vision goggles that lit up the space with an eerie green glow to keep him headed in the right direction. With his gun up and aimed directly in front of him, Reese listened for any sounds to indicate where their target was.

He paused when he came to an intersection between the cargo containers, looked left, then right before holding up two fingers and gesturing for Baz and Trey to take opposite directions. Despite the fact they had the ability to communicate through the microphones and earpieces they wore, he didn't speak, not wanting to risk giving away their position.

Trey went straight, Baz to the right, so Reese moved to the left. He ignored the lightness in his head brought on by the narrow confines of the space and the darkness that shrouded him.

"Clear," Trey whispered into his earpiece. "Headin' to you."

Reese continued forward, keeping an eye out not only for the target but also for his teammates.

A minute later, Baz's voice sounded in his ear with the same reply as Trey.

Because they were both moving toward him, Reese paused again, holding his position to reduce the risk of friendly fire.

Baz and Trey reappeared a few paces behind him, and their presence reduced some of his stress. Knowing they were there was a small comfort.

"Moving," he whispered.

They continued on, weaving their way through the rows of shipping containers. Reese's focus was on what was in front of them, Baz's on what might be above, on the tops of those containers, and Trey's was on the rear.

When Reese came to a door, he stopped, holding up a finger as a signal for Baz and Trey. Stepping back to allow Trey to open the door—an action that required a well-placed foot and a tremendous amount of force—Reese kept his weapon aimed and his focus on the door, already considering what was on the other side.

Trey put his back to the door and pulled a one-leg mule kick, the heel of his foot hitting perfectly at knob level, splintering the wood at the latch. The door swung inward as Trey lurched back to avoid potential bullets sprayed by the bad guys they were searching for.

Using hand signals—two fingers pointed up, then toward the room—Reese silently instructed Baz to lead the way while Reese shifted his attention to their six o'clock, ensuring they didn't have anyone coming up behind them.

"Moving," Baz said softly, stepping into the room, Trey following next, then Reese.

The second he stepped into the room—roughly ten by twelve with no windows and no other exits—Reese's heart rate kicked into overdrive, his breaths became more labored. He did his best to conceal his body's reaction to the confined space while he kept his attention on the door.

"He's not here," Trey said, his words a bit garbled in Reese's head.

He could feel the cold sweat dripping down his back as he fought the memories from assaulting him. This was a safe place; there were no real threats. It was a simulation, a training exercise. At some point, he'd even seen the required exit signs that would lead them to safety in the event of an evacuation.

Even though he repeated that in his mind, Reese knew the panic attack was coming on. His hands had already begun to shake, his breaths choppy.

"Tavoularis, you okay?"

The voice in his earpiece did little to calm his nerves. He knew Ryan Trexler and the Sniper 1 Security team were monitoring them via the sensors in their equipment. They'd be able to see his respirations, his heart rate, even his body temperature.

It did nothing to reassure him. In fact, it irritated him more than anything.

"Tavoularis?" RT repeated, his tone harder than before.

"Fine," he bit out, hating that there were witnesses to his panic attack.

"Clear," Baz called out. "Prisoner's not here."

"Lights comin' on," RT announced.

Reese yanked the NVGs off seconds before the overhead lights clicked on, flooding the area in a white-blue glow, the simulation ending.

Overhead, Reese could see the ceiling of the warehouse, knew he wasn't locked in a six-by-six cinderblock hell, but it didn't help. With his weapon at his side, he marched out of the room, then through the maze of shipping containers that made up the obstacle course designed to put the Sniper 1 agents through their paces.

"We're gonna call it," Brantley announced, his voice streaming into Reese's ear.

"The hell we are," Reese snapped as he joined the others in the command center office where the team was monitoring their actions through a variety of equipment. On one of the screens, he noticed Hunter Kogan, along with Hunter's brothers Trace and Conner—the targets Reese and his team had been searching for—appearing in one of the corridors.

"We're good for today," Brantley insisted.

Reese squared off with the man, hating that he was so defensive, but unable to hide his frustration over the fact Brantley would coddle him like that. If this had been a real extraction, the hostage would've been as good as dead.

"One more time," Reese snarled back at him.

To his shock, Brantley stood his ground, facing off with him. "I said we're done. We've accomplished what we came to do."

"The hell we have." Reese and his team had yet to locate and rescue the hostage, which was the sole objective of the simulated mission.

RT stepped over. "If it's any consolation—"

"It's not." Reese slapped his laser gun on the table, then tossed the goggles alongside it. "Fuck you both."

Without looking back when Brantley called after him, Reese stormed out of the building.

He needed some air.

Hell, he needed a drink, and that was saying something considering he wasn't the sort who sought booze to manage his stress levels. For whatever reason, this particular training exercise had pushed him to his limits.

Reese fucking hated that, for the past three hours, he'd failed every time he attempted to rescue the hostage. Didn't matter that it was all fake, that ultimately RT and Brantley controlled the outcome. It didn't make him feel any fucking better because they didn't control Reese's reaction, the panic that flooded him whenever he was in a dark, confined space.

When he stepped outside into the blazing Texas sunshine, Reese took a deep breath, but he didn't stop walking. He considered making a beeline for the truck parked with a line of other vehicles, all there for the same training exercises Reese had just undergone. Instead, he headed around to the side of the building.

He'd bet good money that no one else would go into a full-blown panic simply by walking into a dark room. It wasn't the first time, either, and he hated that it probably wouldn't be the last.

Pacing along the length of the enormous metal building, Reese allowed his breaths to return to normal. Being outside helped.

He was on another trek away when he heard the door slam shut, knew it was Brantley coming to check on him. It was enough to ratchet up his frustration another notch.

"You okay?" Brantley asked when Reese pivoted and headed in his direction.

"Fine," he snapped. "I don't need you checkin' up on me."

As soon as the words were out, he could see the surprise on Brantley's face. If he hadn't been seconds from that damn panic attack, he would've felt shitty for using Brantley as his verbal punching bag.

"What can I do to help?" Brantley asked, his tone harder than before.

Reese came to a stop, stared at the man. "You can give me some breathin' room."

Brantley held up his hands in the sign of surrender and took a step back.

"More than that," Reese grumbled. "I need some distance. I need the truck keys."

"They're in the truck," Brantley stated, his voice ringing with worry.

"I'll see you back at the hotel later," Reese said, marching away without a backward glance.

Reese found the truck unlocked, the keys under the seat where Brantley usually left them.

A second later, he was behind the wheel, pulling out of the parking lot. He didn't give a shit if he looked like a fucking pathetic loser for walking out or running away. Right now, he couldn't think straight, and he damn sure did not want to see the pity in Brantley's eyes.

He'd seen it enough lately.

"HE GOOD?" RT ASKED WHEN BRANTLEY STROLLED back into the tech room.

Brantley glanced at the man who was technically his new boss. "Fine. We've been at it too long."

When RT didn't respond, Brantley knew Reese's brother-in-law was as worried about Reese as he was.

He couldn't blame the guy. Whatever was bothering Reese was now projecting off of him, and Brantley had a bad feeling that it was more than the panic attacks he was currently having. More than likely, it was a culmination of the tension that had been growing more taut between them and his unease with enclosed dark spaces.

"Well, I definitely like the progress they're makin'," RT said.

Brantley nodded. "I agree."

They had come a long way in the six months they'd been training. It helped that Reese had a military background, having been in the Air Force. Baz was a former APD police detective and Charlie a former officer, so they had proper training from a law enforcement agency. Not counting the newbies, the only team member who was out in the field who didn't have any formal training was Trey. He'd been a security guard, so his training was minimal, but he was proving he could do as good as, if not better than, the rest of them.

As for Evan and Slade, they would have their turn before the weekend was over, and Brantley would get his chance to see their baseline firsthand.

Brantley's skill set—having been a Navy SEAL—was still above and beyond what the Sniper 1 Security team could provide, but he was utilizing the courses and the simulations to keep his mind and body sharp since he'd been forced into retirement after suffering a career-ending injury.

Brantley exhaled, looked out into the warehouse.

RT stepped up to his side. "Why don't y'all lay off the simulation this weekend. Maybe try some team-building exercises that don't require them to snake through container walls in the dark. Might help Reese's mood."

If they were lucky.

"Or better yet, don't work at all. Gather the team, do somethin' fun. Take a breather."

A breather.

Unless that was referring to two minutes to collect his thoughts, Brantley didn't even know what that was. But he wasn't opposed to trying new things, and right now, he feared forcing this training might be doing more harm than good.

"I think we'll do that," he informed RT.

Baz stepped up to his side. "I'm gonna swing by the office and pick up JJ and Tesha and head back to the hotel."

Brantley informed him of the new plan to leave tomorrow before Baz slipped out of the building.

When Trey strolled out from the maze of shipping containers, Brantley gave him a nod. "Mind if I catch a ride back with you?"

His brother looked confused for a second, glancing around as though searching for someone.

"Reese headed back already," he explained.

Trey nodded. "I'll be in the truck."

Half an hour later, after saying his goodbyes to the Sniper 1 Security team, Brantley walked into the hotel room he was sharing with Reese. The digs weren't fancy, but it certainly wasn't the worst place he'd ever stayed. The rooms were clean, the furniture updated sometime in the last decade, plus they had a continental breakfast and a small bar that opened a few hours each night. Since it was cheap and convenient, they'd become frequent guests.

When he heard the shower running, Brantley set his phone down on the dresser and considered joining the man. He knew just how to relax Reese and a shower would be a bonus.

Brantley was tugging off his shirt when his cell phone buzzed. He tossed the shirt to the bed, then glanced down to read the text only to realize it wasn't his phone that was making the noise.

Reese's phone was plugged into the charger, the face lit up with a text message from—

Brantley's chest squeezed when he saw Madison Adorite's name on the screen.

He knew it was wrong to pry, but that didn't stop him from picking up the phone and reading the message she'd sent: *Tonight works for me. I'd love to have dinner with you. See you at seven.*

What the fuck?

He set down the phone, looked at the closed bathroom door, took a deep breath, and willed the tightness in his chest to abate.

Before he could conjure up the energy to confront Reese about it, Brantley changed his mind. He grabbed his shirt, yanked it on over his head.

When he heard the shower turn off, he grabbed his cell phone and slipped out of the room. It was safe to say he needed that breather. Maybe he'd misread the message. Surely the man he lived with, the man he loved, was not going on a date with his ex-girlfriend. It had to be a mistake.

Please, God, let it be a fucking mistake.

CHAPTER TWENTY-ONE

AFTER DRYING HIS BODY AND WRAPPING THE towel securely around his hips, Reese grabbed a smaller one and ran it over his hair as he stepped out of the bathroom and into the compact, single room. He glanced around, almost certain he'd heard Brantley come in.

No one was there.

Frowning, he walked over to his phone, glanced at the screen.

There was a single message notification.

Madison, probably. She was the only person he expected to hear from, and that was because he'd texted her on the way back from the training center, a knee-jerk reaction to that damn panic attack. One he clearly hadn't thought through well. Even as he'd been typing it, Reese knew it was wrong, but his frustrations and embarrassment had pushed him to do it anyway.

Trepidation filled him, but he tapped the screen to pull up the message. Sure enough. Madison had accepted his offer of dinner.

With a sigh, Reese sat down on the edge of the bed. What the fuck was wrong with him? What the hell had made him text her? He had absolutely nothing to say to Madison, knew that having dinner with her would result in mixed signals, and absolutely nothing that would help him resolve his own issues.

For the past few months, ever since Madison had texted him the first time, Reese had been on the fence about talking to her. It wasn't like he was looking for closure. They'd gone their separate ways after Reese had been stupid enough to propose to a woman he hadn't really been in love with. He suspected she had turned him down because she knew that, but they'd never bothered to have a conversation about it. In fact, they hadn't spoken since, other than the continuing chat thread. But those exchanges had been short and uneventful, exactly the way Reese had intended.

Another heavy sigh escaped as Reese stood, carrying the towel back to the bathroom and tossing it on the sink. He glanced at his image in the mirror, let his eyes slide over his bare chest, his abdomen. He paused briefly on the old scars he'd acquired over the years, most of them during his time as a POW. While they were familiar … while he could remember each and every one of them with vivid and painful clarity, Reese wasn't sure he recognized anything else about the man staring back at him. He certainly wasn't the same man he'd been a year ago, back when he'd met Brantley Walker and his entire life had changed.

And he'd be damned if that wasn't the problem. The man he'd been … where the fuck had he gone? How the hell had he changed so drastically in such a short period of time? Those were just some of the many questions he'd been pondering for months now. The ones that were weighing him down, making him crazy, keeping him up at night.

Reese had gone from being single, dating women, and living alone. Sure, his apartment had been shitty and small, but it'd been his. He'd had a decent job managing Walker Demolition, a ton of friends who he'd wanted to spend time with. Now he was in a relationship with a *man*, living with that man, not to mention working with him, too. He had a phenomenal job with the Off the Books Task Force, plus a dog he'd come to love more than anything. And yeah, he still had a ton of friends, but the only person he cared to spend time with was Brantley.

Looking at it rationally, Reese didn't see a problem, but something felt off. Something felt … different. Too different. As though he was missing something, but he didn't know what.

Still standing at the mirror, he took a moment to run a comb over his hair. It was a little longer on top than he liked, but he hadn't bothered to grab the clippers before they left, so he was stuck with it.

Reese ditched the towel around his hips, snagged a pair of boxer briefs. He pulled them on, then retrieved jeans and a T-shirt from the tiny closet. Socks and boots came next. Once he was dressed, he grabbed his cell phone from the dresser, picked up Brantley's truck keys. Even holding them made him feel guilty about where he was about to go, who he was about to see. But he was committed, and Reese wasn't going to back down now. This was the path he'd chosen, and he needed to follow through so he could find the answers he was so desperately searching for.

He snagged the key card from the dresser, then he left. He opted for the elevator rather than march down the long, narrow hall to the stairs. The ride down took all of a second, then he was nodding at the night clerk on his way past the check-in desk and out into the twilight.

No sooner did he step outside than he saw Brantley strolling toward him.

"Hey," Reese greeted, realizing even his voice sounded guilty.

Brantley's eyes narrowed on him, slid down to his boots then back to his face. "Goin' somewhere?"

Reese cut a quick glance at the truck. "I ... uh ..." He met Brantley's gaze. "Yeah, goin' out for a bit. Need to clear my head."

"Want me to go with you?"

Reese turned away, unable to look at him when he lied. "Nah. I need some time to think."

The lack of response told him more than he cared to know. When Brantley Walker didn't have a comeback, didn't engage in an argument, it meant he was retreating.

What sucked was that Reese was making him, and he was too confused at the moment to care.

"Later," Reese muttered as he strolled over to Brantley's truck.

Without looking back, Reese climbed in, shoved the key in the ignition, and turned the engine over. He was backing out when he looked up again, saw Brantley still staring after him. If he hadn't known better, he would've sworn that was pain etched on Brantley's face.

Too late now. He was committed.

BRANTLEY ABSOLUTELY DETESTED THE TIGHTNESS HE FELT in his chest as he watched Reese drive away in his truck. He could've been a dick about it, demanded the guy take an Uber, but he hadn't. He couldn't.

What hurt the most was the fact he'd given Reese an opportunity to come clean, and he'd lied to his face. Needed to clear his head? Not likely. Certainly not while he was on a date with Madison Adorite.

Even thinking her name had shards of pain lancing his heart, which only pissed Brantley off. He rubbed at his temples, feeling the first warning signs of an oncoming headache.

When his truck disappeared around the corner, Brantley marched into the hotel, through the lobby, up the stairs. By the time he reached the room, he was seething. Still, he managed to slide his key card into the slot, unlocked the door. He pulled out his phone as he headed for the closet.

The first thing he did was pull up his Uber app to get a car to the airport. Once that was set up, he placed a call to JJ, popping the pain medicine for his headache and downing it without water.

"Hey, boss man," she greeted with a smile in her voice.

"Hey. Can you keep an eye on Tesha tonight?" he asked, not quite sure why he was so concerned with Reese's dog's well-being.

"Of course. Everything cool?"

"Yeah," he lied. "Reese went out to take care of a couple of things. You can touch base with him in the mornin'."

"Brantley, what's wrong?"

He should've known JJ would hear the anger and frustration in his underlying tone.

"Nothin'. Just a headache, but I'm good. Check with Reese in the mornin', would ya?"

"Why him? Why not you?" she countered.

"Just do it, would ya?" he snapped.

"Of course," JJ said slowly. "Sure."

He didn't bother with more pleasantries, disconnecting the call and shoving his phone in his pocket.

It pained him that he was keeping things from JJ. Being that they'd been friends since childhood, he knew she would've been there for him, allowed him to bounce his frustrations off her. Unfortunately, he wasn't even sure what to say the problem was, so he didn't see the point in bothering her with it.

Dragging his duffel from the closet floor, Brantley proceeded to shove all his shit inside. If he left anything behind, he figured Reese would grab it for him.

Maybe.

Then again, it was possible Reese was off to rekindle a romance with his long-lost love and he wasn't going to give Brantley a second thought.

Fine. Perhaps that was a bit overdramatic. After all, Reese worked for the task force. At the very least, he'd give his notice if he wasn't coming back, so there would be at least that chance for them to have an open, honest conversation about why Reese decided to throw away a damn good thing to go back to a woman he'd admittedly never loved.

Brantley gritted his teeth, swallowing down the anger and hurt.

He retrieved his gun from the holster on his hip, released the magazine, and checked to make sure there wasn't a bullet in the chamber. He preferred not to go through the hassle of checking it in at the airport, so he opened the case he carried it in, placed it inside, then locked it up, then opened the wall safe and tucked it in alongside Reese's.

Alongside Reese's. That was strange. Why had Reese left his weapon behind? That wasn't like him. They were both usually armed whenever they were out. It was second nature, a part of the job.

Brantley frowned, then closed the safe and locked it.

Once he was packed up, he grabbed the pen and notepad that was on the small desk and scribbled a note to Reese.

Caught a flight back tonight.

I hope you found the answers you were looking for.

BW

He tossed the pen down on the paper, stared at it for a moment.

No, he wasn't going to dwell on it. He just wasn't that guy.

His cell phone chimed, signaling his car had arrived. Shouldering his bag, he left the key card on the dresser and stepped out into the hall. He took the stairs and made it outside without encountering another soul.

Once he was situated in the backseat of the little compact four-door, his bag at his side, he considered making a call to Trey to let his brother know where he was going but decided against it. He really wasn't interested in a lecture tonight. He knew Trey would give him shit about running away from his problems, and he would've been right. Brantley simply wasn't in the mood to listen to it.

He should've known his time with Reese had been too good to last. Although they'd endured their fair share of bumps in the road, they'd been going strong for ten months or so now.

At least he'd thought they had.

Apparently their relationship had surpassed its expiration date.

In Reese's defense, Brantley had known he'd never been with a man before. And since they'd gotten together, he'd never caught so much of a glimpse of Reese checking out another man. Not with an approving eye, anyway. It was time Brantley accepted the fact that the guy wasn't gay, he was curious, and now that his curiosity had been sated, he was going back to what he knew.

And since Brantley had no chance of competing in that arena, he was better off cutting his losses now.

If he thought about it rationally, Brantley would admit it was his own damn fault. He was the one who had pushed for the relationship, asking Reese to move in with him after dating for only a month. He should've known better. Considering he'd never had a serious relationship—not since his teenage years, anyway—it made more sense for him to stick to what he knew, too.

With a heavy exhale, Brantley focused his attention out the window.

At least it had been fun while it lasted.

CHAPTER TWENTY-TWO

TWENTY MINUTES AFTER HE'D LEFT THE HOTEL, Reese was pulling into the restaurant parking lot. It was busy for a Friday night but not too bad. There were half a dozen spots available, so he selected one that faced the front of the building.

Once he was parked, Reese sat in the truck, staring out into the night, wondering once again what the hell he was thinking.

He'd contemplated turning around half a dozen times during the short drive but hadn't. Although he knew this was a mistake, that seeing Madison again wasn't going to gain him anything, Reese knew it was necessary. If not for him, then at least for her. He needed to show her he'd moved on, and he figured face-to-face was the least she deserved.

Taking a deep breath, he forced himself out of the truck and across the parking lot. He couldn't remember the last time he'd come to one of these little delis Madison liked so much. Personally, Reese preferred eating at home, something he had in common with Brantley. One of the *many* things he had in common with Brantley.

Reese exhaled slowly, shoved away the guilt. No sense dwelling on it now. He was here, and he fully intended to follow through.

Once inside, he told the hostess he was there to meet someone, and she nodded for him to go back. He found Madison sitting at a table along the wall of windows—exactly where she shouldn't be sitting—with a dozen or so other people scattered throughout. She smiled when she saw him. If he hadn't been frustrated with the fact she was being so cavalier about protecting herself, he would've smiled back.

There was no denying Madison Adorite was a beautiful woman. Stunning was probably a better word for it. Her long, nearly black hair was board-straight and shiny; her dark brown eyes glittered with mystery. There was an air of class and sophistication about her, something he'd always admired despite the fact it made him feel inept.

When she stood to greet him with a hug, he figured why the hell not.

"It's good to see you," she said softly, her voice still raspy and sweet.

"Same." He wrapped his arm around her in a friendly hug, inhaling the soft scent of lavender and vanilla.

She still smelled the same.

Reese waited to see if he felt that stirring of longing or lust he'd previously felt when he was near her. It never came. Not so much as a flutter.

He forced himself back and waited until she took her seat before pulling out the chair across from her.

"You're here alone?" he asked, glancing around briefly, hoping to see a couple of guys watching her back. Reese knew her brother employed a number of enforcers hired to do the heavy lifting as well as to take a bullet for the Adorites if it ever came to it. And it had. A couple of times, in fact.

"I am." She laughed softly. "I don't need a bodyguard, Reese."

He didn't bother telling her that was bullshit. He knew Madison was well aware of the danger she was in simply by being the sister to Maximillian Adorite, the boss of the Southern Boy Mafia. Just sharing the same last name put her, as well as the rest of her siblings, in imminent danger.

Not that anyone could tell Madison that. She'd always been fiercely independent, insisting she lived her life by her own rules, even if she assisted the family when it came to certain legal matters. Since her older brother Victor was also a lawyer and took on the brunt of the family's legal business, Madison was able to pick and choose so that she could keep herself separate as much as possible.

At least that was what she claimed. To be honest, Reese didn't know much about what Madison did. She'd always made a point to keep her family matters close to the vest. Probably one of the main reasons Reese had never truly fallen in love with her despite the fact he had wanted to. He'd never actually felt as though he knew her.

"You look good," Madison said, her eyes raking over his face.

"Likewise. How's the family?" He was hoping to keep the conversation casual.

Her head tilted, her eyes softening, almost as though she was disappointed that he hadn't laid on the charm. "As good as can be expected, I figure. It's been a rough couple of years."

The waitress appeared to take his drink order.

"Bud Light. Thanks." Reese turned his attention back to Madison. "What's been rough about it?"

"Restructuring."

While Madison would share a tidbit about her family every now and then, she was always hesitant to talk about her family's "business." Being that they were a known criminal organization, not all their activities were aboveboard, and to protect them, she rarely spoke about it. Although he understood her desire to protect her family, Reese had never understood why she felt she had to keep it from him.

"So no turf wars?" he asked, hoping to lighten the mood and redirect the conversation.

Clearly that wasn't the right question to ask, because Madison's gaze hardened before she forced a smile. "How're you doin'? Still working at the demolition company?"

The waitress returned with his beer, set the bottle on a paper coaster before inquiring about their order. Reese wasn't hungry, but he didn't want to make things awkward, so he ordered a chef salad and skipped the dressing.

"Still on your health kick, huh?" Madison teased.

He recalled how she'd always given him crap about his healthy eating habits. He'd never thought anything of it because she tended to eat the same things he did. Not like Brantley, who, if presented with the choice between a salad and a double bacon cheeseburger, would choose the burger ten times out of ten. And Brantley made no apologies for it either.

"All right." Madison leaned forward. "What's wrong? I thought you wanted to have dinner with me?"

Reese considered his response carefully. It hadn't been that he'd necessarily *wanted* to, but he didn't think that was the appropriate way to kick this off.

"I'll take your silence as a negative," she finally said, looking incredibly uncomfortable.

Exhaling, Reese propped his forearms on the table. "I'm gonna be honest. I don't know why I came."

Surprise and what might've been hurt glittered in her dark brown eyes. "No?"

He shook his head, held her gaze. "It was a spur-of-the-moment decision."

Madison stared at him momentarily, seeming to study his face as though the answers would be there. "So you're *not* interested in rekindling anything here?"

Reese didn't even hesitate when he said, "No. That's not my intention."

Madison canted her head to the side, her expression shifting to curious. "Are you saying there *is* another woman in your life?" She laughed softly, her gaze dropping to the table. "I should've known. I mean, you're a real catch, Reese. And it's been so long. What we had was—"

"What we had was temporary," he interrupted, not wanting her to make it into something that it wasn't. He knew how easy it was to rewrite history, especially when it came to past relationships. Hell, he'd caught himself doing as much in recent months. Always when his anxiety levels were high, and he was trying to figure out why he felt unsettled.

Madison's gaze bounced up to his face. "Temporary?" She nodded, skeptical. "I guess you don't recall the proposal the way I do."

Reese stared at her. "Maybe not, but I remember your rejection pretty clearly."

Madison's gaze dropped to the table once again. "About that…"

"No," he said quickly. "That's not why I came, Madison."

Well, maybe it was, but now that they were discussing it, Reese realized he didn't want to hash it out. It was the past, and it needed to remain there as far as he was concerned.

They were both silent for a moment, gazing around the space at the other diners. The restaurant was slow tonight. Only a couple of tables were occupied, mostly by couples with small children. Since it wasn't exactly a date-night place, Reese figured it would remain that way.

"So who is she? The woman who's made you forget all about me?"

Reese's gut churned, and his mouth went dry. He knew the respectable answer was to say he wasn't in a relationship with a woman but rather a man. It wasn't a secret anymore. But it didn't come easily for him, and that was what bothered him the most. He still didn't understand how it had happened, much less how to explain it.

"I'm not—" Reese's response was cut off by the crash of dishes.

He looked up to see their waitress had dropped a tray of food—likely theirs—and was staring wide-eyed at the door.

Reese followed her gaze, looked over to see two men brandishing weapons. Acting on instinct, he reached for his sidearm only to realize he didn't have it on him.

Shit.

Keeping his cool, Reese sat up straight, continued to watch. He expected them to head to the register, which was a small booth near the exit where customers paid their bill before leaving. While he waited for them to demand money, Reese attempted to devise a plan.

The couple closest to the door moved, the woman grabbing the little girl, the man ushering the little boy behind him. The cacophony of silverware on dishes had disappeared, replaced by a few squeals and some panicked murmurs.

Reese kept his focus on the two men. Neither of them moved toward the register or even the kitchen. The two meatheads looked around the room, their weapons following their eyes, as though searching for someone. When their gazes stopped on Madison, one guy elbowed the other, pointing in their direction.

Son of a bitch.

"You expectin' company?" he asked, keeping his attention on the big assholes now heading their way.

"What?" Madison glanced toward the door.

"Do you know them?" he asked quickly.

"Never seen them before."

That didn't mean a damn thing. More than likely these guys knew Madison Adorite. Or, at the very least, they knew her brother.

"There's a back exit," he told Madison. "As soon as I get up, that's where you're headed."

"I'm not—"

"Shut up, Madison," Reese snapped, glaring over at her. "You see all these people in here? They're in danger because these assholes want you. That means we've got to keep this simple. I get up. You head for the door."

Madison's mouth opened as though she wanted to argue, but Reese cut her off again.

"No questions, dammit. Go outside. Find a place to hide. I'll find you in a few."

He could see the questions in her eyes, but thankfully, she didn't voice any.

As the meatheads approached their table, Reese slowly got to his feet, stepping around so that he was between Madison and the two assholes.

It took a little finesse, but he managed to move, keeping her behind him as he positioned so she had a direct route to the exit door.

"Can I help you boys?" he prompted, his gaze shifting to the gun now aimed squarely at his head.

The guy's grip was firm, steady, the gun aimed appropriately.

Not an amateur.

"We're just here for the princess," the shorter guy said mockingly.

Despite his short stature, the guy was built like a Mack truck, all beefed up. Unlike his friend, he looked a little twitchy, like this was the first time he'd taken a restaurant hostage at gunpoint.

"Don't make this hard, doll," the big guy told Madison directly. "We all know it ends the same way."

"I hate to break it to you, but she's got other plans tonight," Reese said, taking stock of the situation even as he nudged Madison farther behind him.

Two guys, two guns. One possibly competent, the other not. The only positive was that they both appeared distracted. Probably figured they had complete control of the situation thanks to the weapons. Reese knew he had to get the element of surprise if he stood even half a chance.

"Not no more, she don't," the bigger guy said.

"Look, man, we don't want any trouble," Reese continued, tracking their reactions, the way their eyes shifted, their lips pursed, the sweat forming on the other one's brow.

"If you sit down and shut the fuck up, there ain't gonna be no trouble," the big meathead said, swinging his gun in Madison's direction.

"I can't do that," he said firmly, stepping to the side, putting himself between Madison and a bullet.

The big guy chuckled, glancing over at his buddy. "You hear this one? He can't do that."

Evidently that was amusing because the other guy laughed.

"Ah, there he is now," Reese bluffed, nodding in the direction of the door.

"There's wh—"

The second they turned their heads, Reese took advantage, nailing the big fucker in the face with his fist and sending him flat to the floor. Unfortunately, he didn't knock him out entirely, nor did he knock the gun from his hand.

With his buddy laid out on the floor, the shorter one reacted, lunging in Reese's direction, telling him he was more of a brawler than a shooter.

"Go, Madison!" Reese shouted, elbowing the short guy in the face just as the big guy got to his feet.

All the hand-to-hand he'd endured lately prepared him for the fight that ensued. Unfortunately, his attention was split between the guy's fist and the gun he was still waving. He knew this wasn't going to be a fair fight, but he heard Madison retreating, so he focused every ounce of his frustration on the dickheads, praying she followed instructions.

Reese got in a few good hits, but two on one wasn't working in his favor. He took several punches to the face, a few more to the gut that had him folding over. A couple of knees to the head had him falling to the floor, then they were landing them one right after another, ganging up on him.

He had no recourse at this vantage point, so he blocked as many punches as he could, hoping like fuck Madison made it to safety.

"Hey! Cops!" someone shouted.

It was enough to have them backing off, allowing Reese to move back, get out of range of their rib-cracking kicks. He could feel the blood pouring from his nose, felt some dripping into his eye from a cut on his forehead.

His assailants were both out of breath, making Reese feel a little better. The big guy's eye was already swelling from where Reese had gotten in a direct hit.

Reese knew without looking that there were no cops. Two walls were solid windows, and there wasn't a single red or blue light flashing anywhere.

Luckily, the meatheads were either too stupid or too panicked to notice.

"Where'd the bitch go?" the bigger one bit out.

"I don't fuckin' know," the shorter guy said, backing his way toward the door. "Let's get outta here, man. I ain't goin' down for this shit."

The big guy wasn't quite as eager to retreat, continuing to stare down at Reese. His beady eyes narrowed and flashed with fury. "This ain't over. I will find her. And when I do…"

"I hear sirens, bro," the short fucker finally said, panting like he'd run a mile. "We gotta get the hell outta here."

The big one grinned, and that was when Reese realized the guy definitely wasn't an amateur as he'd hoped.

When the gun lifted, aimed right for his heart, Reese saw his entire life flash before his eyes.

And the one person he thought of before he heard the gun's report and felt the fires of hell erupt in his chest…

Brantley.

ALTHOUGH SHE HATED TO DO IT, MADISON ran when Reese told her to. It was a cowardly reaction to the situation, but it wasn't like she had another choice. No, she didn't know those guys, but she could take a wild guess at who they were, who they worked for. For years now, her brother had been warning her that a rival crew was looking to take over this territory, and they were willing to do whatever was necessary to do it. But Madison hadn't taken it seriously, and the more time that passed, the more complacent she'd gotten, refusing to believe she was in any danger.

And now this.

As she hid in the alley behind the restaurant, pressed up against the wall, hoping to keep out of sight, she tried to come up with a plan to help Reese. It was the least she could do since this was all her fault.

Unfortunately, she didn't have a gun and she wasn't much of a fighter, which meant she'd probably be more of a distraction than anything.

Her back went ramrod straight, and her breath lodged in her chest when she heard a loud pop, the unmistakable sound of a gunshot followed by a few panicked screams from inside the building.

"Oh, God. Oh, God." Her heart slammed painfully against her ribs, and indecision filled her. She had to help Reese.

She looked left, looked right, gauged the distance between her location and the door she had exited.

"You can do this," she muttered to herself, even as her feet remained rooted to the stained and greasy asphalt. "You *have* to do this."

She couldn't leave Reese in there alone, but how could she help him? Never had she felt so incredibly helpless before. Never.

Just as she was about to head back inside—she *had* to—a shiny black Escalade came barreling down the alley, coming to a screeching halt directly in front of her.

Her breaths slammed into her lungs as she recognized the man getting out of the driver's seat.

"Get in, Madison."

She glared at the enormous black man with the shiny bald head and the gleam of menace in his eyes. It was probably the most inopportune time for her body to flare to life at the mere sight of him, yet it did. It always did. Taye Smith, a.k.a. Rock, was the one man Madison had always reacted to like this.

"I'm not goin' anywhere with you, Rock," she hissed, glancing back at the door she'd exited through and gauging the distance.

"You won't make it," Rock assured her. "If you try, I'll throw you over my shoulder and force you into this car."

"I'm not leaving Reese. I can't. He needs help, Rock!"

"The cops are on their way."

Were they? Were they really? Madison had never fully trusted Rock. Not when it came to explanations, anyway. He was a liar because it was a tool of the trade. When protecting a criminal organization, it wasn't like he could tell the truth.

Damn it.

"Till the count of three," Rock growled. "Then I'll throw you in there myself."

He would, too. Her brother's head enforcer wasn't known for his subtlety. At least not when it came to doing Max's bidding.

"Now!" Rock barked.

She could hear the sound of sirens from down the street, prayed the police would be there any minute. They would help Reese; she knew they would.

If he wasn't dead already.

Her stomach clenched, but she did what she'd been taught to do.

She got into the SUV and let Rock whisk her away to safety.

CHAPTER TWENTY-THREE

For a brief moment—very, *very* brief—Trey wondered how much an Uber to Coyote Ridge from Dallas would cost him.

Yes, he was well aware it was a stupid thought, something only irrational, desperate people would even indulge in. Yet he'd had it, and now, as he sat alone in his hotel room, he considered it again. If only he hadn't carted Evan and Charlie up here with him, he could've driven his ass back home tonight rather than wait until morning without worrying about how they were going to make it back.

"You're losin' your fuckin' mind," he muttered to himself, snatching up the remote and stabbing it in the direction of the television.

He simply needed a distraction. Something to watch until he could fall asleep. Then tomorrow, he'd wake up, and they'd head back to Coyote Ridge. Another trip to the training camp from hell out of the way.

Trey heard a door slam outside, and he winced. While the hotel was decent—some would even consider it nice—the one thing it lacked was soundproofing in the walls.

With a sigh, he leaned back against the pillows, stared at the muted television. There was hockey on, so he left it there. It wasn't a sport he was particularly interested in, but he did enjoy a game or two from time to time. It certainly beat the nightly news and all the depressing shit going on in the world.

His cell phone buzzed on the nightstand. In a move that reeked of desperation, Trey snatched it up, read the screen. When he saw Magnus's name, that strange sense of euphoria came over him.

Despite his best efforts to deny it, Trey and Magnus had been indulging in ... well, the truth was, he wasn't sure what to call it. An affair? Fucking? Scratching an itch? Whatever it was, Trey still got chills when he saw Magnus's name on his phone. The good kind. The ones that were a prelude to a mind-blowing, body-rocking orgasm.

"What's up?" he grumbled, playing his role as the man who wished Magnus would go away.

"What're you wearin'?"

He fought back a grin, hated that he even wanted to. "What do you need, Magnus?"

A soft chuckle sounded. "What I want and what I need are in direct cahoots these days."

Trey didn't even try to decipher the riddle. He'd learned that he didn't understand half the shit Magnus said. Considering their age difference, that wasn't exactly a big surprise. Having just had his thirty-seventh birthday back in May, Trey felt ancient in comparison to the twenty-five-year-old he was fucking these days. But the good news was, Magnus had aged a year, too, since their first encounter on New Year's.

"I've got shit to do, Magnus," Trey relayed, ensuring he maintained his put-out tone.

"Yeah, you do."

A knock sounded at the door, and Trey looked up. He was not going to answer because he was tired and wanted to sleep. The only person who would intrude would be his brother, and Brantley had more important things to deal with.

"If you don't have somethin' important to say, Magnus, I've got to—"

"Answer the door, Trey," Magnus said softly.

"What?"

"You heard me. Answer. The. Door."

Confused but curious, Trey got up from the bed and strolled across the room. He planted his eye on the peephole only to see that someone was covering it from the other side.

He unlocked the deadbolt, turned the knob, and opened the door, not caring that he'd just acted like every teenage girl in every horror movie ever made.

Standing in the well-lit hallway was Magnus, wearing flip-flops, a pair of tan cargo shorts, and a white T-shirt with Camp K-9 on the front. He had a day's worth of stubble on his square jaw and a gleam in his hazel eyes.

"What the fuck?" Trey muttered, wondering if he was dreaming.

"Perhaps you should rephrase that," Magnus said, disconnecting the call as he stepped forward, effectively moving Trey backward. "How about *would you like to fuck?* That sounds far more appropriate, considering."

Aww, hell.

"What are you doin' here?" Trey managed even as Magnus closed the door and leaned into him.

"I got tired of waitin' for you to come back."

Was this real? Maybe Trey was dreaming. For the past six months, he'd spent far more time than was appropriate thinking about this man, dreaming about him. It wouldn't surprise him if he was dreaming now. He was tired. It made sense he'd fallen asleep, more so that Magnus had invaded his unconscious mind since he spent so much of his awake time thinking about him.

"If I didn't know better, I'd think you were expectin' me," Magnus said, his mouth brushing over his.

"What?" Yeah, he was well aware he sounded like a dumb ass. A dumb ass on repeat.

Trey sucked in a breath when Magnus's calloused hands skimmed over his bare stomach, his thumbs gliding up the center of his abdomen. His rough palms scraped over his nipples, and Trey wondered if he could come from simply being touched. It was no secret that Magnus knew just how to do it to make it happen.

When Magnus's hands reached his neck, those thumbs hooked under Trey's chin and tilted his head back. Then there was the warm, wet rasp of a tongue on his neck, licking, sucking.

"Fuck, I missed you, Trey," Magnus moaned, gliding his lips downward, over his collarbone. Licking from one side to the other. "Did you miss me?"

"Not even a little," he lied, knowing that was exactly what Magnus expected to hear.

They'd been playing this game for months. While Trey would pretend not to be interested, Magnus would continue to pursue him until Trey would give in. Although in the beginning, Trey had been serious about resisting this man, he now found it impossible to do so. But he also found it easy to continue with this ruse because that was all it was. He refused to want more, and Magnus clearly wasn't looking for serious, so it worked well for them.

"Then it sounds like I haven't been doin' my job well," Magnus said, meeting Trey's gaze before he dropped to his knees.

"What job is that?" Trey asked, his voice gruff.

He sucked in a harsh breath when Magnus yanked Trey's shorts down his legs, freeing his iron-hard cock.

"This one."

"Ahh, fuck," Trey hissed when the blessed heat of Magnus's mouth engulfed his dick, taking him to the root.

Instantly, his fist was in Magnus's hair, tugging roughly as that skilled, eager mouth sucked, his tongue swirling around his shaft.

Magnus pulled back, slowly releasing him, looking up with a mischievous smile. "And practice makes perfect, right?"

"Shut up and suck my dick," Trey growled, jerking Magnus's head forward again as he succumbed to the pleasure.

Oh, hell.

He was in so much trouble.

MAGNUS HAD BEEN JONESING FOR TREY FOR the past three days, but unlike Trey, he didn't have a problem admitting it.

Sure, making the two-hundred-mile drive to see the guy for one night was probably a bit on the desperate side, but when he'd set out three hours ago, Magnus had decided he didn't really give a shit. He was enjoying the hell out of his time with Trey, and what better way to keep the sparks alive than to make a surprise visit?

And boy, did he love these fucking sparks.

Even now, as Trey roughly fucked his face, using him for his own pleasure, Magnus was high on the adrenaline pumping through his veins. It was always like this. Every single time. Even six months in, every time was like the first.

A dark, thundering growl escaped Trey seconds before his hand tightened in Magnus's hair, holding him still.

"Not yet," Trey groaned.

No, definitely not yet. Magnus wasn't ready for Trey to come any more than he was. He knew it only got better from here.

When Trey tugged on his hair, Magnus pushed to his feet. He grunted when Trey slammed his lips down on his, those strong arms banding around him, holding him firmly.

This was the best part of their encounters, as far as Magnus was concerned. That moment when Trey dominated the situation, rendering Magnus putty in his hands. Never had Magnus been with anyone—man or woman—who could so easily take control, and he'd be the first to admit, he'd gotten addicted to it.

"Put your hands on me," Trey breathed against his lips, moving them toward the bed.

Magnus dragged his palms over Trey's naked back, loving the way those muscles bunched and his skin tightened. It hadn't taken long for Magnus to realize this was what turned Trey on the most. He loved to be touched. Good thing, too, since Magnus enjoyed the hell out of touching.

Magnus slid his palms around to Trey's chest, forcing him to step back, to allow Magnus to continue. Trey released him, but he didn't go far. His fingers curled around Magnus's wrists, guiding his hands over his chest, his abs. Magnus paid attention to every inch, enjoying Trey's soft sighs and guttural groans.

As soon as he had Trey distracted, Magnus pushed him down to the bed. He kicked off his flip-flops before crawling over him so he could continue his ministrations while Trey relaxed. Their eyes met and held as Magnus straddled his hips, pausing briefly to tease Trey's small, dark nipples into tight little points.

"Admit it, you missed me, too," Magnus said with a smile.

"Not a chance."

That made Magnus's smile widen. Initially, he'd believed that Trey hadn't wanted anything to do with him. Perhaps the man hadn't. But it hadn't taken Magnus long to dig his way beneath Trey's skin, giving him exactly what he needed that brought them both maximum satisfaction.

Magnus leaned down, nipped Trey's bottom lip. "Admit it," he repeated as he rocked his hips, grinding against Trey's impressive erection.

"No."

Even as Trey said it, the man's hands had already started working the button on Magnus's shorts. The zipper followed. Magnus hissed in a breath as those hard hands curled around his cock. And then he was thrusting into Trey's fists, increasing the friction. He knew Trey wouldn't let it go on too long, so he took advantage when he did.

"Lose the shorts," Trey demanded.

It wasn't easy to do since Trey refused to release his cock, but Magnus managed to get his shorts down his legs, then Trey used his feet to kick them away.

"Now the shirt."

This was easier, although it gave Trey free rein to stroke him more firmly. If Magnus didn't know better, he would think the man was trying to make him come.

He was tossing his shirt to the floor when Trey moved, shifting so quickly it surprised Magnus. The next thing Magnus knew, he was straddling Trey's head, his cock tunneling into that sexy fucking mouth. He gripped the headboard that was mounted on the wall, using it to hold himself still while Trey succeeded in blowing his fucking mind.

"Trey," he growled in warning. "Ah, Jesus … Trey … fuck."

It was too easy to get lost in the sensations, to lose himself to a man who knew exactly what to do to have him dangling precariously from that razor-sharp edge. But what made it absolutely phenomenal was the fact that Trey wouldn't let him go over the edge. Not until he was ready.

Magnus was panting when Trey shifted again, this time manhandling Magnus down onto the bed as he moved over him. Their lips fused once more and everything slowed. The tension remained, but the intensity dropped a few thousand degrees. It was a momentary reprieve for both of them, Magnus knew. A chance for them to pull themselves back, to prepare for what was to come.

"I didn't miss you," Trey mumbled against his mouth.

Magnus smiled. He knew that was Trey's way of admitting he actually had missed him. The man was still in denial and Magnus was content to let him remain there. This was working for them, and to be honest, it was the most intense, the most meaningful relationship he'd ever been in in his entire life. He looked forward to spending time with Trey, and while the majority of that time involved some form of sexual act, Magnus knew it was turning into more. And he also knew to keep that to himself.

"Please tell me you've got a condom," Trey rumbled as he pushed himself up.

"Not on me, no," he teased. "But I might have a stash in the pocket of my shorts."

And by stash, he meant six. When he'd been anticipating this, Magnus figured that was a safe number in the event Trey didn't have any of his own.

"I hope you've got lube," Magnus said, propping himself up on his elbows when Trey got off the bed to retrieve Magnus's shorts.

"Who said I'm gonna go easy on you?" Trey retorted, not bothering to look at him.

Magnus couldn't hide his amusement. "I'm game if you are."

Trey's eyes snapped up. "Is that a dare?"

"Maybe."

Magnus didn't fear Trey anymore. He didn't worry that the man would hurt him when it came to their sexual encounters. They'd been doing this long enough that he realized Trey's main objective was Magnus's pleasure even if he pretended it was completely selfish. Then again, Magnus was the same. His only goal was to watch Trey's eyes roll back in his head.

After rolling on a condom, Trey padded to the dresser, where a black duffel bag sat on top. He rummaged around for a second, then produced a small clear bottle with a flip-top cap. The *click* of the cap being opened was loud in the otherwise silent room.

Magnus's jaw unhinged when he saw Trey stroking himself. The lubricated latex covering him glistened in the dim yellow glow from the lamp.

"Turn over," Trey commanded.

Magnus rolled onto his stomach, spreading his legs, making room for Trey between them. The bed dipped from Trey's weight, then there were hard hands on the backs of his thighs, massaging, kneading.

"Grip the edge of the mattress," Trey ordered as he forced Magnus's knees toward his chest.

Shifting into position, face down, ass up, Magnus curled his fingers over the edge of the mattress and held on for dear life.

A satisfied exhale escaped him as Trey stroked his cock, working him back up to that precipice all over again. But just when Magnus thought the man would impale him, Trey's tongue took over, rimming him, sending shockwaves of pleasure through his entire body.

Trey certainly knew how to make him moan, and sometimes it seemed Trey's sole objective was to do just that.

"Trey…"

Or maybe *that* was Trey's goal. To make Magnus beg.

"God, Trey … I want you inside me."

That guttural rumble from behind him sent chills dancing down Magnus's spine.

When Trey's lips glided upward, along his spine, Magnus didn't know what to expect next. Trey never ceased to surprise him.

A soft growl sounded, then Trey gripped his hips, the mattress rocking as Trey inched closer to him. A hard hand landed between his shoulder blades, keeping Magnus's face in the mattress. A second later, he was impaled by Trey's enormous cock. Pain blazed briefly, morphing instantly into pleasure.

Trey didn't hold back, pounding into him, holding his hips while Magnus tried to remain still, accepting every savage thrust as Trey used him in the most delectable way possible.

Needless to say, when Magnus came, it was once again one of the most exquisite orgasms of his entire life. Made all the more satisfying when Trey followed him right over the edge.

CHAPTER TWENTY-FOUR

BRANTLEY KICKED HIS FEET OUT IN FRONT of him, wishing like hell he was at home and not in this godforsaken airport. The only positive in the whole fucking mess was that his headache had remained manageable. All credit went to the pain medicine that Reese had so kindly thought to pack for him.

Reese.

Damn it.

Not for the first time, Brantley regretted reacting so rashly. He hated airports. All the people, the noise. The coming and going. Granted, that sure as shit beat the waiting he'd been doing for three hours now.

He checked his watch. Make that three hours, thirty-nine minutes.

Why he hadn't thought to call ahead to confirm a flight, he didn't know. Now his ass was keeping the uncomfortable chair warm. And at best, he was on standby for the next flight to Austin. His chances of actually getting on a plane were probably slim to none.

Hell, he could've driven back to Coyote Ridge in less time.

Only Reese had his fucking truck.

Brantley sighed. He scanned the concourse, noticed a coffee shop. Couldn't hurt, right?

Forcing himself up from the chair, he shouldered his bag. He made it no more than a few feet when his phone buzzed in his hand. He glanced at the screen, saw it was an unknown number. He should ignore the damn thing. If it was a potential case, it wasn't like he could do a damn thing about it. His entire team was here in Dallas. Anyone down in Austin would be shit out of luck.

The call ended before he had to make a decision.

Brantley stepped up to the coffee counter. "Large black coffee."

The woman rattled off the price, so he pulled out his wallet, grabbed some cash. As he was passing it over, his phone rang again. This time RT's name appeared.

"Hey, what's—"

"Where are you?" RT demanded.

Brantley waved off the change from the cashier and stepped out of the way. "At the airport. Why?"

"At the air— Never mind. Not important. It's Reese."

Hearing the emotion in RT's voice, Brantley's heart lodged in his throat and he couldn't even force out any words.

"He's at the hospital," RT explained, his tone hard. "He's been shot."

The words registered and Brantley forgot about everything else. He stared, not seeing the people, not hearing the barista call that an order was ready. The only sound was the harsh thump of his heartbeat in his ears and the ragged breaths sawing in and out of his lungs.

"Shot?" he croaked. "What? Why? What the fuck?"

"You need to get here, Brantley. Now."

Brantley forced his legs to move, heading for the exit at a fast clip, doing his best not to knock anyone down in his haste. "Which hospital?"

"Baylor."

That told him absolutely nothing. "I'm at Love Field," he told RT. "How far am I?"

"Half an hour tops."

"Son of a bitch."

"He's in surgery, Brantley," RT said, his voice softer, calmer than before. "We're here now."

"What the hell happened?" he barked.

"Just get here. I'll fill you in then."

"I'll be there as soon as I can."

With his heart lodged firmly in his throat, Brantley hailed a cab.

Twenty minutes later, thanks to light traffic and a determined cab driver—the promise of a two-hundred-dollar tip worked wonders—Brantley walked into the emergency room waiting area.

Not recognizing anyone there, he headed for the nurses' station. "I'm lookin' for a patient. Reese Tavoularis. Can you tell me where he is?"

"Are you family?"

"I'm his partner."

Her eyes softened and he realized she had misunderstood. He'd actually been referring to work, although technically the other had been true up until tonight.

Not that he was going to bother her with those details, because evidently, it worked, seeing as she had turned her attention to the computer, and after he spelled out the name for her, he learned Reese was in the intensive care unit.

Thankfully, she offered decent directions, because his mind was elsewhere and the hospital was enormous. He found it easily, somehow keeping his heart in his chest as he made his way into the ICU waiting room. That was where he found RT with Reese's brother, Z, along with Reese's mother, Cindy, and her boyfriend, Hugh.

RT was the first one up, strolling right to him.

"Where is he?" Brantley asked, scanning RT's face for any bad news that might be coming.

"He's still in surgery."

"How long has he been in there?"

"A couple of hours."

Brantley frowned. "Why the fuck didn't you call me?" he demanded.

"We didn't know," RT said defensively. "I called as soon as I got word."

That made him feel a little better. "He's gonna be okay though?"

"Sounds like it," RT said, his voice steady. "We got a brief update a little while ago. They said they were able to retrieve the bullet and repair the artery it nicked. No doubt he was lucky."

Bullet. Artery. Lucky? *Jesus Christ.*

"What the fuck happened?"

"All we have are bystander reports, but it sounds like Reese was havin' dinner and he confronted two armed men. There was a fight—two on one—that ended in one of the other men shootin' Reese, then they took off before police arrived."

"They *shot* him?"

RT nodded and Brantley saw there was something he was holding back.

"Tell me, goddammit."

RT swallowed, looked away, looked back. "We don't know who he was with, but there was mention of a woman he was havin' dinner with. Sounds like Reese instructed her to run before he confronted the guys."

Brantley let that information bounce off him. He could not worry about the fact Reese was rekindling things with his ex. Right now the only thing that mattered was that Reese was all right.

"Reese was on the ground when the guy shot him," RT explained. "They said the bullet nicked an artery but the trajectory of the bullet was a blessing."

Not a fucking thing about this felt like a blessing.

"He's gonna be all right?" he asked again.

"The prognosis is good, yes."

Brantley's knees weakened and he leaned on the nearest wall to keep himself upright.

"He's strong. He'll pull through this."

Brantley nodded. The words were meant as encouragement, but Brantley didn't want platitudes. He wanted to see with his own two eyes that Reese was all right. At that point, he could leave the man in his family's capable hands and get out of his hair.

Two hours later, a nurse came out to inform them Reese was out of surgery and that they could go back to see him, but only two at a time.

Brantley hung back with RT and Hugh while Cindy and Z went in first. He was effectively wearing the tile flooring thin when Reese's brother returned a short time later, his face grim.

Brantley nearly plowed over Z in an attempt to get an update.

"He's still out of it," Z said softly. "But the doc says he'll be fine. They're keepin' him in ICU for tonight and they'll assess his condition in the mornin', see if they want to move him to a regular floor."

Brantley took a deep breath in, let it out slowly.

"Go on back," Z instructed. "My mom's still in there, but you should be there, too."

Brantley didn't argue, stepping around him.

Z gripped his arm, pulled him up short. "Prepare yourself. He doesn't look good."

That gaping hole in the pit of his stomach widened even as he nodded.

Shoring his nerve, Brantley made his way into the brightly lit wing of the hospital. He followed the signs until he came to Reese's room. There was a male nurse standing at a computer just outside the solid glass wall. From where the man was positioned, he could see in, keeping a close eye on his patient.

On the other side of the glass, Brantley could make out Reese's body in the bed, all the machines and wires, but Cindy was blocking his view of Reese's face.

Figuring it wasn't doing any damn good to stand around, Brantley stepped into the large room, his gaze slowly moving until he could see Reese fully.

His heart thumped painfully hard as he gave him a visual assessment. Reese was connected to machines by a myriad of tubes and wires, all doing whatever it was they did to keep Reese comfortable and alive. As though that wasn't bad enough, Reese looked like he'd gone ten rounds with a freight train. His face was battered and bruised. There was a gash over his left eye, held closed with a white butterfly bandage.

"Hey," Cindy said softly when she looked up at him.

It was obvious she'd been crying and Brantley felt shitty for intruding on her moment.

"Brantley's here now," she said, turning back to Reese as she patted his hand gently. That, too, was bruised, his knuckles swollen and scraped. Looked like he'd gotten in a few good ones of his own.

Reese didn't move, didn't open his eyes.

Brantley couldn't ignore the tightness in his chest or the heat in his sinuses. Seeing Reese like this...

Cindy rose to her feet. "Why don't I give you two some time. I'll see if Hugh wants to grab a bite to eat. I figure it'll be a long night."

He nodded, unable to look away from Reese.

Once they were alone, Brantley moved toward the bed. Aware of the nurse in the hallway, Brantley knew better than to touch Reese. The man wouldn't approve of anyone else knowing they'd had a relationship. So he simply pulled over a chair, eased into it, keeping a safe distance.

Brantley sat there, thinking of all the things he wanted to say but never speaking a word.

The night passed in a sleepless blur while Brantley remained in the hospital room with the beeping machines and the antiseptic smell. From time to time, he would stretch his legs, pace the room, return to his seat. Since the ICU had strict visiting hours, Z, Cindy, and RT were unable to come back, so he kept them updated via text message.

All the while, Reese remained unconscious in the bed, the machines continuing to do their job.

When the doctor came in, Brantley would get an update. When the nurse came in, glanced at the machines to read Reese's vitals, wrote things down, slipped back out, he would simply exhale.

It wasn't until shortly after dawn broke the next morning that Reese finally stirred.

Brantley had been snoozing in the chair at his bedside when he heard movement, opened his eyes to find Reese was looking at him, his eyes puffy and bruised like the rest of his face.

"Madison," Reese said in a gruff whisper.

There was no denying the pain that ripped through his chest when he heard that name. Why he'd hoped Reese would think of him first, he didn't know.

"I'm sure someone'll call her," he assured Reese, sitting up straight and stretching the kinks in his neck.

"No," Reese said, his voice strained from lack of use. "Where *is* she?"

Brantley shrugged. "I don't know if anyone knew to call her."

Reese shook his head, his frustration evident. "They were there for her."

"Who?"

Reese took a deep breath, winced. "They came for her. I told her to run."

It took a second for the information to sink in.

"She's missin'," Reese choked out.

The nurse strolled in, a young woman who looked bright and chipper this morning. The complete opposite of the man who'd been in charge of Reese's care through the night.

"Good morning, Mr. Tavoularis," she greeted. "It's good to see you're awake."

Reese barely gave her a second look, his full attention shifting to Brantley. "Where's my phone?"

"Cell phones aren't allowed in here," the nurse told him with a smile, even as she gestured toward a large plastic bag. "Those are his personal effects."

While Nurse Smiles took Reese's vitals, Brantley rummaged through the bag until he found Reese's phone still tucked into the pocket of his jeans.

"I'll see if I can get ahold of her," Brantley told him as he took the phone with him out into the hall, then back to the waiting room.

He was surprised to find RT and Z both there. They'd clearly gone home, showered, and changed and now looked far more alive than Brantley felt at the moment.

They were instantly on their feet when he appeared, their eyes hopeful.

Realizing no one else knew Reese was awake, Brantley gave them the good news.

"Thank God," Z said on a rough exhale, even as he pulled out his phone, began tapping out a message, probably giving Cindy and Hugh the news.

"He's askin' about Madison," Brantley explained, hating the words as they slid off his tongue. "Said those guys were there for her."

Z's eyes jerked up from his phone, studied Brantley's face. "He was havin' dinner with Madison?"

Brantley nodded.

"Why?"

RT frowned, plowing right over Z's question. "There for her how?"

Preferring to answer the second question, Brantley shrugged as he focused on the phone in his hand. He pulled up Madison's number, dialed.

"Max is a mob boss," Z noted. "There's no tellin' who might be after her. I'm sure he's got a long list of enemies."

"It went to voicemail," Brantley said, ending the call without leaving a message.

"I'll call Max," RT stated, strolling out of the waiting room and into the main hall.

RT disappeared around the corner, phone to his ear, leaving Brantley there to pace, running a hand over his hair. Now that Reese was awake, all the pain and frustration from last night returned.

"Hey." A firm hand landed on his shoulder. "I know Reese'll have a damn good explanation for this."

Brantley looked into Z's eyes, held his gaze. "I'm not sure he does."

"You two havin' problems?"

He hadn't thought they were. Hell, for the past six months, ever since Juliet Prince had been dealt with and they'd started working for Sniper 1 Security, Brantley'd thought they were settling into a nice routine together. Never in his life would he have imagined Reese to be chatting it up with his ex-girlfriend, much less going on dates with her.

"Give him a chance to explain," Z said firmly.

Brantley nodded because it was the right thing to do, not because he was in agreement.

"Any chance you've given the rest of the team a call?"

Brantley's gaze slammed into Z's.

Ah, hell.

BAZ ANSWERED HIS PHONE ON THE FIRST ring.

"Hey, boss man. What's up?"

"Reese is in the hospital. ICU. Here in Dallas. He was shot last night. He's awake and alert now, but I don't have any updates on his condition."

Because Brantley was speaking so fast, his voice low, it took a second for Baz to process the information.

Baz glanced over at where JJ was asleep on the other side of the king-sized bed. "Holy shit."

"I'll be up here for a while, but y'all are welcome to head back to Coyote Ridge whenever you're ready."

He didn't bother telling Brantley to fuck the hell off. Seriously? He thought they would simply pack it up and go home while Reese was in the hospital? Clearly something was off with Brantley to even suggest it.

Since he wasn't sure what Brantley'd been through, he opted to keep his cool. "We'll load up and head up there."

"You mind clearin' out our room, too? I'll call the front desk, tell 'em to give you a key."

"Yeah, sure."

"Be sure to grab the guns in the safe."

"Will do."

"The code—"

Baz interrupted him. "I'll get it from JJ."

When the call disconnected, Baz stared at his phone for a second.

"Who was that?" JJ grumbled, rolling over so she was facing him, her eyes still closed.

She looked so good like that. Sleepy and tousled. In his bed.

"Brantley. Reese was shot last night."

Her eyes snapped open, but she didn't immediately sit up. "What?"

He nodded, assuring her she'd heard him correctly. "He didn't give me details, but he did say Reese is awake and alert and stable."

Her exhale was so loud he wouldn't be surprised if their neighbor heard it.

"Why the hell didn't he call last night?" she bit out, sitting up and brushing her long hair back from her face.

Baz fought the urge to stare at her. He'd always been spellbound by this woman, and seeing her first thing in the morning was something he doubted he would ever get used to even if they spent the next eighty years together.

Tesha, who was asleep at the foot of the bed, rolled onto her back, clearly not ready for the day to start.

Figuring her question was rhetorical, Baz told JJ to get ready while he called Trey. He relayed the brief details Brantley had offered, then told Trey he would meet him at the hospital in a little while.

It didn't take long to pack up what few things he'd brought with him. When JJ was out of the shower, Baz got the combination from her, then left her to finish up while he took Tesha out to do her business. On his way back in, he stopped in the lobby to get a key card from the front desk.

When he walked into Brantley and Reese's room, the first thing he noticed was that Brantley's things were gone. He recognized a couple of Reese's T-shirts, which was how he deduced that the remaining items belonged solely to Reese.

What the hell had happened last night? He knew Brantley hadn't come back to the hotel to pack up his things after Reese was shot. He wouldn't have done it without clearing out Reese's, too.

Using the passcode, he unlocked the safe, found both of their Sigs tucked inside, both cased and unloaded.

Neither of them had been armed last night? He found that strange since they'd all taken to carrying all the time after what they'd been through in recent months. And since they were on duty twenty-four/seven, they needed to be ready at a moment's notice.

"Tesha, I think there might be trouble in paradise," he told the dog as he gave the room one final look to ensure he'd gotten everything.

Back in his and JJ's room, he found her drying her hair, but all of her things had already been packed. She was efficient like that, something he found both amusing and immensely attractive. Hell, everything about the woman turned him on, and he vowed that he would ensure she knew it from that moment on. Baz would not take anything for granted, especially when it came to JJ.

The blow-dryer turned off, and JJ turned to look at him as she ran her brush through her hair one final time.

"You 'bout ready?" she asked.

"Yeah. I got their stuff cleared out. I'll start loadin' it up if you wanna finish up in here."

"Will do."

Baz hefted a few bags onto his shoulders and headed for the elevator. When he was stepping inside, his phone buzzed in his pocket. Without looking at it, he sighed. It was eight o'clock, so he knew who it was. This was about the time that the text messages started every single day. Molly would begin by wishing him a good morning with half a dozen emoticons that made absolutely no sense to him.

However, there was no longer any reason for Molly to be communicating with him. Baz wanted nothing to do with her. It was enough to know that the baby wasn't his, something that actually caused a pain in his chest. Although the situation hadn't been ideal by any means, Baz couldn't deny he'd been excited about becoming a father. At thirty-two, he was more than ready to start a family.

On his terms, of course. The fact that Molly had fucked with his life for the past nine months eliminated the ache and replaced it with fury. She had lied to him.

Huffing his frustration, Baz exited the elevator, strolled through the empty lobby area, and out into the humid, warm morning. The sun was high in the sky already, guaranteeing a scorcher of a day. After piling their bags into the bed of Trey's truck, he pulled out his phone to read the text message.

Molly: *Good morning, Sebastian. I woke up thinking about you. How much I miss you. How I look forward to seeing you.*

Even before he'd learned the truth, Baz had started to wonder if the woman was insane. She sent him text messages like that all the damn time, despite the fact he had never led her on.

As he was staring at the screen, another text message came in.

Molly: *I see you've read my message. No response?*

That had become her new thing about a month ago. Her phone would tell her when he had read her text, and she would immediately respond if he didn't. It was the very reason he would ignore many of them throughout the day, not wanting her to blow up his phone.

Figuring if he didn't respond, the texts would just keep coming, so he shot a quick message back: *I don't think it's a good idea for you to be texting me anymore.*

He watched the little dots bounce as she was typing.

Molly: *What? Why? That's not fair. Are you denying your love for me now? You love me, Sebastian. I know you do.*

Ah, shit. It looked as though responding was the last thing he should've done.

CHAPTER TWENTY-FIVE

"WHO WAS THAT?"

Trey glanced over his shoulder to see Magnus rolling onto his back, his arm sliding over his eyes to block out the light Trey had turned on.

"My brother. Reese is in the hospital."

Magnus peeked out from under his arm, frowned. "Is he all right?"

Trey honestly didn't know. After he'd talked to Baz, Trey had called his brother directly, insulted that Brantley hadn't made the effort. He hadn't appreciated getting the news secondhand, and he told Brantley as much. Of course, Brantley being Brantley, he'd been curt, not willing to answer questions, as though his only objective was to relay the information, not go into detail.

"He's awake, that's all I know."

"Well, that sounds like good news."

Yeah, if he wasn't in the intensive care unit, maybe.

"I'm gonna grab a shower, then head up there," he informed Magnus as he pushed to his feet.

It took effort to walk away from the naked man in his bed. Despite his worry for Reese, Trey wasn't ready for the night with Magnus to be over. He had enjoyed the hell out of having him here, even if he wouldn't let Magnus know that.

What he didn't understand was why Magnus was still there. That wasn't their routine. On the nights Magnus would come over, he was always gone before Trey woke up the next morning, and he'd gotten used to waking up alone. Odd thing was, he was glad Magnus hadn't pulled his disappearing act, but he wasn't sure he wanted to accept it yet.

After padding to the bathroom, he flipped on the shower. While the water heated, he brushed his teeth and shaved his face. He didn't waste time, getting into the shower as soon as he was finished.

Once he was concealed behind the opaque glass, he heard the water in the sink come on, followed by some moving around. He waited to see if Magnus would say anything, and when he didn't, he sighed, focused on sudsing himself up, rinsing off.

A few minutes later, he heard the click of the glass door opening. Trey turned beneath the warm spray of water to see Magnus stepping inside. It wasn't a big space, but clearly that wasn't a problem, because Magnus stepped up to him, pressing their chests together.

"I figured you were in a hurry. Thought we could get this out of the way now."

When Magnus's hands glided up his arms, then over his shoulders, Trey groaned. He fucking enjoyed the hell out of Magnus's touch. More than he probably should.

The taste of mint and man exploded when Magnus's mouth fused with his. Trey didn't hesitate, pulling him even closer and holding him tightly to him.

"Have I mentioned how much I like when you manhandle me?" Magnus muttered against his mouth.

Those lips trailed along his jaw, down his neck, and Trey groaned in response. "Do you?"

"God, yes."

When Magnus went to his knees before him, Trey fisted his hair—who was he to deny the man his pleasure?—holding him firmly in place as he relaxed against the wall.

He watched as Magnus eagerly took his cock in his mouth as though his greatest thrill was sucking Trey's dick. The man was damn good at it, Trey knew that much. The way he worked him with his tongue, careful to avoid using his teeth. Most impressive was how deep Magnus could take him into his throat.

But it was the eye contact that always captivated Trey. The way Magnus stared up at him, as though gauging his reactions to ensure he was doing what he needed to do.

"Magnus," he groaned in warning, pumping his hips, tightening his grip on Magnus's hair. "Goddamn, that feels good."

If it weren't for the fact they didn't have a condom, Trey would've yanked Magnus to his feet and impaled his ass. Instead, he let the sensations of that skilled mouth work him closer and closer to the edge.

"You look so fuckin' good with my dick in your mouth," he growled, still holding Magnus's gaze. "Take all of me." Trey groaned low in his throat when Magnus took him to the root. "Fuck yes. Just like that."

Trey rolled his hips slowly, sinking deep into Magnus's throat a few times, holding back the release that was building.

"Ah, hell," he ground out, retreating slowly then beginning to fuck Magnus's mouth in earnest, holding out for as long as he could, because not only did it feel fucking amazing but he liked the connection he felt with the man. When they were intimate, there was nothing between them. The outside world faded away. No worries, no cares. Only this.

Trey grunted, taking control, holding Magnus's head still as he fucked into his throat. He let out a garbled roar when his orgasm ripped through him, Magnus swallowing every drop.

He should've been replete, sated. Only he wasn't ready for this to be over. He wasn't ready for Magnus to walk out that door. He wanted a few more minutes even if he couldn't tell the man that. Instead of focusing on the shower and getting on with his day, Trey jerked Magnus to his feet and crushed their mouths together.

Pinning Magnus to the wall, Trey reached between them, curling his fingers around Magnus's thick, hot shaft and stroking firmly. Magnus writhed beneath the onslaught, moving against Trey, his tongue thrusting into his mouth while Trey swallowed every moan, every groan.

Although he would've enjoyed watching Magnus come, Trey didn't stop kissing him. He was bruising them both, he knew, but he didn't care. It was exquisite and necessary.

And when Magnus gripped his head tightly, crying out as he came, Trey swallowed that down, too, consuming everything the man would give him.

"Christ Almighty, what was that?" Magnus asked when Trey finally released him.

"Sorry."

"Fuck. Don't be sorry. Promise to do it again."

Trey shook his head, stepping beneath the spray once more. He would never understand Magnus. The guy took everything Trey was willing to give him without complaint. And the fact that he'd made the trip to Dallas simply for a night of sex meant this was turning into something more. Something Trey had no interest in. The idea of getting hurt by one more man didn't sit well with him, and Trey was willing to avoid it at all costs.

"Are you headin' back today?" Magnus asked as he stepped out of the shower and grabbed a towel.

"Gonna go to the hospital first," he answered, flipping the shower water off and opening the door wide.

"Want me to go with you?"

Trey's response was instant. "No. You should head back."

The last thing he wanted was for the team to know he was indulging in this sort of behavior. He went to great lengths to conceal his interactions with Magnus because the last thing he wanted was to get shit from those he worked with.

Magnus was watching him, his expression unreadable. "Okay then."

Trey nodded, took the towel Magnus passed over before turning away from him.

As far as Trey was concerned, their night was over, and it was time they got back to the real world.

The moment JJ set eyes on Brantley in the ICU waiting area, she knew something was wrong. Something more than the fact that Reese had been shot and was now recovering from surgery.

Yes, that was far more than enough to put that irritable look on a man's face, but she could see it in his eyes. The storm clouds were back, the ones that had been there when Brantley first returned to Coyote Ridge after being medically discharged from the navy. It had taken a couple of months and his introduction to Reese to move those storm clouds out.

While JJ knew it would be best to give him a wide berth, it was nearly impossible for her to do that. It was in her nature to want to help those closest to her, and Brantley was the closest thing to family she had these days.

"Why don't we take a walk," she suggested from the chair beside him, hoping to get a few minutes alone with Brantley to get him to open up.

"Don't want to leave," he said, staring down at his phone.

"Brantley…"

His sharp gaze lifted, slamming into her. "Let it go, JJ."

Pain flooded her. An emotional onslaught, not physical. She hated that he could so easily shut her out when she considered him her best friend. But she understood Brantley on a level most didn't. He'd always been the strong, silent type. Even in high school, back when Brantley was dating JJ's brother, Jeremy. She figured that had been part of the allure for her brother, and since she'd had a crush on Brantley at the time, she fully understood the appeal.

It wasn't all that appealing at the moment.

"For a minute," she said harshly. "But that's all you get."

A small smirk tugged at Brantley's mouth before he exhaled and leaned back in the chair. "I'm sorry."

"I know." JJ glanced around the waiting room, taking stock.

RT and Z had gone back to see Reese while Cindy and Hugh were sitting in the corner, both sipping coffee. JJ had heard that Reese's sister Jensyn was on her way to the hospital, having flown in from California this morning.

"What are the doctors saying?" she inquired, keeping the topic neutral.

Brantley sighed softly. "It'll be a long recovery. The bullet nicked an artery, but he suffered more injuries from the fight. A couple of cracked ribs, contusions, and a broken finger."

"Jesus." She glanced over at him. "They did a number on him?"

"Two on one." Brantley wouldn't look at her. "He was protecting Madison Adorite."

"She related to Max?"

"Sister."

"Was she at the training facility?" she wondered aloud. How else would Reese have run into her?

"No."

Hmm.

JJ let the information tumble around in her head. Reese protecting a woman while at a restaurant. A woman related to a notorious mob boss she'd never heard of until she'd become acquainted with Sniper 1 Security. Why in the world would he be doing that? Was it business, was it—

"She's also Reese's ex-girlfriend," Brantley said softly.

JJ's head snapped over, her eyes slamming into Brantley. "And he was ... *out* with her?"

"A date."

No. No way that was true.

That information wasn't processing all that well. No matter how much she shifted and turned it, JJ couldn't get the pieces to fit. She knew Reese was head over heels for Brantley. She got to witness it every single day, had for months now. Those two were still floating on clouds half the damn time with rainbow glitter and sunshine coming out of their asses.

Something didn't add up.

A date? With a woman? An ex-*girlfriend* woman?

"Is that the woman everyone was looking for?" JJ asked, recalling the conversation she'd overheard between RT and Z.

"Yeah. But she's fine. Not a scratch on her." Brantley stretched as he sat up straight. "One of Max's enforcers was there to save the day. Got her to safety and left Reese there to die."

There was pure venom in Brantley's tone. Enough that JJ leaned away slightly as she twisted to look at him. "He's not gonna die, B."

"I know that," he snapped, shoved to his feet. "Doesn't change what they did."

No, clearly it didn't.

JJ watched Brantley walk away. She could practically feel his frustration and his anger. Whether it was because Reese had been shot or because Reese had gone on a date, she didn't know.

But whatever it was, she didn't see it resolving itself anytime soon.

CHAPTER TWENTY-SIX

BRANTLEY KNEW IT WAS TIME TO MAKE his exit. He'd spent the better part of the day with everyone else, waiting to get confirmation from the doctor that Reese was on the mend. They'd finally gotten that when they were told Reese would be moved to another floor where he could be monitored now that his condition had been upgraded to stable.

Now the question was whether or not he told RT and Z that he was bailing or if he simply walked out and waited until someone realized he was gone. The latter would've been the easy route, and he was damned tempted to take it.

Unfortunately, easy wasn't something Brantley experienced all that often, proven when Baz and Trey intercepted him as he was heading for the elevators.

"You goin' to grab somethin' to eat?" Baz asked, carrying two Styrofoam containers and a bottle of water.

Brantley stopped, took a deep breath, and decided to be truthful. "I'm headin' back to Coyote Ridge."

Trey frowned, glanced at Baz then back to Brantley. "Are they releasing Reese?"

"No. He'll be here for a while longer. But he's got his brother and his mom. They'll take care of him."

Brantley could see the concern on their faces, but he wasn't in the mood to break it all down for them. He didn't want to acknowledge the fact that the man he loved had been on a date with his ex when he'd been shot for putting himself between her and a bullet. And he damn sure didn't want to try and explain it to anyone else.

"Why don't I go with you," Trey suggested, looking at Baz again. "Y'all can take my truck back. Leave Reese's here. He might need it."

"I'm good, Trey," Brantley insisted.

"The hell you are." Trey grabbed Brantley's arm when he attempted to move past. "Take my keys," he told Baz.

"I don't suppose you'd mind takin' Tesha," Baz said quickly. "Right now she's outside with Hugh because they won't let us bring her up here."

"We'll take her," Brantley grumbled, jerking away from Trey and resuming his trek to the elevator.

"You wanna tell me what's goin' on?" Trey insisted when he stepped into the elevator seconds before the doors closed.

Brantley kept his attention on the number pad. "No."

"Why the fuck are you leavin' Reese in the hospital?"

Brantley didn't respond because he'd been serious with his answer. He did not want to talk about it.

"He just had life-saving surgery," Trey hissed.

Grinding his teeth, he stared straight ahead, ignoring his brother.

"Goddammit, Brantley."

Thankfully, the doors opened into the lobby. Brantley made a beeline for the exit, keys in hand. He stepped outside, got blasted with a gust of Texas heat, and wondered if fall would ever get here and whether or not it'd been this hot every day. He honestly couldn't remember much of what had happened over the last couple of months, much less the weather.

"I'll bring the truck around," he told his brother, lengthening his stride in an attempt to get away. "You get Tesha."

He heard Trey issue a few choice curse words, but he didn't stop. He headed for the parking garage where RT had said they'd parked his truck after one of their agents had retrieved it from the restaurant Reese had been at with Madison.

Not for the first time, he wondered whether they'd been having a good time before they were interrupted by a couple of fuckups who'd been on a finders-keepers mission with one of Max Adorite's siblings as their prize. He hadn't bothered to ask Reese for details because he didn't think he could handle them. He did not want to know that Reese and Madison had been making eyes at one another while sharing a bowl of pasta or whatever the fuck they ate when they went out.

His stomach twisted, the knot taking up permanent residence there.

Not sure exactly where his truck was parked, he used the key fob to honk the horn, following the sound until he located it on the third floor of the garage.

Once he was inside, he started the engine, cranked up the a/c, and sat silently for a moment. He considered leaving Trey here. His brother would do better to catch a ride back with Baz and JJ. Brantley was in no mood for company, and he knew Trey was going to badger the shit out of him until he broke. That or he knocked the idiot unconscious, which was a very appealing idea.

Unfortunately, Brantley felt responsible for Tesha, and he didn't like the idea of her having to wait outside of the hospital until Reese was released. That or having to go home with one of Reese's relatives. They would be good to her, he knew, but Brantley wanted Tesha with him.

Holy hell. Were they going to have a custody battle over a dog?

Forcing the thoughts away, Brantley put the truck in Drive and headed for the exit. He paid the parking attendant and swung back around to the portico where he'd left Trey. Thankfully his brother was alone with the dog so Brantley wasn't forced to explain to anyone else why he was bolting. If they didn't know already, surely Reese would give them all an update as to the change in their relationship status soon enough.

"I expect you to sit there and shut up," Brantley told Trey as he buckled himself in. "Don't ask questions, don't share your feelings. Just shut the hell up."

Trey nodded, his eyes scanning Brantley's face, clearly trying to figure him out by his expression.

It wasn't hard, he figured. Right now, Brantley was on the verge of a mental breakdown, and he was in no mood to get all emotional with his brother or anyone else. He wanted complete and total silence.

A mile down the road, he decided silence sucked.

So he turned on the radio and tuned Trey and Tesha out.

TREY WAS THANKFUL THE DRIVE FROM DALLAS to Coyote Ridge was only three hours. And that was when a sane person was driving. When Brantley was behind the wheel, they could cover ground at a faster clip, coming in at a little under two and a half.

Two and a half hours of listening to country music while Brantley pretended he was the only person in the vehicle. Trey had attempted to engage in conversation more than once only to be frozen out completely. Needless to say, he didn't give up easily, so he'd put forth the effort right up until Brantley kindly dropped him off at his house. He was just lucky his brother had stopped long enough for him to get out, rather than throwing him from the moving vehicle.

Once in the house, he shot a quick text to Baz letting him know they'd made it and checking in to see when they'd be returning. He'd learned that Baz and JJ had gotten on the road an hour after they had, so it wouldn't be long before they'd hit the town limits. Baz promised to drop off his truck as soon as they did.

Which meant until that time, Trey was stuck at home.

Alone.

On a Saturday.

Fucking great.

Because he'd spent the majority of the day at the hospital, he opted for a shower, thinking it might be a good idea to head over to Moonshiners when Baz returned his truck. He could go to the bar, grab a couple of beers, and do his best not to think about reaching out to Magnus to see what the man was doing.

Did he want to know?

Hell yeah, he did.

He'd felt shitty since that morning when he sent Magnus on his way like he was a dirty little secret.

Trey figured technically he was. It wasn't like Trey had any desire to spread the word that he was fucking a twenty-five-year-old who he had absolutely nothing in common with aside from the fact they both enjoyed what Magnus did to Trey with that skilled mouth. And how Magnus enjoyed how Trey dominated him whenever they were naked. That was the extent of their similarities, and Trey knew nothing more was going to come of it.

So why the fuck was he constantly thinking about Magnus? Why the hell did he dream about the man, waking up with his fucking cock hard and aching in his fist damn near every morning? It was getting old, and Trey knew he needed to do something about it quick before he got in too deep to dig himself out.

Trey glanced at his cell phone.

Now was as good a time as any, wasn't it? There was no reason he could think of to see Magnus anymore. Last night had been ... it had been phenomenal. Like a grand finale, the be-all end-all of more-than-one-night stands.

Before he could come up with an excuse, he grabbed his phone, pulled up Magnus's number, and typed up a quick text: *Thanks for last night, but it's getting more complicated than I wanted. It was fun while it lasted.*

Trey deleted back to the beginning. Started over.

Made it back home. Reese is doing well. Thanks for making the trip last night. Had fun, but I think it's time we call it quits.

He stared at the message. It sounded polite yet apologetic. Plus he had let Magnus know how Reese was doing, so it qualified as considerate, too.

Yes.

Perfect.

And yet he couldn't bring himself to hit send.

With a heavy sigh, Trey hit the button to turn off the screen then tossed the phone on the counter. He would wait for Baz to bring his truck, then he'd hit Moonshiners. A few hours out and about would help him clear his head, bring things into perspective.

At that point, he could figure out how to let Magnus down gently.

CHAPTER TWENTY-SEVEN

"What the fuck were you thinkin'?"

Reese rested his head back on the pillow and stared over at his brother. It wasn't the first time Z had asked him that question since he'd regained consciousness, and like the other times, Reese had no answer for him.

Honest to God, he had no fucking idea why he'd taken Madison to dinner. No clue why he'd texted her. Hell, he didn't know why he hadn't deleted that goddamn text back when she'd first texted him a few months ago. Nothing he'd done in the past seventy-two hours made any damn sense to him.

"You know he's gone, right?"

Frowning, Reese lifted his head, stared harder at Z in an attempt to understand. The move made the muscles in his chest pull, causing searing pain to charge up through his chest, so he relaxed once more.

"Brantley," Z clarified. "He went back to Coyote Ridge."

Son of a bitch.

Reese looked up at the ceiling, took a deep breath, and wondered if the pain in his chest was from the bullet wound or from knowing Brantley was likely gone for good.

"Why the hell would you do that to him?"

Reese didn't bother to tell Z nothing had happened with Madison. It wouldn't matter. It was the principle his brother was having a hard time with, and Reese couldn't blame him. He didn't understand it himself, and if their roles had been reversed, if Brantley had gone on a date with an ex—say, maybe Cyrus—Reese would've felt the same way.

"Tell me this," Z urged. "Are you and Madison gettin' back together? I hope the hell not because she left your ass there to die, Reese. She fuckin' bolted."

"I told her to," he rasped, his throat gravel-rough.

"Maybe. But she left you there to die."

Reese closed his eyes, wishing like hell Z would give him some space. As it was, he'd had a revolving door of visitors ever since they moved him out of intensive care, and he wanted to be alone. He *needed* to be alone.

Preferably at home. In fact, more than anything, he wanted to walk right out of this hospital, hop in his truck, and head back to Coyote Ridge. More so now that he knew Brantley had left.

Brantley had left.

Fuck.

What the hell had he done?

Two hours later, Reese woke up, groggy from the pain meds that had pulled him under.

He didn't open his eyes right away, listening for the sound of breathing, something to tell him whether or not he had company. He figured he did since they couldn't seem to leave him alone. It was the very reason he'd succumbed to the drugs, let them pull him into the black hole of oblivion for as long as possible.

Unfortunately, it hadn't lasted long enough because he could still feel the pain in his chest, knew that he was a long way from recovered.

Worse than that, he knew that Brantley really was gone.

Stay Tuned

I hope you enjoyed the sixth installment of the Off the Books Task Force. Although it looks like they're in limbo now, I promise there's more to come for Brantley and Reese. As well as for JJ and Baz, Trey and Magnus, and the rest of the task force. Each book in this series is a full-length novel involving a new case and the continuation of the relationships between them all. And I promise not to keep you waiting long for each installment.

If you enjoyed *Secrets*, please consider leaving a review.

About Nicole Edwards

New York Times and *USA Today* bestselling author Nicole Edwards lives in the suburbs of Austin, Texas with her husband and their youngest of three children. The two older ones have flown the coop, while the youngest is in high school. When Nicole is not writing about sexy alpha males and sassy, independent women, she can often be found with a book in hand or attempting to keep the dogs happy. You can find her hanging out on social media and interacting with her readers - even when she's supposed to be writing.

Connect with Nicole

I hope you're as eager to get the information as I am to give it. Any one of these things is worth signing up for, or feel free to sign up for all. I promise to keep each one unique and interesting.

Nic News: If you haven't signed up for my newsletter and you want to get notifications regarding preorders, new releases, giveaways, sales, etc, then you'll want to sign up. I promise not to spam your email, just get you the most important updates.

Nicole's Blog: My blog is used for writer ramblings, which I am known to do from time to time.

Nicole Nation: Visit my website to get exclusive content you won't find anywhere else, including sneak peeks, A Day in the Life character stories, exclusive giveaways, cards from Nicole, Join Nicole's review team.

NN ON FACEBOOK: Join my reader group to interact with other readers, ask me questions, play fun weekly games, celebrate during release week, and enter exclusive giveaways!

INSTAGRAM: Basically, Instagram is where I post pictures of my dogs, so if you want to see epic cuteness, you should follow me.

TEXT: Want a simple, fast way to get updates on new releases? Sign up for text messaging. If you are in the U.S. simply text NICOLE to 64600. I promise not to spam your phone. This is just my way of letting you know what's happening because I know you're busy, but if you're anything like me, you always have your phone on you.

NAUGHTY & NICE SHOP: Not only does the shop have signed books, but there's fun merchandise, too. Plenty of naughty and nice options to go around. Find the shop on my website.

Website:	NicoleEdwards.me
Facebook:	/Author.Nicole.Edwards
Instagram:	NicoleEdwardsAuthor
BookBub:	/NicoleEdwardsAuthor

ACKNOWLEDGMENTS

Of course, I have to thank my wonderfully patient husband, who puts up with me every single day. If it weren't for him and his belief that I could (and can) do this, I wouldn't be writing this today. He has been my backbone, my rock, the very reason I continue to believe in myself. I love you for that, babe.

Chancy Powley – As always, you keep me going, and I thank you for that.

Jenna Underwood – I always look forward to the random notes in the mail. They make me smile. As do the phone calls (even if I can't always answer).

I also have to thank my street team – Nicole Nation Street Team – Your unwavering support is something I will never take for granted.

I can't forget my copyeditor, Amy, at Blue Otter Editing. Thank goodness I've got you to catch all my punctuation, grammar, and tense errors.

Nicole Nation 2.0 for the constant support and love. You've been there for me from almost the beginning. This group of ladies has kept me going for so long, I'm not sure I'd know what to do without them.

And, of course, YOU, the reader. Your emails, messages, posts, comments, tweets… they mean more to me than you can imagine. I thrive on hearing from you; knowing that my characters and my stories have touched you in some way keeps me going. I've been known to shed a tear or two when reading an email because you bring so much joy to my life with your support. I thank you for that.

By Nicole Edwards

The Walkers

Alluring Indulgence
Kaleb
Zane
Travis
Holidays with The Walker Brothers
Ethan
Braydon
Sawyer
Brendon

The Walkers Of Coyote Ridge
Curtis
Jared (a crossover novel)
Hard to Hold
Hard to Handle
Beau
Rex
A Coyote Ridge Christmas
Mack
Kaden & Keegan
Alibi (a crossover novel)

Brantley Walker: Off The Books
All In
Without A Trace
Hide & Seek
Deadly Coincidence
Alibi (a crossover novel)
Secrets

Austin Arrows
Rush
Kaufman

CLUB DESTINY

Conviction
Temptation
Addicted
Seduction
Infatuation
Captivated
Devotion
Perception
Entrusted
Adored
Distraction

DEAD HEAT RANCH

Boots Optional
Betting on Grace
Overnight Love
Jared (a crossover novel)

DEVIL'S BEND

Chasing Dreams
Vanishing Dreams

MISPLACED HALOS

Protected in Darkness
Salvation in Darkness
Bound in Darkness

OFFICE INTRIGUE

Office Intrigue
Intrigued Out of The Office
Their Rebellious Submissive
Their Famous Dominant
Their Ruthless Sadist
Their Naughty Student
Their Fairy Princess
Owned

PIER 70
Reckless
Fearless
Speechless
Harmless
Clueless

SNIPER 1 SECURITY
Wait for Morning
Never Say Never
Tomorrow's Too Late

SOUTHERN BOY MAFIA/DEVIL'S PLAYGROUND
Beautifully Brutal
Without Regret
Beautifully Loyal
Without Restraint

STANDALONE NOVELS
Unhinged Trilogy
A Million Tiny Pieces
Inked on Paper
Bad Reputation
Bad Business

NAUGHTY HOLIDAY EDITIONS
2015
2016
2021

Made in the USA
Coppell, TX
27 July 2022